An outpost on the edge
of the world

A Knight on the run and in
pursuit of the truth

Feuding dragon overlords
bent on conquest

An unstoppable army, united
by a sinister leader

. . . and one lonely city caught
in the middle of it all.

THE LINSHA TRILOGY

City of the Lost

Flight of the Fallen
(2004)

Return of the Exile
(2005)

THE LINSHA TRILOGY

CITY OF THE LOST

Mary H. Herbert

CITY OF THE LOST

Distributed in the United States by Holtzbrinck Publishing. Distributed in Canada by Fenn Ltd.

Distributed to the hobby, toy, and comic trade in the United States and Canada by regional distributors.

Distributed worldwide by Wizards of the Coast, Inc. and regional distributors.

DRAGONLANCE and the Wizards of the Coast logo are registered trademarks of Wizards of the Coast, Inc., a subsidiary of Hasbro, Inc.

All Wizards of the Coast characters, character names, and the distinctive likenesses thereof are trademarks of Wizards of the Coast, Inc.

Printed in the U.S.A.

Cover art by Matt Stawicki
First Printing: August 2003
Library of Congress Catalog Card Number: 2002114365

9 8 7 6 5 4 3 2 1

US ISBN: 0-7869-2986-3
UK ISBN: 0-7869-2987-1
620-17976-001-EN

U.S., CANADA,   EUROPEAN HEADQUARTERS
ASIA, PACIFIC, & LATIN AMERICA   Wizards of the Coast, Belgium
Wizards of the Coast, Inc.   T. Hofveld 6d
P.O. Box 707   1702 Groot-Bijgaarden
Renton, WA 98057-0707   Belgium
+ 1-800-324-6496   + 322 457 3350

Visit our web site at **www.wizards.com**

Dedicated with love to two very patient people:

To Betsy H. Schmick,

Although my sister claims I grew up
in an altered state of consciousness,
and although she does not like
fantasy, I love her anyway. She is one
of my biggest fans and best friends.

To Guy M. Houser,

My little brother does like fantasy
and has faithfully read every single
one of my books and stories. He, too,
is one of my biggest fans and best
friends.

Arrow in the Dark

Sometimes the only thing separating life from death is timing, that split second on the threshold of mortality when the rock is only a foot above your head, the horse's hoof is inches away from your face, the sword blade is swinging toward your torso, or the runaway wagon full of ale barrels is only a single rotation of the wheels away from your body. In that fraction of a moment, life and death become as one, and only luck, instinct, or perhaps fate will decide your next state of being.

Linsha pondered this as she studied the large tear in her old blue shirt. Really, this dependency on timing was becoming all too familiar to her. On their own accord, her eyes followed the line of the tear across her left breast to the fletched tail of a crossbow bolt protruding from the rotting masonry of the old wall beside her left shoulder. A tatter of blue fabric clung to the shaft. One step more, one fraction of a second faster, and she would have been—

Hooves clattered over the rubble, and an adolescent male head peered cautiously around another crumbling wall about twenty feet away. Linsha heard him gasp.

"What have you done now?" More hooves clashed on the ruined paved road and a large male centaur trotted into Linsha's view. The horseman was big, muscled from years of fighting, and colored such a dark bay he looked almost black. He took a single look at the woman pinned by her shirt to the wall and his face suffused with anger.

"Leonidas!" he bellowed, rounding on someone behind the wall. "How many times have I told you not to loose a bolt until you are certain of your quarry?" He sprang forward and wrenched the offending crossbow out of the hands of the hapless shooter.

Linsha closed her eyes to the gloom around her and her ears to the voice of the annoyed centaur. She concentrated her attention inward to the wild pulse of her heart and the jangled rush of relief, delayed fear, and outrage. Focusing her mind on her body's instinctive reactions, she calmed her racing heart, restored her breathing to normal, and sent her emotions spiraling into a calm repose. It was a technique she had learned from her mother who had to use it often when dealing with her father, Palin.

She opened her eyes, extracted the bolt from her shirt and the wall, and walked over to the large centaur who was still berating a smaller one. Two others had joined them and stood silently at a respectful distance. All four horsemen were heavily armed and wore war harnesses decorated with the brass emblem of the Dragonlord Iyesta, ruler of the Missing City.

Linsha tapped the bolt against the lead stallion's burly arm to get his attention. "I'm all right," she said lightly. "Really. Nice of you to ask."

Leonidas, she now saw, was a young male, a buckskin with dark legs and mane and a coat the color of sand. He was still in the gangly stage between colt and stallion, all legs and knees and elbows. A wisp of a pale beard attempted to age his youthful face.

The lead centaur turned, the irritation still plain beneath his thick black beard. "Lady Linsha, I do apologize. We did not know you were out here. But that is no excuse—," he twisted back to Leonidas. "You do not shoot until you see your target! Do you want to explain to Lord Commander Morrec how you shot his officer in broad daylight?"

The young centaur blanched. Lord Barron uth Morrec, Senior Commander of the Circle of the Knights of Solamnia in the Missing City was well known for his temper and his dedication to his officers.

"No, Caphiathus," he mumbled. He shot a nervous glance at Linsha. "I'm sorry, Lady Knight." He hesitated and jerked a hand at the darkening ruins around them. "I am not accustomed to this. It still unnerves me."

Caphiathus snorted a hearty sound that was not entirely contemptuous. "Then the next time we bring you, weanling, we will be certain you leave your weapons behind, so none of us find a bolt in our hindquarters."

Linsha decided to take pity on the young centaur. "Broad daylight" was a rather optimistic description of the settling twilight around them—and the bolt had missed after all. She could still remember the odd feelings and sensations of unease she felt the first few months she had spent in the Missing City. It took some time to get used to this place.

"At least he said 'the next time,' " she told the buckskin.

"Lady Knight, why are you out here alone?" Caphiathus said. "It is hardly safe for us, let alone a person unattended."

For an answer Linsha strode back to the crumbling

remains of the building she had been standing beside when the ill-aimed bolt almost ruined her day. Squatting on the bare ground, she pointed to a faint foot track that passed by the ruin before disappearing in the windblown dirt and gravel of open ground. All four centaurs bent over for a look.

"I saw someone in the market this morning. A stocky man I've never seen before. He loitered around the booths, but he talked to no one and he bought nothing. He spent a great deal of time looking at the city walls, the gates, and the city patrols. I didn't like the looks of him, so when he left this evening, I followed him." She studied the footprints then glanced up at the horsemen. "Whoever he is, he does not wish to be found. He knew he was being followed, and he lost me."

Caphiathus did not question or even doubt her assessment of the situation. Until three years ago, Linsha Majere had been a member of an ultrasecretive clandestine circle in Sanction, living a life as a petty thief and con-artist on the streets of one of the most diverse and volatile cities in Ansalon. If she said she did not like the looks of someone, she had ample experience to back up her suspicions. The centaurs who patrolled the environs of the Missing City had learned early to trust her.

The big bay straightened and gazed out where the edge of the old city faded into the gathering darkness. "Whoever he is, he's gone now. But perhaps we know where to look for him. We found evidence of a camp in the Scorpion Wadi that looked fairly recent. We will check it again. In the meantime, if you are finished here, Leonidas can make amends and carry you back to your citadel."

Linsha recognized a dismissal when she heard one. She nodded and rose to her feet. She had worked with the centaurs long enough to recognize the worry and tension that edged their leader's voice. It was a tension they were all feeling these days. There wasn't much she could do out here now, anyway. The trail was cold, and the night swiftly approaching. She should probably report back to her commander.

When the silence seemed to last longer than it should, Linsha cast a glance at the young centaur, who walked over to her. If nervousness were magic, Leonidas would have been radiating like a mage's glow light.

She hid a pale smile. Yes, she was third in the chain of command of the Solamnic Knights in the area. Yes, she had something of a reputation as a warrior and a clever gatherer of information, and yes, she was a frequent visitor to the Dragonlord Iyesta's lair. But she wasn't *that* fearsome. Wordlessly, she offered the crossbow bolt back to the young stallion.

Taking it between long, nimble fingers he snapped it in half, then in smaller pieces, and then tossed the bits to the ground. The centaur, like an adolescent released from an expected tongue-lashing, relaxed. Bending his gangly legs, he lowered his back so Linsha could easily mount, and when she was astride, he turned and jogged southward to the occupied quarters of the Missing City.

Linsha looked back over her shoulder to Caphiathus and called out, "Let me know what you find!"

His response was muddled in a clatter of hoofbeats as the three centaurs wheeled around and cantered away along the old road.

<hr />

Beyond the vanishing traces of the ancient city, a low swell of hills rose from the scrubland and looked down on the fading ruins. Early darkness pooled in the folds and crannies of the hills, hiding rock clusters and clumps of scrub pine and shrubs that clung to the meager shelter of the gullies.

The darkness also hid two men. They crouched in the cover of a thick stand of brush and watched the meeting of the Knight and the centaurs in the rubble of the city a hundred yards away.

"There, that woman," said one man, pointing downward. "She spotted me in the marketplace."

"And followed you here," the second man added. His voice was level and emotionless, but the first man shot him a nervous look.

"I got the information you wanted," he said.

The second man nodded once. He was tall and lean and wore the long, voluminous robes of a plains tribesmen. A hood camouflaged his face in shadow and hid the cold expression on his features.

The two men watched from their hiding place without talking as the centaur patrol left the lady Knight and cantered into the hills. The noise of their hooves pounded close by the watchers then dwindled when the horsemen headed north toward the Scorpion Wadi. Moments later the last centaur carried the Knight back toward the city and the ruins were left deserted once more. The darkness closed in.

The robed man rose to his feet and stepped out of the shelter of the copse. "Tell me," he ordered.

The other man followed. "Give me the rest of my fee."

A bag of coins appeared in the tall man's hand, but he held it back in his fist like a trap.

The spy gave him a surly look and casually stuck a hand in his belt near a hidden throwing knife. "There is a caravan from Morning Dew. It's due in about four days. In time for the festival. The spring crops have been good this year, so the farmers are looking forward to some bartering. The Legion is not expecting reinforcements until autumn."

"What about Elder Joachem? You met with him two days ago to get the date of the shipment of supplies and weapons."

"Had to get rid of him," the spy said with a sneer. "He was getting too greedy."

"Sloppy," snarled the robed man. "That is the third city dweller you have disposed of. I thought I hired a professional. I wanted no deaths to draw unnecessary attention."

"Sloppy!" he hissed. "That old man got nosy. He wanted more coins, more answers. He thought I was part of a smuggling ring and—"

"There are more subtle ways of dealing with the curious," said the tall man in a tone as cold as a glacier. His left hand shot out, snatched the spy's shoulder, and with surprising speed and strength, wrenched the man around and locked his body against his. The spy had no time to retaliate. The man's right hand slid under the spy's jaw, grasped the side of his head in a grip like a vise, and snapped it sideways. A moment later the spy became so much carrion.

He carried the body into the thicket and dumped it under the heavy undergrowth. Perhaps the centaurs would find what was left after the desert scavangers feasted. Perhaps not. It would not matter before long. Settling his hood carefully about his face, he strode down the hill and moved purposefully toward the lights of the city.

"And there are less subtle ways of dealing with the stupid."

Evening in Mirage

2

Linsha, naturally at ease on horse-back, leaned her weight back, re-laxed her legs, and eased her seat into the rhythm of the centaur's pace. For the sake of good manners, she would not touch his human torso unless he gave his permission.

"Have you been out with the patrols for long?" she asked.

Leonidas shook his curly head. "This was my first night," he said. "I just came here a few days ago to join my uncle Caphiathus."

He had been in the Missing City only a few days? Linsha pondered. That explained a great deal of his nervousness. "At least this won't be your last," she said with a chuckle.

The centaur brightened, and his words came tumbling out. "Oh, yes. Thank you, Lady. Another uncle once had a crossbow bolt that missed his ribs and pinned the edge of his vest to a tree."

"How fortunate for him," Linsha murmured.

"Yes," Leonidas said with a perfectly innocent face. "It was the other twelve bolts that put him off his feed."

Linsha couldn't help but laugh. She could not decide if this centaur was simply naïve or if behind that awkward, coltish exterior was a sense of humor and thoughtfulness that went deeper than his uncle gave him credit for. She played with the idea of trying to read his aura. It was a mystic ability she had that enabled her to sense a person's true nature, good or evil. It was one of the things she had learned during her brief time with Goldmoon at the Citadel of Light and the strongest of her few mystic talents. Lately though, her ability to use even this simple magic of the heart had faltered and failed, and more often than not she ended up with a strange tickle around her neck and a foolish look on her face. She decided to keep an eye on him instead, especially whenever he had a crossbow in his hands.

Leonidas's smooth trot quickly carried them out of the deserted fringes of the ancient ruins and into the streets of the North District. Buildings rose up around them, flowering gardens filled corners and yards, and the pale glow of lamplight began to gleam in windows. The tall, elegant figures of elves walked by carrying golden lamps that shed light on the well-tended sidewalks. A noblewoman strode past, her long, silvery hair bound in complex braids. At first glance, everything seemed normal. It wasn't until one looked carefully at the forms filling the streets that their translucency became apparent.

Strangest of all, to Linsha's mind, was the silence. There were no voices, no footsteps other than their own, no sound of laughter or music or stamping of horses' hooves, no rumble of wheels or the sound of water in the fountains. Here in this part of the city where the living had not come, there were only the phantoms and the endless wind that blew from the plains.

Linsha felt a faint shudder in Leonidas's hide. She could hardly blame him for feeling skittish. The Missing City was one of the oddest places she had ever visited. Centuries ago, before the first Cataclysm, the city had been a thriving community by the name of Gal Tra'kalas built by the Silvanesti elves on the shore of the Courrain Ocean. Some time during that first world-shifting catastrophe, something happened to the fair elven city that changed its physical existence forever. The city itself was utterly destroyed, leaving only ruins. But strangely, over these ruins lay a spectral copy of the old city, inhabited by ghostly figures who appeared to live normal lives completely unaware of the other world around them.

Several griffin riders who flew over the ruins shortly after the Cataclysm reported ". . . the city is haunted by fiends, who took the form of our brothers and sisters. The city, too, is reborn in an unholy mockery of life, for though rubble litters the place, the likeness of every building and barn still is visible."

The elves thereafter shunned Gal Tra'Kalas. No Silvanesti came to confirm the presence of the ghostly city. No one, save maybe a few nomads, travelers, or brigands stepped foot on the broken ground of the dead city, and it remained empty for generations, shimmering like a mirage on the edge of old memories. It wasn't until after the Second Cataclysm that a brass dragon and a group of civilized people rediscovered the city of the lost and made it their own.

With darkness gathering quickly around them, Leonidas slowed to a careful walk. The images of the city looked real enough to the casual glance, but they often hid the reality of the ruins beneath the ghostly surface. Heaps of rubble, collapsed cellars, jagged walls, and decrepit roads still lay underfoot to trap the unwary.

The centaur made a sudden swerve that caused Linsha to clamp her knees tighter around his ribs and grab for the swath of mane on his withers. "Sorry," he mumbled. "There was a woman there."

There was a woman, a willowy beauty who passed completely through the centaur, taking no notice of him. Her long, pale hair blew in a breeze neither Linsha nor Leonidas could feel.

"I hate that," the young stallion grumbled. "They're just like ghosts."

"But they're not ghosts."

"I know. I've heard the stories."

So had Linsha. The city of Gal Tra'Kalas was not dead; these elves were not undead. They just existed in a different world that somehow overlapped the world in which Linsha and everyone else lived.

Leonidas's tone said he'd heard all the words and didn't believe any of them. Linsha resisted the impulse to pat his shoulder.

"Once you get used to it, the place is rather interesting and very complex. If you pay attention, you'll start to recognize people and see the passage of their lives."

Leonidas sighed and stepped carefully around a child running along the street. "I suppose so. I don't know that I'll have time to get used to it any day soon. Uncle Caphiathus says we are to go on a long patrol tomorrow for three weeks."

Linsha straightened. "Three weeks. That's a little unusual."

"That's what I've heard from others. Before the patrols went out for only seven days at a time then took three days off. Now their range has been expanded, too. Uncle didn't say why." He twisted at the waist so he could look at Linsha over his shoulder. "I've heard that

Iyesta is growing nervous, that there are rumors of invasion. Maybe even Malys is coming."

It was Linsha's turn to feel a cold shudder slide through her bones. The very name Malys was enough to send even the most normal-thinking folk looking for a deep cellar with a strong, fireproof door. But Malys, she knew, was not Iyesta's biggest worry. There were three other dragons closer to the brass's realm that were more likely to cause trouble—Thunder, a conniving blue dragon to the west, and black Sable to the north. Farther west, just beyond Thunder's domain, the great evil green Beryl brooded over her vast realm. How Iyesta had managed to hold her thriving realm for this long was a marvel to Linsha. It was a constant struggle, she knew, for Iyesta to protect the populace that had grown under her care, to defend her borders, and to keep her enemies constantly off guard. The brass had to bully, cajole, charm, beguile, outwit, outtalk, and outmaneuver every dragon that looked her way. She had the most efficient spy system on Ansalon and a loyal army of centaurs, humans, and elves who patrolled her borders and guarded her lair and city. Her only allies were a few metallic dragons who sought refuge in her realm and the mysterious bronze dragon, Crucible, who had a lair somewhere near Sanction and who, with the help of Lord Governor Bight, did what he could to keep Sable distracted.

Iyesta had kept her lands free of tyranny, desolation, and terror, and she had worked tirelessly to help her people survive. For twenty years, she had been successful, but lately Linsha had sensed something change. A faint hint of of a new danger edged the air like the smoke of a distant grassfire. There was nothing Linsha could identify, only a taint in the background that set off a small but persistent alarm in her head. She wished she could put a form to her unease, so she could convince others to pay attention.

"Keep your eyes open," she said to Leonidas. "I don't think Malys will be our problem."

He nodded and said nothing more for the moment. Sounds of traffic, voices, and busy footsteps began to intrude into the silence. Interspersed with the phantom buildings, solid buildings began to appear, built in the identical elven fashion. The rubble and ruinous remains had been cleared away here, and the streets were smoothed and paved with new stone, making movement easier. Leonidas broke into a slow jog. More people, different races this time—solid and very much alive— bustled about real taverns and shops among the ghostly elves, paying little attention to the images of the older city around them. It was, as Leonidas pointed out, very disconcerting.

Yet Linsha found it all fascinating. She had heard of the Missing City years ago when she lived in Solace with her parents and grandparents. The Legion of Steel, which had its base in Solace for years, had been looking for a site to set up a base of operations in the southern continent away from the attentions of the two Knightly orders. The abandoned ruins of the Missing City had been chosen not only for its location on the sea, but for the symbolism of its identity. For an order that wished to remain invisible, to work quietly and unseen among the people, the irony of building a site in the Missing City was too good to pass off. The Legionnaires who constructed the outpost deliberately crafted their solid buildings to match exactly the translucent buildings of Gal Tra'kalas, forming a site that blended like a mirage into the spectral city.

Shortly after the original outpost was founded, the dragon Iyesta arrived and made her lair in the old city.

Under her protection, other people found the peace and quiet of the city to be a haven. The population grew and spread into the other quarters of old Gal Tra'kalas and moved beyond the ghostly walls. A thriving port lined the harbor and the citizens did a small but brisk trade with other cities along the Silvanesti coast and into the Bay of Balifor.

While many still called the new city the Missing City, the more pragmatic inhabitants—usually those who lived on the outside of the phantom town—thought the name was silly. Everyone knew how to find the place, only Gal Tra'Kalas was sort of missing, so why not give it a new name to reflect its new image? People started calling it Mirage, and the name stayed. Now, the name Missing City referred to the sites within the ruins, while Mirage named the sections outside the gates. Newcomers often found this confusing, but the residents enjoyed their dual city and its odd history.

"Lady," Leonidas said politely. "Where do you wish to go?"

They had reached the area of small shops and businesses called Little Three Points where the Northern District, the Artisans' District, and the Port District met in a triangle of tree-lined streets. Sounds normal to the night life of a busy city drove away the silence. The scents of olive trees, sage, and blooming jasmine perfumed the night air and competed with the smells of cooking food, dung fires, animals, and, in the summer heat, public latrines.

Linsha drew a deep breath of appreciation. She was and always would be a city girl. Although she enjoyed rambles in the country on a sunny day and would tolerate a trek through the wild lands, she loved a populous city and all its wondrous varieties of buildings, peoples, foods, streets, and landmarks—including the numerous inns and taverns. Her stomach rumbled, reminding her she had not eaten since late morning. As much as she would like to invite Leonidas to her favorite outdoor tavern for a pint of ale and a meat roll, she knew he was anxious to return to his uncle, and she should return to the citadel. Knight Commander Remmik was in charge of the watch this day, and he had no patience with her. She was already several hours late reporting for duty. If only Sir Morrec had not left on a brief journey to the Silvanesti Shield. His absence tended to turn Sir Remmik into a martinet.

"Please take me to the Solamic Citadel," she said to Leonidas.

The centaur turned east and trotted into the Port District, the most populated and busiest section of the Missing City. It was here where the Legion had built most of their original buildings in the old Silvanesti style, and here where most of the city's commerce took root. Open-air markets filled empty lots. Shops of all varieties, warehouses, and offices grew into the spaces where the ancient businesses stood. In fact the new bustle of the city so nearly matched that of Gal Tra'kalas that a person had to be careful not to mistake real people or buildings for the phantom ones and walk headlong into one.

This very real problem eventually convinced the Legion—and later the Solamnics—to move their headquarters outside the Missing City into the newer district of Mirage. The Legionnaires appreciated a place where they could rest and relax without phantoms, while Sir Remmik wanted the Solamnics to be more visible.

The last vestiges of twilight lingered in the western sky when Leonidas and Linsha reached the old city wall. Long ago the wall had enclosed all of Gal Tra'kalas, until the event that destroyed the fair city. In the past few years the Legion and the Knights had slowly rebuilt large sections of the wall in strategic places, but there was not enough material or labor or time to complete the massive project in the near future. All they could do was keep rebuilding and hope for peace.

Linsha spoke a few words to the guards at the city gate, called the Legion's Gate in honor of its builders, and the centaur carried her through into the streets of Mirage. As they passed the new piers of the city's harbor, Linsha ran a hurried eye over the quiet waters. Several freighters lay at anchor, their sails tightly furled and their lamps lit for the night. Not far away, the small fleet of fishing vessels that called Mirage home were settling down for the night and preparing for a well-earned rest. Linsha looked past the boats and beyond the small breakwater to see if Iyesta or even Crucible was there to enjoy a bath in the warm summer evening, but the brass was nowhere to be seen and the secretive bronze had not visited the Missing City in weeks. Linsha's hand strayed to the bronze dragon scale that hung from a fine chain around her neck—a gift from a friend she had not seen since Yule a year and a half ago.

Oh, well. It was worth a hope, she thought. A word from one of the metallics would have freed her from the tongue-lashing she knew she was going to receive. She sighed. Her hand dropped from the dragon scale, and her attention returned to the city around her.

Leonidas had relaxed even more. Now that he did not have to be constantly alert for ghostly buildings and people, his gait smoothed to a fluid motion that was a pleasure to ride, and the knots of muscle in his back, neck, and shoulders eased away beneath his golden-brown skin. His face lost its look of intense concentration, making him look even younger.

"I have never been to a place like this before," he said. "I think I like Mirage better than the City."

Many people did, Linsha knew. The buildings of Mirage did not copy the Silvanesti architecture of the phantom city, so more than anything else they revealed the changing character of the new city. Many newcomers moved into this district and built as they preferred, using the few natural resources from the plains and the sea. Quite a few of the new arrivals to Mirage were refugees fleeing the terrors of the dragon overlords—kender from their devastated homelands, Silvanesti elves trapped outside their beloved forest by the Shield, centaurs and men from the Plains of Dust held by Thunder and the lands drowned by Sable. They came and built with stone, mud bricks, shells, and plaster. The result, while eclectic, was pleasing. The streets were neat and orderly. The storefronts were in good repair and painted in muted colors that complimented the natural colors of the beach, rock, plain, and sea around them. Trash and debris were cleaned regularly, drunks and derelics and gully dwarves were removed, and everything was meticulously maintained.

Part of this civic-minded responsibility was due to a zealous city council and a dutiful city watch, and a part of it was due to Iyesta herself. The big brass liked cleanliness, organization, and efficiency, and woe to anyone who tried to disregard her wishes in the capital of her realm.

Trotting quickly now, the centaur bore Linsha through the streets, past the small, unobtrusive Legion command post to the edge of Mirage where a low rise of hills lifted from the beaches and overlooked the city. On the highest point Sir Remmik had built the epitome of Solamnic fortresses, a masterpiece of smoothly crafted walls, powerful towers, and perfectly placed defenses.

Only two years old, the walled stone ediface loomed over the open hilltop, guarding both the harbor and the city like a silent, vigilant giant. Outside the high stone walls, the ground all around had been cleared for training fields, a parade ground, and pens and corrals. Within, the fortress was a self-contained citadel for a garrison of seventy-five with its own well, kitchens, smithies, stables, barracks, storerooms, brewery, jail, and a central keep with a hall large enough to seat the entire circle for a feast.

Leonidas stared up at the smooth walls of the gate tower to the glow of torches high on the ramparts above. "This is very impressive," he remarked as he came up the sloping road to the heavily guarded gate.

"Yes," Linsha said. "Sir Remmik is very proud of it. I believe he paid for much of it himself."

From somewhere in the scrub trees at the base of the hill came a long, haunting cry of an owl. Linsha heard it and nodded with satisfaction. Good. Varia was back.

Leonidas paid scant attention. He continued to study the imposing building, then tilted his head and his lips curved in a slight frown. "Has he ever fought dragons?"

Linsha chuckled. The centaur saw with a keen eye. He recognized the difficulty she saw in the citadel. While the Legion of Steel kept an unobtrusive profile in the area, the newly arrived Knights of Solamnia had come barging into Mirage like a saber rattling, over-zealous lordling trying to win accolades for himself. Considering the volatile and offensive nature of the enemies around them, Linsha would have preferred a little less pomp and a great deal more circumspection.

Unfortunately, circumspection was little known to the Knight Commander. Although Sir Remmik was second in command of the Solamnic Circle in Mirage, Sir Morrec admittedly had little taste for the daily grind of organizing and supplying a garrison and building a fortress. More often than not he gave full authority to Remmik, who was not only a talented engineer, but a brilliant organizer and supplier. Because of him, the Solamnic garrison had the finest fortress on the Plains of Dust, bulging storehouses, well-crafted armor and weapons, and an attitude that said to the people of Mirage, "Now that we're here, everything will be fine."

Linsha wasn't so sure.

A few steps before the main gate, Leonidas came to a stop and offered Linsha his hand. She lifted her leg carefully around his waist, took his hand, and slid to the ground. Before she let go of his fingers, she pulled him closer. "You are right that something is stirring," she said softly. "Be careful, and if you need help or you need to get word to someone, let me know."

The centaur's deep brown eyes stared into hers for a long moment, and Linsha saw that her guess had been right. Young and gawky he might be, but intelligence and understanding flowed in him.

"Thank you, Lady." He bowed to her and turned away into the night. The sound of his hoofbeats faded down the hill.

Linsha listened for a short while, then squared her shoulders, saluted the officer of the guard, and strode in to make her report to Sir Remmik.

Jamis uth Remmik

3

Sir Remmik was making his rounds with his scribe and two torchbearers when Linsha found him. For some time he deliberately ignored her as he examined the storeroom locks, issued flour, meat, and rations of ale for the morning meal to the cook, checked the barracks and stables, and took a final head-count for the night. Linsha followed him wordlessly, hoping the grinding of her teeth was not obvious over the sounds of their tramping feet.

It was not until he inspected the guardposts that he nodded to Linsha. He frowned at her torn shirt and disheveled appearance. His own uniform was beautifully tailored and immaculate. He moved on, expecting her to follow as he stopped to speak to each sentry and visit each guardpost on the walls, in the towers, and at the gate.

"These Knights were promptly at their stations," he said to her at last, his expression cold. "They were not galavanting about the city ignoring their duty."

Galavanting? Linsha fought to keep her expression unreadable. The insulting pompous scarecrow. She did not deserve his condescending reprimand; she was no untrained recruit. She was a Knight of the Rose, third in rank in the Circle, and a highly experienced operative.

"Sir Remmik, there was a stranger in the market. I followed him. I suspect—"

She stopped. What exactly did she suspect? But the Knight gave her no time to consider. His hand chopped off any further explanation. The two younger Knights holding the torches clamped their jaws tight and looked anywhere but at Linsha.

"The Knights of *this* garrison know their duty and how to follow it," Remmik stated in short, sharp words. "You would do well to forget your slovenly habits from your previous clandestine assignment and remember what you are." He stood straight, his back pikestaff straight.

Once again, Linsha thought irritably, here it comes.

"Let honest pride be felt in possessing that truest virtue of a Knight—obedience," he intoned as if chanting a devotional incantation.

And there lay the crux of the matter. Obedience. Knight Commander Jamis uth Remmik believed in nothing but himself and the Solamnic Measure. He was a high ranking Knight of the Crown, and for him there was only the law, the Oath and the Measure, the obedience of Knighthood. To him, Linsha was an anathema, an undisciplined rogue, a troublemaker, and Sir Remmik couldn't abide troublemakers.

Much of his animosity stemmed, Linsha knew, from an incident that happened four years ago when she had been brought before the Solamnic Council on charges of treason and disobeying orders after she helped the city of Sanction and saved its governor, Hogan Bight, from assassination. The three commanders of the Clandestine Circle in Sanction had ordered her to disregard the clear threat against Lord Bight and let him face death. She had refused. After the crisis, she had turned herself over to the Council in Sancrist to clear her name, but politics being what they were, she languished in prison for weeks while arguments passed back and forth between the authorities. It wasn't until Lord Bight sent an officer of his guards to Sancrist to inform the Council that he was in the debt of the Solamnics for Linsha's courageous actions and that two of the three Solamnic officers had regrettably died in a raid on their secret headquarters. The Knights of Neraka were suspected.

It hadn't taken long for the surviving officer to drop the charges against her, and the issue never came to trial. Linsha was quietly cleared and reassigned to a garrison where she could put her considerable talents to use—and where she was far from the center of Solamnic activity without being truly exiled. She was far from home and family, far from the seat of her honored order, and far from those few she could call friends.

Yet Linsha did not allow those facts to dismay her. She chose to remember instead that she and Lord Bight were still alive, that she had cleared her name with the Grand Master, and she had kept her honor intact. Sir Remmik could go blow up a drainpipe.

"Yes, Sir Remmik," she said in a bland voice. "Obedience. I will work on it."

His dark eyes narrowed into black slits in the flickering torchlight. The man was older than Linsha by ten years and intelligent enough to recognize that tone of voice. He knew she would not make a sincere effort to become the Knight he thought she should be. But beyond berating her in front of other Knights, there was little he could do. She was of equal rank in the

Order of the Rose. Only his seniority and his expertise with planning and supply put him ahead of her in command of the garrison. He would need a severe breach of conduct on her part to inflict any form of punishment on her—and she knew it.

Linsha watched as these thoughts paraded over his face in a quick procession of grimaces. Although he was only slightly over her height, he still managed to look down his long nose at her.

Why was it, she wondered, that there were some people in the world who shared an instant and mutual animosity with each other? No rational explanation. No obvious reason. They just grated on each other's self-control from first sight. This man was an excellent example. No matter what she tried, she could not banish the dislike that reared up every time she and Sir Remmik came face to face.

"Clean yourself up, Knight," he snapped. "You are duty officer tonight. Tomorrow, Iyesta asks for you to come to her lair at sunrise. Dismissed."

Linsha quelled the burst of pleasure that threatened to show on her face. A visit to the brass's lair was always enjoyable. Of course, it meant no sleep in the morning.

She jerked her head in the barest nod and turned on her heel without bothering to salute. Let him go salute himself. He probably practices saluting in a mirror so he can be perfect.

Linsha strode into the darkness away from the infuriating man and entered the barracks attached to the main keep.

Going into her small niche, she lit an oil lamp on the narrow table that was one of only three pieces of furniture in the room. A narrow bed crowded against the left wall and a wooden chest sat at its foot. Linsha had learned early to travel light and forego the encumbrances of too many personal items. Her room was bare and utilitarian; it contained all she needed to sleep and dress.

She tossed her torn shirt in the chest for one of those cold winter days when when she had nothing else better to do than mend clothes, then she pulled out her uniform. Remmik's words came to her again. *Slovenly. Galavanting.* By the absent gods, that man was a fool. For the sake of this garrison, she hoped nothing would happen to Sir Morrec that would put Remmik in charge.

Linsha toyed with the idea of a transfer as she pulled on the blue pants and the blue and silver tunic. Had she served enough time here for the Grand Master to consider her request? Would her request even make it past Sir Morrec? The old man liked her and respected her abilities. One of his greatest strengths as a leader was his skill in bringing out the best efforts of his Knights and allowing them to do their work. She had to admit, even as much as she despised him, Sir Remmik performed excellent work and was superbly placed for his abilities. It was just a shame he was such a rigid, unforgiving, unpleasant example of a Solamnic Knight.

Linsha paused and ran a thumb over the ornate embroidered crest on her jacket—a crown over a kingfisher perched on a horizontal sword decorated with a rose. The design had been sewn, at Sir Remmik's request, in silver threads on all the uniforms of those serving the citadel. It was rather flashy, Linsha decided, but the symbols of the Solamnics represented almost two thousand years of dedicated service and sacrifice. They were the emblems of an Order she had dedicated her life to serve. To serve with honor. How honorable would it be to request her way out of here?

No, she would not request a transfer. That was only the wishful thinking of a tired, out-of-sorts mind that had seen death in the point of a crossbow bolt only a short hour ago. Linsha laughed at herself. After all, the Measure promised that all who made the supreme sacrifice for the sake of their country would be rewarded in the afterlife. Maybe learning to put up with Sir Remmik would earn her at least a day of celestial feasting or something.

A sharp tap disturbed her thoughts, and she hurried to the window slit and opened the wooden shutter. A large owl, delicately patterned with creamy bars and spots, sidestepped through the narrow opening and walked carefully onto Linsha's outstretched wrist. Agate black eyes stared down at the woman and a soft raspy voice said, "You could have opened the window. There is no perch out there."

"I'm sorry, Varia," Linsha said, her voice hushed. "I was distracted."

A throaty chuckle vibrated in the owl's throat. "Remmik again. I watched you follow him around like a disobedient squire."

"It was his idea of punishment."

Linsha lowered the bird to eye level and gently laid her face against the owl's pale breast feathers. The warm smell of bird, pine trees, sun, and desert wind filled her nostrils—the familiar scents of an old friend.

"It is good to see you. You have been gone too long."

Varia nibbled Linsha's auburn curls and bobbed her head a time or two in her own greeting. Her dark eyes gazed unblinking into the woman's green ones. Two tufts of feathers grew on either side of Varia's round head like horns; they rose and fell according to her mood. Now they were flat in contentment as she

25

settled comfortably into place.

Varia was similar to the elusive talking Darken Owls in that she could communicate with humans, and she was an excellent judge of character, but she was the size and coloration of a normal owl. Linsha had never learned if Varia was one of a kind or part of a species somehow related to those Darken Owls. Not that it truly mattered to her. Varia had found Linsha during a reconnaisance ride into the Khalkist Mountains nearly six years ago, and after a careful scrutiny, the owl had attached herself to a companion worthy of her friendship. Linsha had been surprised, then delighted, and they had been together ever since. Even during Linsha's incarceration by the Solamnic council, Varia had found shelter in the hayloft of a nearby stable and patiently waited for her to be released.

"I do not have much to tell you," Varia said in her whispering voice. Although the owl was a virtuoso of sounds from faint whispers to demonic screams, no one in the garrison knew she could talk. The other knights thought Linsha simply had a fondness for pet owls, an ignorance Varia preferred and Linsha found useful.

Linsha sat on the edge of her bed and lowered the owl onto her knee. She knew she should be hurrying, but Varia had been gone for three days on what she liked to call a spy flight, and Linsha was anxious to hear her news. She stroked a fingertip down the bird's soft, spotted chest. "Tell me."

"Everything looks normal. I flew a path around the city from the cliffs near Barddeath's Creek, over the Scorpion Wadi, up past Sinking Wells, as far as the edge of the Silvanesti Forest, and south again to the big bluffs at Kirith Head. I saw nothing out of the ordinary. There are a few nomads out there. The drovers are moving their herds out into the summer pastures. Centaur patrols are everywhere. I saw a small band of elves camped near the Shield keeping watch, and a small caravan from City of the Morning Dew is headed this way."

"How does the country fare?"

"The best I have seen it. The grasslands are green and lush. The wells and oasises—"

"Oases," said Linsha.

"What?"

"It's oases, not oasises."

"You humans." Varia ruffled her feathers and gave a long blink. "Anyway, the *oases* are full. The herds of cattle and goats do well. I heard a farmer say this could be an excellent harvest for the olives, grapes, and corn." She clicked her beak appreciatively. "Which means, of course, it will be a good season for mice."

When Linsha did not respond, Varia tightened her talons lightly against the woman's knee until her gaze focused once again.

"What exactly are you looking for?" asked the owl.

"Nothing," Linsha admitted. "Something. I don't know. Maybe I am just turning into a nervous old woman. For some days I've had this odd feeling that something is wrong. I feel as if someone is watching me. I see enemies in the marketplace. I hear rumors of disaster. I see shadows everywhere. Am I imagining things?" She didn't want to ask, "Am I going crazy?"

Varia tilted her head in a thoughtful way. "This is a city out on a limb. Iyesta works very hard to keep Mirage safe, but any day another dragon could sweep over and chop that limb off. That is not fancy."

"I know," Linsha murmured. She thought of the centaurs and the tension on their faces, their longer patrols, and the array of weapons they carried. Perhaps their increased activity was nothing more than the orders of a new leader trying to prove his vigilance. Maybe the man in the marketplace had not been a spy but a mere brigand or sellsword checking out the territory. Maybe these feelings of gloom were nothing more than homesickness or loneliness or a growing irritability with the whole situation. After all, she *was* getting older whether she liked it or not, and she had spent the past ten years in one tense and dangerous situation after another. Someday she wanted to go back to Solace to see her family, eat a meal at the Inn, visit her grandmother's grave, and just rest for a while.

Linsha felt her thoughts begin to run in circles. She could "maybe" herself to death and still go nowhere. She either had to find some solid evidence to back up her imaginings or she should relax and let things be as they were.

Not tonight though. She had wasted enough time and angered Sir Remmik enough for one day. With care and some reluctance, she lifted the owl to a perch she had installed close to the open window. Varia fluffed her feathers once then settled down for a nap before her evening hunt.

"I am summoned to Iyesta's lair tomorrow. Do you want to come?" Linsha asked as she moved toward the door. When Varia gave her a sleepy yes, Linsha added, "Meet me in the stable then, at sunrise."

A tired hoot was the only reply.

Linsha spent the rest of the night in the Solamnic headquarters in the keep. The room was spacious enough for several desks, rows of shelves, and a large fireplace. It was comfortable enough even in the winter, well protected by stone walls, and centrally located so the officer of the watch could supervise the changing of the guards and be available for any emergency, late night advice, or minor disasters.

During the long, quiet hours before dawn Linsha read several reports left for her by three of her contacts. As an erstwhile member of a clandestine circle, Linsha had learned how to make contacts, find snitches, and gather information not readily available to a circle of armed Knights. She knew the beggars who would watch the docks for a few coins, the fearless boys who would follow a suspect through the busy streets, the courtesan who sold her favors to the captain of the City Watch, the maid of the city's busy mayor, the stable lads in the militia's stables, and more importantly, those Legionnaires who were friendly to the Solamnic Knights. With charm, friendliness, a sincere interest, and a knack for finding just the right price, Linsha had set up a network of information gatherers in and around the Missing City that rivaled Iyesta's in its efficiency.

It was mostly because of this network that Linsha began to see little things that did not make sense. A patrol of Iyesta's militia was massacred, and no one could find out who was responsible. Another esteemed elder in the city council had disappeared, leaving his family behind. What did that make now? Two elders and a merchant who had disappeared lately without a trace. Then there was a shipment of iron bars ordered by one of the local blacksmiths that was stolen. Strangers were seen prowling around the streets for no obvious reason and then mysteriously vanishing. Did any of these things tie in together?

Most alarming of all, to Linsha's mind, was the silence emanating from Thunder's neighboring realm.

Stenndunuus, or Thunder, was aptly named. Loud, clashing, and brash, Thunder was one of the most malevolent of the minor dragonlords. He coveted Iyesta's grasslands and fertile river valleys, but he was too wary of the aggressive brass to challenge her face to face. Instead, he constantly threatened and plotted and voiced his hatred for her at every opportunity. Lately though, he had been very quiet, and very little news had leaked out of his realm. Linsha wondered if the big blue was up to anything, or if he was just laying low to keep out of the attention of *his* neighbor, Beryl.

At least there was one dragon neighbor who seemed to be complacent for now. Since the end of the Dragon Purge a few years ago, black Sable had spent more and more of her time in her lair in Shrentak where she indulged in her passion for experimentation and the study of parasitic beings. Her gruesome and revolting creatures had grown so numerous of late that no one in Iyesta's realm ate anything brought out of Sable's loathsome swamp or went anywhere near it. Although Sable was still a threat to Iyesta's territory, Linsha did not believe Sable was planning anything more complicated than her next meal or another addition to her foul zoo.

A slight smile came to Linsha's face at the memory of one creature she had seen delivered to the great black. During her brief duty as a bodyguard to Lord Governor Bight in Sanction, she had accompanied the governor through secret tunnels and passages under the mountains to trade a particularly nasty creature called a cuthril slug to Sable for information. She remembered her incredulity at the exchange and Lord Bight's secret smile. She remembered, too, trying to explain this trade to the Solamnic Council. Few people could understand why Hogan Bight would make the effort to leave his city to take Sable a slug. Why did he do it? Why did Sable leave him alive?

It wasn't until Linsha came to the Missing City and became friendly with Iyesta that she understood better the reasons behind Lord Bight's occasional meetings with Sable. By luring her into face-to-face contact, Lord Bight was able to gather information from the dragon and spread his own news and gossip that kept her distracted and wary and too uncertain to move either north toward his domain or south toward Iyesta's. From her place in the Plains of Dust, Iyesta did the same thing. Using lies, rumors, the occasional mention of Malys's name, and a show of her own force, Iyesta had kept Sable away from the Plains for years and made her too wary of exposing her backside if she turned and attacked Sanction. A few herds of cattle sent periodically to Shrentak helped sweeten the precarious stalemate.

If only, Linsha thought for the countless time, there could be someone on the western side of Thunder to help keep him in line. Unfortunately, there was only Beryl, and she was too vicious and untrustworthy to pin any hopes on her. If she weren't so busy plotting against the elves in Qualinesti, she probably would have looked to her east and tried something devious against Thunder already.

Linsha threw the reports on her desk and sighed. The political and draconic connections across Krynn were endless, mind-boggling, and tangled like a hag's knitting. Even the wise could not sort them all out. If someone was plotting against Iyesta, or the Knights of Solamnia, or the Legion, or the city, or anyone for that matter, Linsha could not see yet who it was. She was too weary and too morose to think clearly this early morning.

Tired of her own thoughts, Linsha climbed the steps

to the high wall and watched the sun rise beyond the red hills. People born before the Chaos War thirty-eight years ago told her the sun had changed when the gods departed and the war ended. It was strange, smaller and paler than before. Yet it was the only sun she had ever known. It seemed adequate enough to her. After all, what could you do about a burning sun far beyond your grasp? Complaining didn't change anything. Even the mages in the height of their power could not change the sun. There were just some things you had to accept.

An image of her father came into her mind as he had been the last time she saw him. He had made a special journey to Sancrist to visit her in the Solamnic prison. Palin had been strong then, still filled with his magic, and his presence had been a blessing to her. He had listened quietly to her tale of Sanction—and she had told him almost everything—and when she finished he hugged her close and approved of her decisions.

She'd heard since then that life had not fared well for him. Last year she received a message from her brother, Ulin, that their father had been captured by the Dark Knights. She wanted to go home then, but by the time she arranged for an emergency leave and transportation she received another note telling her he was alive and home again. The last word she had from Solace told her of her grandmother's death. She wondered how her father was faring. Where was he? How was he adjusting to these changes in his life when there were no gods to pray to? He had always told her that he truly believed the gods would return some day. What would he tell her now?

She watched the cool gold light of day swell and fill the sky, sweeping like a tide over the city, bringing it to life. The faded gray and black of night passed into brilliant colors—the blue of the bay, the red of the hills, and the green of the fields and meadows. Traffic began to fill the streets of Mirage, and at the gate of the Citadel, a silver horn blared a greeting to the new day. Around her, the banners of the Knights of Solamnia filled and fluttered from the battlements in the new breeze. It would be another warm day, a delightful day to a city accustomed to cold winters and short summers; a perfect day to prepare for the Midsummer Festival that was just a few days away.

Footsteps behind her brought her out of her pensive thoughts and she turned to face a young Knight striding toward her.

"Lady, there is a beggar at the gates who wishes to see you," he told her without a blink. The Knights of the garrison were used to greeting odd people at the gate for the Rose Knight.

"Send an escort to the stable to meet me. I will ride to the overlord's palace in twenty minutes."

She turned back to the wall and stared silently at the brightening skies. To the north lay the vast expanse of the Plains of Dust. Beyond those miles of grassland, savannah, and desert was Sanction and Solace. An odd yet fitting choice of names for two places she desired to be.

A flash of light caught her eye from somewhere just beyond the distant ragged edges of the ruined city. Bright and yellow as brass, it caught the morning sun, dipping and soaring on the wind fresh from the sea. Linsha smiled. The big brass dragon was out enjoying a morning flight. Knowing the dragon as she did, Linsha assumed she had some spare time before Iyesta would be back in her lair and waiting for her. Linsha watched the dragon fly for another moment or two, then left the wall and returned to the headquarters to turn the watch over to the day officer. There was no time left for brooding thoughts or endless reflections on things she could do little about. Morning had come, and with it were a myriad of things she had to do before she could snatch a little sleep before reporting for duty again. With luck, Sir Morrec would be back today and she could get a little respite from Sir Remmik's pompous lectures on the subject of obedience.

With a lighter heart Linsha walked to the gate to meet her visitor.

The Beggar and the Dragon

4

Linsha recognized the hunched and ragged figure waiting for her at the gate. She gave him the briefest nod and continued walking past the guard towers and along the path to the garrison's main stables located in the large field to the north of the citadel. There was a stable available in the fortress itself, but it was small and its stalls were limited to horses used for message delivery and errand-running. Most of the Knights who had their own horse for personal use kept them in the bigger stable where the horses could be released into nearby pastures for exercise and fresh grass.

Knowing the beggar would follow her, Linsha continued along the path to the barn and walked into the dim interior. The stable lads were already up and hard at work cleaning stalls and feeding horses, but they had not reached her horse's box yet. She waved one lad off who offered to help and fetched her own brushes and saddle. She poured a small scoop of fragrant grain into the horse's trough and began to brush his coat while he ate his breakfast.

A horse of the desert lands, Sandhawk was as chestnut red as the rust-colored hills at sunset and as patient and enduring as the desert itself. Linsha had bought him shortly after her arrival in the Missing City, and thus far, she had been pleased with him.

The gelding tossed his head once, and then went back to his oats as the beggar limped into the stall. Linsha looked over the horse's back and grinned at the man as she continued brushing the chestnut's dusty coat.

"That's one disguise I haven't seen yet," she said with a chuckle.

"My biggest mistake was buying these clothes from a real beggar. They came complete with fleas." He scratched his neck and with the same motion pushed his broad brimmed hat back from his face. Lank, dark hair fell forward, partially hiding a livid scar that marred the man's nose and left cheek.

Lanther had been a handsome man once. Linsha could see the strong lines of his nose and cheekbones under the weathered and scarred skin, but years of sun and desert wind and battles fought with sword and knife had taken a hard toll on his features. His eyes were a vivid blue, a dark blue like sapphires or perhaps the color of a thunderstorm at twilight. Those eyes twinkled at Linsha as the man crossed his arms and leaned against the stable wall.

"I heard you rode a centaur into town last night. What did you do to earn that honor?"

"Well, since you are the first to ask me that question, I will tell you. He was apologizing for ripping my tunic with a crossbow bolt."

Lanther's eyebrows slowly rose toward his hairline. "He shot at you?"

Linsha put the brush away and picked up a hoofpick. "Accidently." She leaned against Sandhawk's side and carefully picked up his front hoof. "I went out beyond the ghost city into the outer lying edges of the ruins and bumped into a patrol. Their newest member shot before he realized what he was doing."

"You weren't hurt?" he asked.

"Just my tunic."

His eyes narrowed. "What were you doing out there?"

"Tracking someone," she replied from behind her horse. "The kind of man that makes my hackles rise."

"Did you find him?"

"Lost him at the edge when the centaurs appeared."

Linsha moved to the horse's back hoof and slowly picked it clean while she waited for Lanther to tell her why he had come. He was a deliberate man and a patient one, two traits that had stood him in good stead. He had told her his story once of his work in the New Swamp. How, as a Legionnaire, he helped people trying to escape from Takar in Sable's realm, providing them with food and guiding them back to the safety of the plains. Sable's minions trapped him one day, until he fought his way out, and badly wounded, made his way across the miles of stagnant water and foul marsh to the small tribal village of Mem-Ban on the edge of Iyesta's domain. There he recovered with the aid of the tribesmen. Unfortunately, his leg was too crippled to return to the swamp. He was sent to the Missing City to join the cell there and to work with Iyesta's spy network. He had been one of the first Legionnaires to approach Linsha shortly after her arrival in the city, and together they had formed a steady friendship and a workable link between the Legion and the Order.

When he did not say anything after a while, Linsha peered at him around the back of Sandhawk's rump and saw through the hairs of the horse's tail that Lanther was trying to scratch his shoulder blades on the boards of the stall wall. He looked so uncomfortable and ridiculous that a chuckle slid out before she could stop it.

"You laugh," he grumbled. "Some day you'll have to use a disguise like this and the little demons will be all over your succulent flesh."

Linsha, who had been forced to use a disguise like that once, jerked a thumb at the horse trough visible just outside the stable door. "So take a bath. There're horse blankets in the tack room."

He made a disparaging noise. "No thanks. I'll find my own bath. I came to tell you that Sir Morrec's company has been delayed near the forest. They won't be back until tomorrow. One of your messengers is on the way here, by the way."

Linsha nodded, resigning herself to another day of Sir Remmik's dictatorial attitude. She didn't bother to be surprised that a Legionnaire was telling her of her own commander's business. The Legion often brought her news before her own Order received it.

Lanther paused as if waiting for her full attention. "We have found information on the elder who is missing," he said. "We received a tip last night that the man is dead. We are searching for his body."

Linsha hissed in irritation. "That makes three missing, doesn't it? Who is doing this? And why?"

"I wish we knew. It would be most strange if these three deaths are mere coincidences."

The two fell quiet for a time, busy with their own thoughts while the work of the stables went on around them.

After a while Lanther stirred and set his eyes on Linsha's bent back. "By the way—" he paused to savor the moment of delivery—"your brother was in Flotsam."

She shot straight up, startling her horse and dropping the hoof pick. "What? When? How do you know?"

A grin spread across Lanther's scarred face, easing the usually tense lines around his eyes and mouth. "One of our members in Flotsam sent a report to Solace and to Falaius to report the death of one of our older members. Falaius was a friend of hers."

Falaius Taneek was a desert barbarian turned Legionnaire who commanded the Legion cell in the Missing City. A tough but fair man, he had gained Linsha's respect quickly and opened a cordial and diplomatic liason between the Legion and the Solamnic circle. He would have known how pleased Linsha would be to hear news of her brother.

"What was Ulin doing in Flotsam? Was my father with him?"

"There was no mention of Palin. Only Ulin and someone named Lucy Torkay."

Linsha leaned her arms over her patient horse's back. "Lucy? Did the report say why?"

He shook his head. "It only said they were there last spring to look for her father. Apparently, he was a local brigand who had stolen the town's treasury. Seems your brother and this Lucy saved the town."

An image of her tall, lanky brother filled Linsha's mind like a warm draught of spring wine. He was her only sibling and a friend and companion of childhood. It had been too many years since she'd seen him last, and she missed him deeply. "Saved a town, did he?" she murmured, bending over to retrieve the pick. "He would."

She said nothing more as her thoughts revolved back to her place in the Missing City. She wished Ulin was there so she could ask him about the forebodings that discomfited her mind, but he was far away, probably back in Solace by now. There was only Lanther. He had been her friend for over a year, and if anyone in this city could understand her misgivings it might be him.

Still she stayed quiet while she thought of the right words. There were many things she wanted to ask him, but she wanted to phrase them in the right words. "Lanther," she said, "you have been in Missing City for two years. You know this city as well as a native and you know what the Legion is doing." She paused, then went on. "Have you noticed anything different lately? Does the Legion suspect something or have any apprehensions about this city?"

If he was surprised by her questions, he did not allow it to show in his expression. "No," he said slowly. "Why?"

"Something is bothering me. You may laugh, call it woman's intuition, but I have survived many years on my gut instincts. I can't put a shape to it." She lifted her hands in a gesture of frustration. "It is like a whiff of smoke on the wind. Strangers in town who make my skin crawl. Dead or missing civilians. Militia on alert. I see no link in any of it, and yet I feel something is wrong."

Lanther, a survivor of many undercover operations and battles in hard places, did not laugh at her admission. "I will ask around," he said. "Discreetly."

Linsha went back to grooming the gelding. She had to be content with that. At least Lanther did not ignore her like Sir Remmik or try to brush her off with light statements and a joke. If he said he would ask, he would do just that. Something might come of it.

A clatter of boots and voices outside announced the arrival of Linsha's escort—three Knights who would ride with her to see the dragonlord. They crowded into the aisle in front of the stalls, calling for their horses.

Lanther stayed to visit while Linsha blanketed and saddled her horse. He talked of inconsequential Legion activities and the city council's plans for the Midyear street festival in Little Three Points, then with a wave, he swung his dingy cloak around his shoulders and limped away down the hill toward the streets of Mirage.

Linsha watched him go. She liked Lanther very much, admired his courage, his convictions, and his determination. He had a roguish sense of humor and a cool charm. And yet, in some things he was still an enigma. He rarely talked about himself but preferred to listen to other people and, like many Legionnaires, he liked to work alone.

She wondered if the Legion knew she had been summoned to Iyesta's lair. She decided they probably did. There was little that escaped the Legion's notice.

A whisper of wings stirred the air by the manger, and Varia landed noiselessly by the chestnut's head. Sandhawk had been trained to disregard the owl. He flicked an ear at her and continued eating. She said nothing while the stable boys were close by, simply sitting and staring down at Linsha like any normal, trained pet owl. Once the bridle was on the gelding's head and Linsha was leading him out the door, Varia glided down and out the wide double doors.

The Knights, young and—to Linsha's mind—inexperienced, hooted at the owl and laughed among themselves as they mounted their horses and fell in behind the Rose Knight. With a shake of her head, Linsha kneed the chestnut into a canter and let the escort follow as best they could.

Iyesta's lair lay in the ruins of the old city in an area of the garden district kept deliberately untouched and unsettled by the servants of the great brass. Long ago it had been the palace of an elf prince. Much of its former beauty could still be seen in the graceful lines of the crumbling walls and arches and in the splendor of its vast expanses of halls, roofless chambers, stables, overgrown gardens, and patches of wild woodlands. The dragon had chosen the throne room, the only chamber large enough to hold her, and had ordered its roof repaired and its interior returned to its former grandeur. Everything else she'd left alone, partially as camouflage for her lair and partially because she liked the contrast of the old ruins set against her neat, well ordered city.

Iyesta was a dragon of contrasts herself. The largest brass dragon in Ansalon, she had a achieved her gargantuan size by preying on evil dragons during the Dragon Purge, yet the extent to which the other dragonlords, especially the five great overlords, disrupted life on the Ansalon horrified her, and she worked actively to undermine their authority. She could be charming, gregarious, a skilled conversationalist, then be viciously aggressive in the defense of her realm.

Because of her efforts on the behalf of the people under her care, she was held in high esteem by those in the brass clan and by other metallic dragons. Several dozen young metallics, mostly silver, gold, and brass accepted refuge in Iyesta's city and helped guard her borders or aided in her operations against the overlords. Three young brass dragons, born of the same egg, had earned a special place as Iyesta's personal attendants and made it their duty to guard her throne room when she was in residence. Usually, at least one of those young brasses sat out in front of her lair every day and screened the petitioners who came to see her.

This morning though, Linsha was surprised to see the large double doors were open and the space was empty. The wide expanse of courtyard before the chamber was in an uproar. Iyesta crouched in the large space bellowing orders as troops of her militia, palace guards, and others Linsha couldn't readily identify ran around in frantic haste trying to obey her. Two other dragons, a young gold female named Desiristian and a silver male Linsha knew as Chayne were winging in for landing nearby. The Knights reined their horses to a halt beside the smooth, paved road that led to the palace. A half-elf, serving in one of the dragon's loyal regiments, came to meet Linsha and take her horse.

"What's going on?" Linsha asked as she handed Sandhawk's reins over to the guard.

The half-elf looked worriedly toward the palace. "Her ladyship is furious. Dathylark, Korylark, and Thassalark are missing, and she's worried sick. I don't know what she's planning, but she's sending out search parties in every direction to find them."

Linsha whistled softly under her breath. All three missing? The brass triplets were inseparable and telepathically bonded. It did not seem possible that something could happen to all three of them. Maybe they had left on a secret mission of their own without telling Iyesta. If that was the case, Linsha pitied their hides when they returned home.

Linsha turned the three Knights of her escort. "You three wait here," she ordered.

She walked with deliberate care along the sweeping carriage way up to the old palace, giving the dragon plenty of time to see her through the gates of the courtyard. Soldiers and servants of the dragonlord recognized Linsha and made no move to stop her as she walked through the gates. She stopped perhaps twenty feet away from the huge brass and waited for Iyesta to acknowledge her. There was certainly no point in trying to shout over the dragon's thundering ire.

While Linsha waited she stared up at the huge brass and felt again her deep awe and admiration for the big dragon. Iyesta was well named Splendor. Over three hundred feet long, she was gracefully built with a short neck, a long, arched back and a tail nearly a third of her length. She carried a wingspan of more than four hundred fifty feet and had a delicate head with a mouth of curving teeth. Her scales had the warm, burnished look of polished brass that gleamed like golden fire in the morning sun.

"You're late!" Iyesta's voice thundered.

Linsha bowed into the blessed silence that had fallen over the court. The scurrying servants and soldiers fled to obey their orders while the other two metallics waited respectfully nearby.

"I did not realize there was a deadline, your lordship," Linsha said without apology. "I was told to report to you in the morning. It is still morning."

Iyesta dipped her head until her large eye regarded Linsha from a few feet away. Her eyes were golden brown, tinged with a smoldering red and gleaming with ancient intelligence. Her spiralled horns gleamed gold in the sunlight. Her lip curled up over her curved teeth like unsheathed simitars.

The Rose Knight did not move a muscle. Iyesta's delicately shaped face alone was taller than a man. When Iyesta peered down, all Linsha could see were nostrils and curved teeth. She stared patiently up at the huge dragon's eye and waited.

Iyesta gave a snort that nearly blew Linsha off her feet. "You are right, Lady Knight. Excuse my impatience. This morning has been . . . long. My friends are missing, and we cannot locate them."

"How long have they been gone?" asked Linsha.

"They were here yesterday. Dart was sent on an errand for me. The other two left suddenly last night with no explanation. We do not know what to make of it."

Three missing brass dragons. If it had been any other metallic in Iyesta's realm, Linsha would not have given it a second thought. None of the metallics who lived under Iyesta's care were bound to her by anything more than respect and loyalty. They came and went as they pleased. Except for the triplets. Three parts of a whole, they were completely devoted to Iyesta and to each other. One or more attended her at the palace all the time. That they should leave and not return without some message did not bode well.

"Do you wish me to return later?" The words were barely said when a small shadow swept over the courtyard and Linsha looked up to see Varia glide in to land on Iyesta's folded wing. The owl had no fear where this dragon was concerned.

"We are going to speak to Thunder," Iyesta replied, a deep rumble of anger in her chest. "You are still in uniform. Come with us. We can talk on the way."

Linsha felt her mouth drop open. *Ride* a dragon? To speak to a blue? This was an opportunity too good to miss.

"Who will carry me?"

"I will."

Without giving herself time to change her mind, Linsha hurried to the escort and gave them orders to return to the Citadel. The half-elf agreed to keep Sandhawk until her return.

Iyesta crouched to the ground, dropped her shoulder, and stretched out her taloned forefoot so Linsha could climb onto her back.

Since the climb was a high one over the brass's slippery scales and Linsha did not want to show too much delight and enthusiastic scrambling, she clambered up the dragon's shoulder with as much decorum and care as she could muster. The dragon's wing joints and the base of her neck were massive, and it was all Linsha could do to spread her legs over the curve of the dragon's shoulders to find some sort of seat. When she was finally situated on Iyesta's back, she flashed a quick grin at Varia and settled the owl against her stomach. Both of them took a firm grip of the dragon's heavy neck ridges.

Iyesta launched herself into the air with a fierce thrust of her hindlegs, nearly snapping Linsha's neck, and spread her massive wings into the wind. The gold and silver dragons swiftly followed her into the sky. Their wings beat hard to lift them above the turbulence of warming morning air into the cooler, calmer heights. Once they reached a comfortable elevation, all three dragons leveled out and veered northwest toward the desert wastelands of Thunder's realm.

flight to Thunder's Realm

5

Linsha sat lost in delight as the dragon soared on amber colored wings. All her senses strained, she sought to catch every sensation of that glorious flight. The feel of the cold wind on her skin, the sharp smell of dragon mingled with the dry, slightly spiced scents of the desert, the sound of Iyesta's wings beating on the powerful wind and the creak of her wing bones; the vast colors of reds and browns and pale greens passing by below and the cerulean blue arching overhead.

It was some time before Linsha realized she was hearing another small sound, a faint humming noise that sounded like a cross between a chortle and a buzz. She tilted her head to look down at Varia. The owl was pressed close to the shelter of her body where the wind would not tear her away, and the faint noise emanated from her throat. Linsha realized the small bird was purring in delight. How many birds flew this fast in their lifetimes?

She glanced down to the land far below and saw they had left all pretense of grasslands behind and were over the barren lands of the Plains of Dust. Until the arrival of the great Overlords, Sable and Beryl, the entire expanse rolling lands of the Plains were a tundra-like, desert waste land, bitterly cold in the winter and warm only during the short mild summers. However, when the Overlords arrived and began using their vast powers to change the land and its climatics to their will, climates were affected in other areas as well. The harsh conditions of the Plains of Dust were tempered by the warmer winds off the hot Bay of Balifor, the spread of Sable's vast swamp to the east, and forestation of Beryl's realm to the west. The edges of the plains turned to savannahs and grasslands, particularly in Iyesta's realm east of the Torath River. The center of the plains, though, remained barren, rocky and arid.

The heart of the Plains lay below the flying dragons like a vast rumpled reddish carpet worn by the tides of endless weather and shaped by the ceaseless wind. Linsha looked down, wondering how any dragon could tolerate the bleak, lifeless expanse of that desert. Yet one dragon did. Thunder kept a jealous vigil over his empty realm and discouraged all but the brave and foolhardy from wandering into his territory. The few daring merchants or barbarians who could survive the crossing of the the blue's domain usually found greater rewards in Iyesta's realm. The foolhardy who wandered into the desert never wandered out.

Linsha asked a question she should have thought of sooner. "Iyesta," she called loudly, "why are you going to see Thunder? Do you think he had anything to do with the disappearance of the three young ones?"

The dragon took so long to answer, Linsha wondered if she hadn't heard the question over the rush of the wind. She considered repeating her query when the brass tipped her head around and said, "I sent Dart on a reconnaissance flight over Thunder's territory to look for something. I've heard rumors. . . ."

Linsha felt a chill that had nothing to do with the wind. "Rumors of what?"

"Just hints. Bits and pieces of news. Rumors of something that may be only Thunder's wishful thinking."

"What?"

"I have heard that Thunder has a new general. That he is raising an army. That he plans to expand his realm."

"He is always planning to expand his realm. But he lives in mortal terror of you and Beryl and Malys. He is too frightened to make a move so aggressive."

"So I believe. But I wanted to check. A traveler told me of seeing men and ogres gathering near Thunder's lair. I fear he may be trying to build an army, so I sent Dart to look. He should have been back last night."

The worry was so palpable in the dragon's voice that Linsha felt it like a blow to her heart. The chill in her thoughts turned to ice.

"Do you think Thunder may have captured Dart and the others and holds them in the hope of trapping you?"

"Of course. That is why Chayne and Ringg are with me. Thunder would not dare take on the three of us. No, I do not wish a fight with Thunder this day. I only want to talk and observe."

Considering that she was the only human in the group, Linsha was relieved to hear that.

"Why did you send a summons for me last night? Did you plan then to go to see Thunder?"

"I did not decide until this morning," Iyesta called back. "No, I have received news from Sanction that I thought you'd like to hear."

49

Linsha leaned forward, her eyes squinting into the wind. "Crucible?"

"He sent a message. He sends his regrets. He cannot leave Sanction at this time because the Solamnics have a plan they're about to try. He did not say what this plan is, but he wants to observe the results."

"Oh." Linsha tried to quell a pang of unexpected disappointment. She knew it was chancy to invite the big bronze to Mirage for the Midyear Festival, but she had not seen him in some time and Iyesta had given her enthusiastic support.

"He also said," the brass added, "that Lord Bight sends his greetings to you."

There it was again, that odd note in Iyesta's voice that sounded like she was trying not to laugh. It crept into her tone everytime she mentioned Lord Bight. Did she find Hogan Bight that humorous?

Varia chuckled, too.

"All right," said Linsha. "What is it? What do you find so funny? I like Lord Bight, arrogance and all."

Iyesta said soothingly, "So do I, Lady Knight. He is a man of many talents."

The owl said nothing but clamped her beak shut and turned her eyes away from Linsha's face.

"There!" Chayne trumpeted. "The blue's lair is there!"

There were no clouds in the sky to obstruct their vision or to hide their arrival. They could clearly see the high, jagged ridge of hills that thrust up from the rolling landscape where Stenndunuus, or Thunder, made his lair. A wide, open flatland spread out from its base for nearly half a mile before falling away into eroded hills and dry gullies.

"What are those?" Linsha asked, staring down at clusters of indistinct figures she could see on the ground far below. The tiny figures seemed to be scrambling out of sight into caves and fissures in the ridge like a colony of ants suddenly disturbed. "I thought Thunder's land was virtually depopulated."

"It was," Iyesta said, disapproval obvious in her tone.

Gold, silver, and brass spiralled down to the ridge. Iyesta often made visits to talk to Thunder and used her naturally gregarious and pushy nature to keep him on edge. During their talks—that is Iyesta talked endlessly while Thunder stamped and growled and hurled insults—she would spread rumors and drop bits of information guaranteed to lead him into useless fits of rage or panic. He was terrified of the larger dragonlords and bitterly envious of their power. Iyesta took ruthless advantage of his fear and played on his desires and weaknesses to insure he stayed on his side of the Torath River.

A roar of fury burst from the ridge and Thunder exploded out of his cave. Winging furiously, he rose up to meet his three visitors, his anger crackling around his muzzle in small bursts of electric fire. Dragonfear, an overwhelming sense of awe and terror, radiated from him like heat waves. Linsha felt the fear hit her harder than a physical blow. Her head reeled and her hands shook. She sank down over Iyesta's neck ridges, almost frozen with terror.

For one horrifed moment Linsha feared his anger would get the best of his common sense and he would use his lightning against them, but Iyesta, Chayne, and Ringg floated down past him and landed on the flattened space on the ridge top.

A muffled squawk came from under Linsha's chest. She suddenly realized she was crushing Varia against the brass's scales. She forced herself to sit upright and focus her attention on the owl and the brass dragon beneath her. With something else to concentrate on, she drove away most of the effects of the dragonfear. But her heart continued to pound like a drum.

Linsha threw a quick look over the edge of the ridge and saw that the flatland below was totally empty. Nothing moved on its flat surface. Not a figure of any sort could be seen.

"Iyesta, you worthless worm!" the blue bellowed as he swept over their heads. "Take your tarnished, dung-eating slugs and get out of here. This is my lair, my realm!"

His hideous horned face swiveled around to watch them while he landed on the only space left, directly in front of the patiently waiting brass.

Like a cat, Iyesta crouched on her belly, crossed her front legs, and made herself comfortable. Linsha and Varia stayed silently in their places, hoping to appear to be part of the dragon. "It is a pleasure to see you, too, Stenndunuus," Iyesta said.

True to his name, Stenndunuus pounded the rocky ground with his taloned feet. He was nearly as big as Iyesta, but with a shorter tail and a stouter body, and his massive weight made the ground shudder. He spread his leathery blue wings in a posture of dominance and hissed. "I said be gone. I do not wish to waste my time bandying words with the likes of you."

Iyesta laughed, a gentle pleasant sound that reminded Linsha of an adult chuckling at the antics of a recalcitrant child. "That is all right, Stenndunuus. We will not stay long. We were just flying by and thought we'd say hello. Perhaps you would like to hear the latest news."

"No!" screeched Thunder, his dark eyes blazing with fury. "Go away! How many times do I have to say it?"

"Thunder acts as if he's hiding something and just got caught," Linsha whispered to Varia.

"He is," the owl told her softly. "I can see him radiating guilt and worry like a heated ingot. He is up to something."

"Do you happen to have something to eat?" asked the brass. "We are quite hungry from our journey."

Thunder trembled all over. Smoke leaked from his nostrils.

"No? Oh, well." Iyesta shuddered delicately. "Goodness, it is chilly here today. Are you still having problems with those pesky whites to the south, Cryonisis and Frisindia? Their Icewall must be quite a nuisance to a heat-loving blue like you. You know, if you asked Sable, maybe she could help you . . ." She went on at length discussing the other dragonlords and their latest activities until Thunder was nearly pop-eyed with rage and impatience. He stamped about in the narrow space rumbling threats and insults until he raised quite a dust cloud. Still Iyesta chatted on amiably as if she were carrying on a conversation with a dearest friend.

Linsha wondered how much longer Thunder would bluster before he erupted.

At last Iyesta decided she had toyed with him enough. She rose to her feet, stretching her legs and rustling her wings. With suddenness of a pouncing cat, she sprang forward, crowding him to the very edge of the ridgetop where the rock dropped away into a sheer cliff. Her large head pushed close to his, and her voice took on an edge of steel.

"Before we go, I want to ask you one question. Do not mislead me. A young brass in my favor wandered close to your realm by mistake. Two of his siblings came to look for him. They are missing. Do you know where they are?"

A snarl hissed from Thunder's ugly snout. "No. And they'd better not come near me, or I will shred their scales from their worthless bodies."

Iyesta glared down at him, her curved teeth inches from his neck. "If you have lied to me, I will kill you."

In this close proximity to the big blue, Linsha could look at his reptilian face and see the malevolence burning behind his fear. His ears were flat against his head, and his lips were curled back in a silent snarl. His eyes flicked once toward her, acknowledged her presence, and added her to the collective hate that burned in his mind like acid. The dragonfear beat at her again until she wanted to shriek. She was a mere human, and she had seen him cowed before the big brass. Linsha knew he would have seared her with lightning if she had not been escorted by three dragons.

Iyesta sat back on her haunches and hid her anger behind a benign expression. "It has been good to see you again, Stenndunuus. We must have another little chat soon."

She sprang forward, spread her wings, and soared into the sky. The gold and silver followed, and in less than a minute, all three were airborn. They did not immediately turn east but soared north at a leisurely pace until Thunder's ridge was long out of sight. Only then did Iyesta veer toward her realm.

All at once she shook herself as if to rid her body of some evil dust or debris. "He's lying!" she bellowed. "I could see it all over him. His aura was shot with streaks of bright yellow!"

The only answer she received was a long-drawn cry dwindling beneath her. She realized abruptly her shudder had been a mistake, for her rider, without straps or harness, had been shaken loose. "Chayne!" Iyesta shouted.

Swifter than an eagle, the smaller silver male spotted the falling Knight and dove after her. The woman was curled in a ball and falling fast, yet he snagged her jacket with his forefoot and carried her up to place her gently back on Iyesta's broad shoulders.

Only when her feet touched the brass's body and Linsha was sure of her seat again did she uncurl her arms from around the owl. The woman and owl looked at one another with huge eyes.

"Thank you," Varia hooted gratefully.

Linsha smoothed a few ruffled feathers back in place. Staying curled around the owl— and not shrieking in terror—had been one of the hardest things she had ever done. She feared if she had released the bird at that speed, the force of the wind could have snapped Varia's wings. Besides, keeping her body curved protectively around the owl and her eyes screwed shut had helped keep her mind off the fact that they were plunging to the ground. Perhaps this flight hadn't been such a good idea after all.

Iyesta curled her head around, her face contrite. "I am very sorry. I did not mean to do that."

Linsha took several deep breaths and managed a shaky smile. "I know. My thanks to Chayne." She breathed another lungful of cold air and tried to still her pounding heart. "So tell me again why you wanted to bring me? What did you hope to accomplish?"

In spite of her effort to be calm and reasonable, the words came out sounding peevish.

"I know now Stenndunuus is gathering an army of sorts. I know he knows something about Dart, and I think he has done something to the young brasses. Yet I can prove nothing. If I move against him, I could upset

Sable or Beryl—or worse, Malys." She shook her head, this time being very careful not to unseat her wind-tousled rider. "Now you also know. You saw the soldiers on the ground. You can warn your Knights and, if you will when we return to the Missing City, tell the Legion."

"Sir Remmik will not cooperate." It was a statement of fact.

Iyesta knew the Solamnic officer and did not argue. "Sir Morrec will. Bring him to me when he returns. I will hold a council. My militia must go on alert. We must plan how to deal with this new problem."

"What about Dart and his brothers?"

Iyesta turned her head to the front, but the wind blew her words back to Linsha. "We will keep looking, but I fear they are dead."

Thunder watched the bright shapes in the sky until they dwindled to the north and disappeared, then he vented his rage on the ridgetop. He stamped and pounded and tore great chunks of earth and rock from the ground. His lightning breath seared across the ridge in blast after blast of white-hot fire. Clouds of dust and steam gathered around him until anyone looking up at his lair from below would have thought a thunderstorm had suddenly blown in.

When at last he calmed down and the last echoes of his thundering roars rolled across the desert and the lightning ceased to scorch the ground, a cautious head poked out of entrance to Thunder's cave.

"Your lordship," a wary voice called.

Panting, Thunder turned around and sprawled on the torn ground, facing the east. "You may come out," he growled. "I won't sear you."

A man-like figure, tall, dark-haired, and well-muscled walked from the cave and bowed low before the dragon. Blue tattoos covered his bare upper body, and his ears were pointed like an elf's. "My lord, what do you wish to do now? I am certain the metal dragons saw us."

"Of course they did. Those blasted wyrms can see a steel on the ground from five hundred feet up. Your sentinals failed in their duty, Gathnor."

"I will have them punished, my lord."

"You will have them used for target practice. I thought your people were better trained than that."

The tall officer's face reddened in anger. The metallic dragons had flown swiftly and with the morning sun behind them. No one but another dragon could have seen them sooner. But he wisely held his tongue.

Thunder glared eastward. "Send word to the general. Tell him to prepare his troops. Iyesta is too well informed. We will have to move quickly."

"Yes, lord. It shall be as you say."

Yes, Thunder thought, it shall be as I say. His power was growing—in ways Iyesta could not imagine. Soon, he would be free to move against her. Her minions would be slaughtered. She would die in hideous pain and despair, and then he would claim her fertile river valleys, her grasslands rich with fat cattle, her villages, and her city. Everything of hers would be his, and he would grow fat on the bodies of the dead. Foremost among those to die, he decided, would be the Solamnic Knights. They were a blight on the world. Especially that woman on Iyesta's back, wearing the blue and silver uniform of the Knighthood. That woman had seen him retreat before the brass; she had recognized his fear. With those short reddish curls and the lean build, she would not be hard to spot again. He would find her and destroy her in some fitting manner.

Meanwhile, there was much to do. The bodies of those young brasses had to be disposed of, his army had to be equipped and prepared to march, his own preparations had to continue. He sprang to his feet and soared off the cliff, his blue scales gleaming azure in the sun. Not much longer now. If all went well, not even Malys would care to dispute his ascendency over the Plains.

Into the Labyrinth

6

Linsha was very quiet when the three dragons returned to the Missing City. The effects of the dragonfear and the surge of terror during her fall had worn off, leaving her drained and exhausted. She did not notice at first that the silver and gold dragons veered away toward the brass's lair, leaving Iyesta alone to fly along the northern boundary of the ruined city.

"Why does she go this way?" Varia's soft, raspy voice prodded Linsha back to the moment. She started out of a half doze and stifled a huge yawn. She glanced down and saw the spectral images of the city away to her right. Farther ahead afternoon sunlight sparkled on the waters of the southern Courrain Ocean. To her left the semi-arid grasslands tumbled and twisted, thrust up and down, and surged away on its endless journey to the northern horizon.

Iyesta spoke before Linsha could ask. "I want to take you someplace, Rose Knight, to show you something that few know about. Normally, I would not reveal this to any human, but I have learned much good about you this past year, and I have heard others praise your sense of justice and your courage. I think I can entrust this secret to you."

"Why?"

"I would like another to know about this. Circumstances change. Accidents happen. Wars begin. There may come a time when I need your help."

Linsha tilted her chin up. She did not need further justification. Iyesta was her friend and had always treated her with respect and consideration. "I give you my word as a Solamnic Knight that I will keep your secret safe."

"Not as a Solamnic," Iyesta demanded. "I want your word of honor. It is stronger and more binding than your vows of Knighthood."

Linsha opened her mouth to argue then closed it. Memories of Sanction flitted through her mind and of weeks spent in a Solamnic prison. "On my honor," she promised.

Iyesta dipped her wings and curved down over the city. She glided back to the west somewhat until her shadow passed over the empty, abandoned remnants of the outerlying ruins. For some unknown reason the images of Gal Tra'kalas did not extend this far out, leaving the verge of ruins to sink forgotten back into the dust.

Linsha recognized the foundations of the scattered outbuildings where she had run afoul of Leonidas and his crossbow. There was no sign of the centaurs, nor any indication of any patrol, guard, traveler, or wandering undesirable. Out here beyond the habitation of the city dwellers and the insubstantial images of the Missing City, the landscape looked bleak, forlorn, and empty.

A broad open space appeared beneath the big

dragon, and she came to land, furled her wings, and dipped her shoulder so Linsha could slide off. Varia flew down, dipping and hooting her thanks.

"One moment," said Iyesta. "This will be easier."

Linsha backed away to give the dragon some room. Although she had seen this a few times, the transformation never ceased to amaze her.

Iyesta folded her wings tightly against her body, curled her tail around her feet, and pulled her head in close. Closing her eyes, she stilled and focused her mind inward. She hummed a few nameless notes—which Linsha knew was not part of the magic, it just seemed to be the dragon's way of counting the seconds—then, a dazzling haze enveloped Iyesta from nose to tail. The haze shimmered and coruscated with brilliant sparkles of fiery yellow, gold, amber, and orange—the colors of the fire that smelt brass.

Linsha shielded her eyes and watched through the shelter of her fingers. The haze brightened then shrank, apparently taking the dragon with it. Brighter and smaller it became until it hovered in front of Linsha in a vaguely human-sized glow of sun-bright light. She had to screw her eyes shut against the searing radiance, then in a snap the light vanished. Linsha blinked, opened her eyes, and saw a woman standing in the dragon's place.

Linsha smiled. The woman, smiling in return, raised a hand and tilted sideways as if she had lost her sense of balance. Linsha hurried to her and helped her sit down on a nearby lump of rock.

Iyesta's human face lit in another bright smile that beamed from her full mouth, danced in her huge topaz colored eyes, and colored her golden brown skin with a pink hue. Her face was one of the most expressionable Linsha had ever seen on a human or anyone else, as if all the exhuberant emotions felt by the big dragon would not be contained and projected from her mobile features with blithe delight.

"The world always looks so different from down here." Iyesta laughed. "I don't have time to do this often enough to get used to two little legs and an upright body."

The owl, who had been watching the shapechanging from the air, came to a fluttering landing on Iyesta's knee. She stared up into the woman's face and cooed her approval. "Finally, I get to see all of you up close instead of bits of you."

"Small creature, you are so soft." Iyesta brushed her fingers over Varia's head, tickling the owl on the back of the neck and rubbing her palm over the owl's russet back feathers. "Tactile sensations are something we dragons do not get to enjoy when we assume our true shape."

Linsha watched them both. Varia's "ear" feathers lay flat on her head and her eyes were half closed while the woman stroked her wings and chest. She knew other metallics could shapechange like this, and she mused for just a moment about the bronze dragon, Crucible. Did he ever shapechange? She suspected he liked to change into a certain tabby-colored tomcat—bronzes had a quirky affinity for small furry animals. But what, she wondered, would he look like if he changed into a human shape? She was about to ask Iyesta if she knew, when the dragonwoman lifted Varia to her shoulder and climbed to her feet. She took a few tentative steps and this time stayed upright.

"I can walk now. We should go. There is not much time left in the day, and I recall you have duty tonight."

Linsha groaned and all thought of Crucible backed away into the pantry of her mind for another day.

Night duty, and she still hadn't had any sleep. She rubbed her eyes and fought back another yawn. If she had to face any more of Commander Remmik's lectures while in a sleep-deprived state of exhaustion . . . well, she might not be responsible for her actions.

Iyesta read the look on her face and chuckled. "We will hurry. I will see that you are back to get some sleep before the sun sets. Come. This way."

With the owl riding on her shoulder, Iyesta strode toward the faded, tattered outskirts of the ancient city. As a woman, she was taller than Linsha by a head, long legged, graceful, and sinewy as a cat. Her brass scales had turned into a garment of sorts that clung to her skin like fine silk and resembled a sleeveless, long shift that hung just to her knees. She wore no jewelry, carried no weapons, and bore nothing more than the owl on her shoulder. Yet she moved with an unspoken authority and sense of self that bespoke danger to any person stupid enough to accost her.

Linsha followed curiously. She had no idea where they were going or why, but she had no fear in Iyesta's company.

Not far from where Linsha met Leonidas the night before, Iyesta came to the faint outline of a crossroad where long ago a road from the Plains converged with a road from the city. A few stone pavings still marked the workmanship of the long-dead elves. Beside the north road sat a jagged row of low pedestals that had once held up some sort of small statues. The statues were long gone—stolen, broken, or buried under centuries of dust—and only their bases remained.

"At one time, this area was a garden, I was told," Iyesta said. She swept an arm out toward an area of sand and rock just to the east of the crossroads. "There are the ruins of a large house near that rise."

Linsha had to take her word for it. There was nothing around her that hinted of a garden of any sort—just scrubby sage, tough sword plants, some skinny clumps of grass, and a few of the cold-resistant cacti that somehow survived the hard winters on this end of the Plains of Dust. Wordlessly, she walked behind Iyesta toward an outcropping of the weathered stone.

From a distance, the outcropping looked like a solid mass of rock thrust up from the soil and exposed by the ceaseless winds. When they drew closer, however, Linsha saw the mass was really a pile of shaped stones collapsed together like a stack of children's blocks and left to meld together through centuries of sun, wind, ice, and rain.

Iyesta walked up to the base of rock before turning to Linsha. "Please stay close behind me when we go down. There are several guardians in the passages. If they see you with me, they will know you are permitted to pass."

Iyesta passed Varia back to Linsha, then hooked her fingers around the edge of a large block of stone and pulled it sideways as easily as opening a door.

Linsha peered at the dark entrance and whistled appreciatively. The stone had hidden a doorway neatly carved and shaped behind the pile of rocks. A stone stairway led down into the darkness.

Linsha laughed. "Don't tell me. The Missing City has mysterious underground tunnels, too."

Iyesta half-turned, her eyes sparkling. "Of course. What old city doesn't? There are always old sewers, foundations, old storage rooms, ancient waterways, secret tunnels, or hidden labyrinths under any self-respecting city. Come and see mine."

The dragonwoman stepped aside and gestured to Linsha to move quickly into the gloom. Linsha hurried to obey. She stepped down the broad stairs, brushing her fingers on the damp, cool stone. Behind her, she heard Iyesta pull the huge stone back into place. The light dimmed, but it did not vanish completely. Cracks and small gaps in the crumbling heap of stone allowed some sunlight to leak into the stairs.

Iyesta went ahead, leading the way down. The light faded into gloom then brightened again where the steps came to an end in a large chamber. Linsha, close behind Iyesta, reached the bottom of the steps and stopped, her eyes wide with interest.

Outside, the afternoon sun had reached the right angle to find a certain crack in the old ruin that let its light into the old chamber like a buttress of pale gold energy gleaming on a standing pool of amber water.

"Centuries ago this was a well," Iyesta said. "Then someone had the idea to put a building around it and use it as a bath. Now it just collects rainwater for whatever lucky lizards can find their way in here."

Linsha saw handiwork that went into transforming the well into a bathing pool. Remnants of an old tile floor could still be seen under years of dirt, and the cracked remains of an old bench sat against a far wall. The pool itself had been shelved and shaped to provide both a shallow end and a deep end for bathers of all sizes. This would have been a delightful retreat in the heat of summer.

"Does anyone else ever come here?" she asked.

Iyesta's smile turned chilly. "It would not be wise. The creature that lurks in that pool now will not tolerate any tresspassers larger than lizards, unless they are with me." She turned away, passed the pool, and walked to the back of the chamber where another, smaller door led to another narrower set of steps.

Linsha took a long, slow look at the water. She could

see nothing obviously wrong with it. It was clear and colored amber from the minerals in the rock around it, and it did not seem to harbor anything dangerous. Just as she turned her head, though, something moved in the corner of her vision. She snapped her head around and, for a brief moment, saw a head seemingly formed by water drop back into the depths of the pool.

"What was that?"

"A water weird. She has a nasty temper, so don't try to pass her without me."

Linsha looked again but did not see the creature. A water weird! She knew a little about them from her father and grandfather. They were elementalkin and did not exist naturally on Krynn. Any water weird found in this world had been summoned by magic. As a result they tended to be irritable, homesick, and vicious. If this creature was any indication of what lay below, Linsha planned to stay very close to Iyesta.

The dragonwoman followed the second set of stairs down past an old chamber that may have once been used for storage. They passed this and continued further down, deep into the earth and rock below the ruins. The light passed away behind them while the dark pressed close. Linsha was forced to use her fingers and feet to feel her way down the long, winding staircase.

Neither Iyesta nor Varia had trouble seeing in the dark, but after the third time Linsha tripped over a broken stair, the dragonwoman remembered her human companion would need some help. Speaking a quiet word, she formed a cool, gentle flame of light that hovered over their heads and lit their way with a bluish glow.

At the bottom of the stairs, a tunnel pushed forward into the earth. Wide and spacious, it was well crafted and still in good repair even after centuries of neglect. The air was cool and smelled old to Linsha's nose, as if it had not been circulated in many years and still carried the dust motes of the First Cataclysm.

Iyesta went forward without hesitation. Linsha followed. The tunnel ran straight and true for perhaps fifty paces then branched left and right. Iyesta turned right. Almost immediately, the tunnel turned left and intersected with another tunnel. This was no simple water system or escape route. They had entered a labyrinth of passages under the city. It was a maze deliberately planned and constructed for some secret purpose. The tunnels were wide and well constructed, paved with stone and arched overhead. She tried to keep track of how they were going, but the twisted turns and numerous intersections that looked so much alike soon lost her. After a while all she could do was follow Iyesta and hope fervently that she was not left behind in this darkdrowned maze.

Although the flame helped light her way and Iyesta guided her through the labyrinth, Linsha found her hand straying to her sword time and again. The tunnels were silent and looked empty, but once or twice she sensed something move in the dark. Another time small hard feet pattered down a side tunnel just as they went by, sending tiny echoes of sound skittering through the empty spaces.

"What is down here?" she asked, but the dragonwoman simply smiled and said nothing.

They walked for what Linsha estimated was nearly an hour before Iyesta turned into a broad tunnel and gestured to Linsha to go before her. The lady knight looked ahead and saw a golden light glowing dimly on the wall at the end of the passage. The air was warmer here, and rich and moist like the air from a hot house.

67

Linsha glanced curiously at her companion then walked along the tunnel to where it turned left and opened into a huge cavern. One look into the cavern stopped her in her tracks. Varia hooted softly in appreciation.

The cavern was enormous, carved millennia ago by sea water when the coast was younger and the seas were higher. The elves had found the chamber, enlarged it, and set it in the center of a labyrinth that stretched under the streets of their fair city from one end to the other. There were no records left that told what the elves used the cavern for, but Linsha stared awestruck at what the brass dragon laid in its protective depths.

Across an expanse lay a mound of sand brought carefully down to the cavern and piled into a nest. Half buried in the sand Linsha counted eighteen dragon eggs, each mottled in browns and golds and each looking warm and healthy. On the far side of the nest, she could see the bulk of another dragon curled protectively around her side of the mound.

She started to walk in, but Iyesta held her arm and stopped her. "The guardian sleeps, and I do not wish to disturb her. Her name is Purestian. It is her duty to guard these eggs until they hatch."

"Are they yours?"

"No. They are hers. I gave her a safe place to stay—and my oath that I would protect the eggs."

"When will they hatch?"

"In around sixty years. If all goes well, my realm will be their home, and they will be as my children."

Linsha beamed. Children had never been a strong wish for her, but the pride in Iyesta's voice was infectious. She studied the cavern from the graceful curving roof to the wide sandy floor.

"Where is the light coming from?" she whispered. "And why is it so warm in here?"

"Purestian and I used spells to set glow lights in the roof. They keep the eggs warm. I come down here once in a while and renew them. Come. We must go." She walked back up the corridor.

Linsha took one last look at the gleaming eggs. She knew what an honor Iyesta had bestowed on her by showing her the nest, and she knew, too, what a responsibility that knowledge laid upon her. She stayed deep in her own thoughts as the dragon led her back to the surface of the city by another long, circuitous route.

It wasn't until they stepped out into the slanting sunlight of the late afternoon that Linsha spoke out.

"You have shown me your eggs and taken a chance that I will not reveal your secret. But what do you expect me to do?"

The dragonwoman touched a finger to Linsha's tunic where the bronze scale hung beneath the fabric. "You and Crucible and the golds and silvers in my realm are the only ones who know the eggs are there. You are also the only one who knows yet that the blue is plotting war. If something happens, I trust you to do what you can to protect the eggs. I would not ask this of another two-legs. Only you have the honor and the instincts to protect my children."

"But what if I need to get down there and find them again?" Linsha protested. "I will defend them as I would my own kin, but I need to know how to get to them."

"Crucible can take you. Or, if he is not here, you can enter through that door." She pointed to the ruinous building they had just left.

Linsha glanced around for the first time and realized they were in an overgrown section of the palace where Iyesta made her lair. A brilliant light suddenly flared beside her, and she scrambled out of the way as the brass returned to her dragon form. The dragon's shadow fell over her.

Iyesta dipped her great head and scraped her cheek over a crumbling stone lintel. A small scale as bright as polished brass fell to the ground.

"If you take this," Iyesta said, "it will help you find your way and protect you from the guardians. Don't forget to warn the Legion."

Iyesta then departed back to her lair and left Linsha standing bemused in the hot sunlight.

With care Linsha picked up the round scale. It was slightly smaller than the one Lord Bight had given her and of a brighter, more reddish tint. Pleased, she turned it over in her hands. She would find a jeweler and have this one edged with gold to match the bronze scale, and it would hang on the gold chain around her neck—a precious gift with a heartfelt obligation; an obligation she hoped fervently she would never have to fulfill.

She stretched her tired limbs and took a deep breath. The weariness she had fought off the past hours came trudging back. There were only a few hours left until she had to report for duty. In that time, she had to return to the Citadel, clean her uniform, find something to eat, and get some sleep. She would have to hurry.

Perhaps it was the heat and bright light after the hours in the cool darkness; perhaps it was her exhaustion. Whatever it was that dragged at her heels, Linsha found she could not hurry. Still deep in thought, she collected her horse and rode, slower this time, back through the busy streets of Missing City. Her mind was so rapt in other matters that she did not notice when Varia left her to seek a more congenial and comfortable place to nap.

Nor did she notice when a stooped beggar in a wide

brimmed hat fell in beside her horse. He limped alongside the ambling Sandhawk for two blocks before Linsha jerked herself out of her reverie and noticed him.

"I could have slid a blade between your ribs and been long gone," Lanther told her.

Linsha gave herself a mental shake. He was right. She needed to be more alert. "My fault," she said with a yawn. "It's too hot, and I haven't slept lately."

He regarded her critically, noting the dark circles that framed her clear green eyes and the smudges of dirt that marred the blue of her uniform. "Busy day with Iyesta?" he asked, his expression unreadable.

"She's very upset. The triplets are missing."

"Missing? How do you misplace three dragons?"

Linsha rubbed her temples with her free hand. She could feel a headache gathering momentum in the back of her head. "Iyesta believes Thunder is involved somehow."

Lanther made a rude noise. "That incompetent? She has him terrified of his own shadow. He wouldn't do anything to rouse her ire."

"Maybe not, but she took Chayne, Ringg, and me to see Thunder this morning." She glanced down to see his reaction.

The man was good, she had to admit. The surprise had already vanished behind his usual mask of imperturbability.

"What did you learn?" he asked.

She shrugged. "That Thunder is hiding something. We're not sure what, though. We saw what looked like more than a few men scurrying to get of sight. And Thunder was more tense and brash than usual."

The Legionnaire hooked his hand around her stirrup and let the horse take some of his weight off his bad leg while he walked. "Did they look numerous enough to be an army?"

"Hard to tell," said Linsha, taking care with her words. "We did not see more than a few hundred I'd guess. Of course, there is no telling how many made it out of our sight before we noticed them."

"A few hundred," he repeated. "Were there any other dragons around? Other blues? Thunder's inimical personality has hardly attracted hordes of underlings."

"No." Linsha stared into the distance. She understood where he was taking his questions. They were the same questions she had asked herself. Plainly stated, she knew there simply was not enough evidence to be certain that Thunder was plotting war or had even harmed the triplets. He might be planning to cause trouble in some petty way, but unless he had an army of thousands and the help of other dragons, he did not stand a snowball's chance in the desert of defeating Iyesta and her militia, her guards, and her companion dragons. He would be insane to attempt it.

"So what is he up to?" she said softly. "Where are the triplets?"

"Two excellent questions," said Lanther.

"And no answers." She reined Sandhawk to a halt and stared at the man without really seeing him.

He chuckled, a rare sound from him. "Go back to your castle. Get some sleep. Let the next few days take care of themselves. Thunder will not attack in the next day or two. Maybe things will look clearer after a good meal and a long sleep."

She gripped his hand briefly. "For a flea-bitten beggar, you have some good ideas. Iyesta asked me to pass on her concerns to the Legion, so please tell Falaius what I told you. Let us see what we can do to unravel this mystery."

"I will alert the Legion. We need to coordinate with the militia, too. Let me handle that."

"Into your competent hands I leave it." Grinning, she reached into her belt purse, pulled out two coins, and flipped them into his hands. "Buy yourself a bath."

With a wave, she kneed Sandhawk into a trot and turned his nose toward his stable.

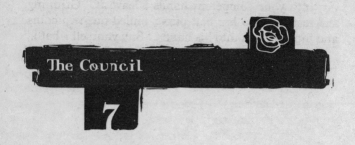

The Council

7

rue to Lanther's word, Sir Morrec and his escort, looking dusty and weary, returned late the next day from their conference with a group of exiled elves outside the Silvanesti shield. The Knights rode into the Citadel and dismounted in front of the main hall. At the top of the stairs by the door stood Sir Remmik, his hands clasped behind his back, his expression carefully arranged into a pleased welcome.

Across the yard, Linsha watched gladly as the Solamnic commander dismounted, handed his reins to a groom, and saluted the officer of the watch. The old man looked well, she thought. Of course, he usually did. For a man in his sixth decade of life, he had more energy and enthusiasm than many of the younger men under his command. While the other Knights walked stiffly around to work out the kinks of a long day's ride, Sir Morrec bounced up the stairs and greeted Sir Remmik with a hearty slap on the back.

Linsha stifled a laugh at the look that passed over the fastidious Crown Knight's face. Sir Remmik's time of sole command was over for now, thank the absent gods, and he would subside back into his normal duties and be the charming, competent organizer Sir Morrec believed him to be. The pompous dictator in his mind would retreat back into the shadows until the next time Sir Remmik found himself in command.

"Good riddance," Linsha muttered. She was more than ready for things to return to normal. Well, as normal as things could get around here. She needed to apprise Sir Morrec of the latest developments and Iyesta's request for a council.

Little had changed since yesterday—that she knew about. Iyesta had put her militia on alert, and she and the other dragons had swept the length of the realm searching for the three missing dragons. Thus far, their search had been fruitless. Lanther had brought word to Linsha that the body of the missing elder had not yet been found, but the city was peacefully about its business of preparing for the Midyear Festival in two days' time. There was nothing else suspicious happening that anyone had been able to discover. The Legion was taking Iyesta's worries seriously, of course, within cautious reason. Falaius had sent out more operatives to try to infiltrate Thunder's so-called army, but he warned Linsha not to expect news in the near future. It took time to gather information from an enemy encampment so far away.

Her odd feeling of uneasiness still lingered in the back of her mind, but it abated somewhat with the homecoming of Sir Morrec and the other Knights. Probably, she reasoned, because she knew if disaster struck, she greatly preferred the Knight Commander to be in charge than Sir Remmik. Now that he was back, he would help her put things in perspective. She thought about talking to him immediately, then changed her mind. Sir Remmik would demand his time for at least the next hour to tell him about every minute of every day that he was gone, then the Knights would want to eat. She would talk to him then, before she reported for night duty.

A messenger found Linsha before the hour had expired and asked her to attend the Knight Commander at his meal in the hall. Tidying her uniform, she made her way to the main keep to report to Sir Morrec. As she suspected, Sir Remmik sat beside him, talking ceaselessly while the man tried to eat.

Sir Morrec glanced up when she entered the hall and gave her a warm greeting. He gestured to the table laden with platters of food and to an empty chair across from him. Linsha preferred not to ruin her appetite by dining near Sir Remmik, but nevertheless she accepted the commander's invitation and sat down. She nodded coolly to the second-in-command without actually looking at his face, and then held a wine glass out for the winebearer to fill.

Sir Remmik sat back in his chair, his expression cold, and launched into a detailed description of Linsha's alleged transgressions that occurred while Sir Morrec was absent. Knowing he had planned this deliberately, Linsha ignored him and helped herself to a few small servings of the fish and vegetables that lay on platters close at hand.

Sir Morrec finally held up his hand to stem the flow of words. He watched Linsha eat her meal for a minute, then asked, "Is any of this true?"

Linsha lifted her eyes from her food and met his straightforward gaze. "Most of it. The situation in the Missing City has taken several interesting turns, and I have been trying to get a clear idea of what is going on." She decided to omit any petty or childish remarks on the subject of Sir Remmik's obssessive and shrewish demands.

"Tell me," the Knight Commander said over his glass of wine.

In less time than Sir Remmik had taken, Linsha told her commander about her suspicions, the intruder she followed, the centaurs, the reports from her contacts and the Legion, her flight to see Thunder, the missing brasses, and Iyesta's rage and concerns. The only part she did not mention was her journey through the labyrinth to see the eggs.

Sir Remmik glared at her as if he suspected she was making it all up, but Sir Morrec sat still, his long elegant features bathed in firelight, and watched her intently without interrupting her.

When she had completed her report, he asked, "What more does Iyesta plan to do about this?"

"I don't know. I have not talked to her today because she has been searching for the triplets. Yesterday, she decided to call a council of her militia, the Legion, and the Solamnics. She is only waiting for you to return."

The briefest spasm of dismay crossed the Knight's face. Although he quickly dampened it, it was there long enough for Linsha to notice. "I have just returned from a lengthy journey. I have a great deal to do. When does she wish to have this council?"

"I'm sure she would hold it now if she was available. Sir, I would not put this off. Iyesta is deeply concerned and furious. We need to plan a defense for the city, coordinate our efforts with the Legion, offer our services to the militia, and extend our efforts in learning the truth behind these rumors."

Sir Remmik could not contain himself any longer.

"Utter nonsense," he snapped. "Just because a few brass dragons decide to leave the realm and Thunder has actually managed to gather a few men long enough to masquerade as an army of sorts doesn't instantly spell disaster."

"I agree, sir," Linsha said, fighting to remain cool. "But it could spell the possiblity of disaster. I don't believe the three brasses left of their own accord, nor do I believe Iyesta will take Thunder's posturing lightly. We need to be prepared."

"We are prepared," the Crown Knight insisted. "These Knights are the best trained, best supplied fighting men on the Plains. They are magnificent. Nothing can defeat them."

"There is more to preparation than a stocked fortress and a strong Knight," Linsha said. "We cannot fight here alone. We need the Legion, the centaur patrols, the tribesmen who ride the desert, the militia who guard the city's walls. We need Iyesta."

Sir Morrec steepled his fingers. "Will it not serve for you to attend this council in my place?"

Linsha had expected this. Although she greatly admired Sir Morrec for his fearlessness, his compassion, and his open-minded attitude toward the city and the Legion of Steel, he had one weakness: a deep-seated resentment toward dragons of all colors. A survivor of the Chaos War, the Dragon Purge, and several dragon attacks, he carried an antagonism toward all things relating to dragons and would do almost anything to avoid any contact with one. He tried to control his animosity and had even developed a grudging respect for Iyesta, but he usually left most of the Solamnic dealings with the brass up to Linsha.

"Not this time, Sir Morrec. We need to show a unified face to the dragon and the city."

Reluctant though he was to face dragons, Sir Morrec understood his duty. Without further hesitation, he nodded once and helped himself to more mutton. "Of course. Make the arrangements."

Satisfied, Linsha finished her meal and hurried to relieve the duty officer. She sent a message to Iyesta's lair, notifying her of Sir Morrec's return and asking for a time for the council. By dawn she had her reply. Midafternoon. She was expected to attend.

When her duty finished after sunrise, Linsha spoke briefly with Lanther outside the stable and confirmed the Legion, too, would be in attendance. Varia told her the area was quiet and Iyesta had settled into her lair for some needed rest. Linsha retired to her own bed, content in her mind that for at least the morning she could sleep in peace.

Midafternoon lolled around hot, sultry, and redolent with dust and flies. Linsha, Sir Morrec, and an escort of six Knights rode to Iyesta's lair and arrived just as a contingent of centaurs trotted into the courtyard.

Someone called out to Linsha.

She looked over the shining hides and strong torsos and recognized the young buckskin, Leonidas. She waved a greeting to him before his stern uncle hushed him.

"Another friend of yours?" Sir Morrec asked as he dismounted.

Linsha pointed to an imaginary tear in her tunic. "The centaur with the crossbow."

His eyebrow lifted. "Indeed. You certainly make friends in odd ways."

Linsha did not comment. Her basic philosophy was one learned from her grandfather: You make friends where you can find them, because you never knew when a friend could offer invaluable aid, or even save your life.

Leonidas was not the only friend she saw in the group gathering in Iyesta's courtyard. There were several other centaurs she knew and liked, Lanther, Falaius, and three Legionnaires she had worked with since her arrival in Mirage, and various acquaintances from the city council.

A fair-haired half-elf named Mariana Brownstem she met with occasionally caught her eye and nodded. The lean half-elf wore the uniform of a militia captain and stood protectively at the edge of the crowd. She kept her eyes moving over the people and her hands close to her weapons.

Linsha wanted to mingle among the people, listen to their worries, and gather what news she could, but she knew Sir Morrec wanted his escorts together. It made a stronger impression. She watched all the faces and the way people moved their bodies. She studied the dragon's guards who stood about the courtyard, and she noted the emotions that flowed from person to person. She did not need her talent to read auras here. The tension that flowed in the courtyard was thick enough to pour over porridge. Linsha looked forward to learning what Varia overheard. The owl was already ensconced out of sight in some tree.

Fortunately, Iyesta had made arrangements to help make people comfortable. In the west end of the courtyard in the shade of three large trees, trestle tables and benches had been set up. Covered plates of sweet cakes and fruit waited beside cooled flagons of a light, fruited wine, ale, and for the strong of stomach, the Plains equivalent of the Khurish kefre sweetened with milk and honey.

As there was no sign of Iyesta and the doors of the throne room were closed, those attending the council made their way over to the tables and helped themselves while they waited for Iyesta to come. Sir Morrec and the Solamnics, looking resplendent in their blue and silver uniforms, claimed half an empty table for their own in the deepest shade and with the best view of the courtyard. They drank sparingly and ate only enough to be polite. Linsha barely touched anything.

When most of the people were seated and quietly talking among themselves, silver Pallitharkian and gold Dooiriotian appeared and took their places by the palace doors. Without fanfare, they opened the double doors together and bowed their heads as Iyesta emerged. Her shadow darkened the courtyard. In almost perfect unison, the gathered people bowed low before her.

Linsha was impressed. The great brass had obviously cleaned and polished her already beautiful scales until they dazzled with gold fire in the sun. She stood resplendent, the embodiment of power and grace and authority, and stared down the length of her snout at the people with her large gleaming eyes. If this doesn't brace up the confidence of the population of the realm, Linsha thought, nothing could.

The huge dragon took her place front of the gathering, folded her wings, and lowered her head to hear what would be said. The other two dragons took up positions beside and slightly behind her.

"Lord Mayor," said Iyesta. "Let us begin."

For the next several hours, the leaders of the civil and military orders in Mirage discussed the latest news of Thunder's perfidity and all it could mean to their city. Many people believed like Sir Remmik that the rumors of Thunder's army had been blown out of proportion and that there was really little to worry about from the blue. Sable, they said, or Malys was the greater danger. But the naysayers did not argue that the Missing City needed more preparation. They made further plans for defense, including strengthening the city walls, increasing the food supplies in the warehouses, forging more arms, and stepping up the training of new recruits in the militia. More scouts would be sent out to watch every inland approach to the city, and the centaur patrols would be doubled.

Iyesta listened to the talk and added several changes to the plans, but most of the time she merely listened, observed, and occasionally offered her approval.

Linsha said little during the long discussions. She, too, sat and watched and listened and made mental notes to continue further discussions with specific people over the next couple of days. There were questions she wanted to ask that she knew would not be answered before a large group and suggestions that she could make more tactfully over a mince pie and a beer at the nearest tavern. To be honest, it was a relief to see other people finally shared her feelings of apprehension. Maybe now that the city was alert, things could get done and her unsettling intuitions would settle down and go away.

She poured herself another drink and tried not to sigh too loudly. The air was still and stiflingly hot under the trees. It gave her a headache that pounded behind her eyes and threatened to split her skull with increasing pressure. She rested her head in her hands and rubbed her temples, but nothing seemed to help. After several hours of talk, she stopped listening and turned her attention inward to the pain. All she wanted to do was go back to the Citadel, take some feverfew, and go to sleep.

The sun was an hour from sunset when Iyesta brought an end to the council. Weary, hot, and thankful it was over, the humans, centaurs, elves, and half-elves made their farewells to the brass and went their separate ways. Most were satisfied at the progress that had been made. All they needed was time and effort to complete the plans.

Sir Morrec, gritting his teeth, stayed until most of the guests were gone then went to Iyesta to pay his respects. The big dragon accepted his remarks gravely, and her red-gold eye stared at him unblinking. Iyesta knew how Sir Morrec felt about dragons, but she liked the man nonetheless.

After the Solamnics left Iyesta's lair they rode without speaking. Linsha and Sir Morrec led two columns. The first part of their way passed through ruinous areas of the old city left deliberately unsettled by order of Iyesta. The phantom images of Gal Tra'kalas hovered around them, showing pleasant homes, flowering gardens, and elves preparing for evening.

Linsha watched the scenes around her for a little while, hoping the idyll peace would ease her headache, but it seemed to only grow worse. She felt breathless as if the air were thick and heavy and too difficult to breath. She had to force herself to sit straight in the saddle and not slump over her horse's neck. The stillness of the evening around them became oppressive. The horses' hooves echoed with an uncanny sound through the ruined streets.

A sudden gust of wind swept around them causing Sandhawk to tremble and toss his head. Linsha calmed the horse with her hands and knees, but her eyes stared in surprise at the ghostly scenes around her. The gust of wind that startled her horse had stirred the phantom trees and whipped up swirls of ghostly dust and debris in the vision of the elves' old city. That wasn't supposed to happen that she knew of. The old familiar feeling of apprehension suddenly bit her.

Another gust blew over them, a sucking wind from the east that stirred the sunken heat and sent dust devils dancing. In Gal Tra'kalas, a young elf maid ran by with her hand clutched to her head scarf and her eyes wide with dismay. A phantom dog dashed along the street, barking furiously. Other figures could be seen hurrying for shelter, closing windows, and rushing children under shelter.

"My lord," Linsha heard one of the Knights call out. "You should see this."

As one, the group reined to halt and followed the direction indicated by the Knight's hand. They looked up beyond the ruins, beyond the images of the Missing City, to the western sky where the sun sat like a fiery egg on the edge of what looked like a sullen black mountain range of jagged, soaring peaks. On the nearly flat and treeless grasslands around Mirage, the phenomenon was startling.

"Kiri-Jolith's glory!" one Knight exclaimed. "What is that?"

"Maybe it's a dust storm," said another.

"An eruption of volcanoes?" ventured a third.

"Could Thunder be doing that?"

After the long meeting they had just endured, the blue dragon was close on everyone's mind, but Linsha, eyeing the odd-looking formations, doubted he was involved. For one thing, the clouds seemed to be expanding. Already the gray-black mass stretched from north to south and billowed upward at a frightening rate.

Worried, she said, "Sir Morrec, I don't think Thunder has the power to do something like that, and I don't believe that is a dust storm either."

The Knight Commander squinted hard at the sky. "It reminds me of the thunderstorms we've seen sweep across the plains . . . but I've never seen one quite like that."

Around the riders the light dimmed and turned an odd gray-green color as the sun, already on its descent, was overwhelmed by the towering banks of cloud. The Knights watched the seething mass approach with frightening speed. "Sir," said Linsha. "We should return to Iyesta's lair. That storm looks ferocious."

The old Knight waved aside her warning. "I agree we should seek shelter, but at dusk storms always look worse than they really are. We'll ride on to the Citadel. We should have time to reach it." He raised his hand and waved on the squad before she could protest. They moved out at a quick trot.

Dismayed, Linsha urged Sandhawk on. The chestnut snorted nervously and balked, his eyes rolling in fear, then he lunged forward. It took all of Linsha's strength to keep the horse from bolting.

The other Knights' horses were terrified, too. Their heads tucked down, they fought to snatch their bits and escape from the coming storm. They pawed the ground in their agitation, and their ears lay flat on their heads.

The wind abruptly veered from the west, and the earlier gusts strengthened to a cold, hard gale that whipped grit and dust into the Knights' faces and threatened to tear them from their saddles. The sky darkened to black. By unspoken consent the squad sped into a canter in spite of the risk of the rough road and the panicky horses.

Linsha looked up once and saw the churning, roiling mass of clouds had almost overtaken them. She peered around desperately for some place where they could seek cover, but they were still in an empty area of the ruinous city. Only ghostly buildings rose around them in mocking illusions of shelter. Strangely enough, she could see the coming storm was still affecting that city as well. Its streets were being whipped by the same wind and the inhabitants ran for cover.

"Sir!" Linsha yelled to Sir Morrec. "We need shelter now! We won't make it to the Citadel."

To add emphasis to her plea, a blinding bolt of lightning exploded across the sky followed two seconds later by a crash of thunder that made the ground tremble.

The horses reared and screamed in terror. Most of the Knights fought to stay mounted. One threw up his arms and crashed to the ground where he lay motionless on his back.

Over the milling chaos of frantic horses and scared men, the lightning streamed again across the sky. In that split second moment of time, Linsha happened to be looking toward the fallen Knight when the electric white light filled her entire vision.

She blinked and the light was gone, but for that second she saw something long and thin protruding from the man's chest. She forced Sandhawk to a trembling standstill and tried to look for the other Knights. The fallen Knight needed help, but she could see little in the increasing blackness that surrounded them.

A horse neighed to her right, and she could hear cursing and the scrape of horses' iron shoes on stone. In the wail of the wind it was hard to hear anything. Was that a scream or just an effect of the wind?

Just then another furious bolt seared down and struck the ground close by with a jarring impact. The concussion slammed her off her horse. Sandhawk, freed of her weight, galloped away in hysterical terror.

Linsha lay flat on her back, her body one large ache and her lungs heaving to pull in some air. Somewhere close by, she heard more voices and the frantic cries of horses. Something didn't seem right. Most of the voices were frightened, surprised, and full of panic. Others sounded fierce, and one screamed something in a language she did not understand. Her aching head reeled. How many people were out there?

She staggered to her feet and fumbled for the short sword she wore at her side. "Sir Morrec!" she cried into the howling wind.

"To me!" came a reply from her right.

Another sudden blast of lightning broke through the clouds, and in the glare of the stark light, Linsha saw her fellow Knights—mostly now on foot—locked in struggle with a strange foe. They were being attacked by tall, muscular, human-looking warriors—warriors Linsha had never seen in the Missing City. The illumination burned out and thunder rocked the sky.

Linsha's shaking hands finally found a grip on her sword and wrenched it free. She had not seen Sir Morrec in that glimpse of fighting men, but he had to be close by. She had heard his voice.

All at once, the tempest broke. With a rapidity that stunned the senses, the world became a driving, battering vertical wall of rain and stinging sleet. Linsha was drenched in an instant. The lightning now came thick and fast followed by such thunderclaps the whole sky shook with the rolling roar.

Linsha fought her way toward her companions. Although the shouts and cries had lessened, she knew the men were close by. She just had to find them. To her dismay, the solid curtains of rain made that very difficult. She could see almost nothing, even when the lightning lit the landscape again. Rainwater filled her eyes and her mouth. The sleet stung her skin. The wind pummeled her like the fists of the gods and tried to drive her to her knees. She ducked her head against the deluge and pushed forward.

Without warning, her foot caught on a heap of rubble and she fell sprawling on the muddy ground. The impact knocked her sword out of her hand and sent it sliding into the impenetrable gloom.

"Linsha!" a voice cried in despair.

"My lord!" she screamed.

A black figure, indistinct in the violent darkness lurched toward her. A sheet of lightning whipped through the clouds overhead and in its instant light, Linsha saw the gleam of a sword in the figure's hand. With desperate strength, Linsha hauled herself to her hands and knees and scrabbled in the mud for her sword. Her trembling fingers found nothing but gravel and muck.

She heard a noise above the wind and rain that sounded something like a boot scraping over stone, and she instinctively rolled to her left. A sword blade whistled by her shoulder, burying its tip in the ground.

Another voice shouted angrily out of the black storm. Linsha could not understand the words and yet the voice sounded vaguely familiar in its tone and depth. She struggled to her feet, tilted her head against the lashing rain, and drew her dagger. It felt small in her hand, but it was better than nothing.

She could not see the dark figure—in fact, without the lightning she could not see more than two feet in any direction.

Movement caught her eye. A swift shape flitted through her vision and out again, hidden by the torrents of rain. She twisted toward it, her hand clenched around her dagger. Lightning exploded in ropes of fire over the Missing City, and in the sudden incandescence, Linsha saw her enemy not more than four feet away from her, its sword tip lowered. She grimaced in the painful light and tried to wipe the rain out of her eyes. It seemed to her the figure raised its sword and came at her. With her lips pulled back in a silent grimace of fury, she lunged forward, her dagger raised to attack. Her body swerved past the man's guard and her blade sank into his chest. She heard a grunt of pain and felt him sag beneath her.

Too late she saw on the edge of her vision a second shape, blacker than night, spring at her. Pain exploded in her head and face. Her legs lost all control, and she staggered sideways. She tripped over something bulky and collapsed in a heap on the cold, unyielding ground. Rain pounded on her body. Her thoughts reeled in a jumble of images and disjointed thoughts.

In the last fleeting moments of consciousness, she heard voices again, this time speaking directly above her head. They seemed to be arguing in some language Linsha had never heard. They would kill her; the small thought emerged through the fog of pain in her brain.

But they did not. One speaker stamped away, his feet squashing the rain-soaked earth. The second speaker paused a moment, then reached over her and pulled Linsha's dagger out of her nerveless fingers. She tried to move, to speak, to indicate in some way that she resented this intrusion but could not. A heavy lassitude settled over her. Her muscles could not even tense as she waited for the pain of the dagger to slice into her flesh.

Instead, the figure raised her arm and dropped it gently over her face as if to shield her features from the pounding rain. Through the haze of pain that crept through her head, she felt a hand brush her skin. The fingers felt cold and hard as if encased in steel. She felt a pressure on her temple, then a color she had never seen before exploded in her head like a lightning blast, and she was gone, out of it all.

The storm closed down around her.

Midsummer's Day

8

She woke to more voices. Several spoke from above and around her—strong, disembodied voices that spoke Common and seemed terribly upset about something.

"There they are! Over here!"

"Oh, bloody Chaos, all of them?"

"Iyesta will have our guts for bow strings."

"We couldn't help that storm last night. The whole city is in a shambles."

"It wasn't a storm that killed them."

Killed them? Linsha wondered. Killed who? But curiosity wasn't enough to pull her fully awake.

"What do we do, Caphiathus?"

"Do not touch them. Leave them here for now. Azurale, gallop to the Citadel to tell their commander to bring litters. He will want to see this. You, Leonidas, stay here to guard the bodies until the Solamnics come."

"What are you going to do?"

There was a heavy intake of breath. "Tell Iyesta."

Like a frog in a pond that has risen for a quick look,

Linsha's consciousness slid slowly back under the depths. The voices went on around her unheeded.

Some time later a louder, more persistent noise finally penetrated the heavy gloom in Linsha's mind. Hooves, most of them shod with iron, clattered up the road in a rapid staccato that cut through the bonds of her unconscious sleep. She woke slowly, one layer of thought at a time, while the sounds around her increased and became more demanding.

Horses pounded around her and wagon wheels groaned to a stop somewhere close by. Voices intruded into her awareness.

"They're over here, sir," she heard someone call.

Leonidas. The name swam out of the depths. She knew him. She tried to open her eyes, but a weight pressed down on her face.

"Holy gods," said a voice close by in a cool tone that belied the emotion of the words.

Another name surfaced from the muddy waters of her mind—Remmik.

"Are they all here? What happened? What evidence have you found?" The questions shot out like arrows, fast and pointed.

Linsha felt irritation hit her like a bucket of cold water. The unfeeling bastard. There were dead around somewhere. How dare he use that tone. The curiosity that failed to rise inside her before came welling up, bringing her mind awake and filling her muscles like a tonic. She realized the weight on her face was her own arm. It felt as unwieldy as a log, but she managed to pull it off her eyes.

"She moved!" Leonidas yelled. "Sir Remmik, she's still alive!"

Hooves clopped on the ground by her head and gentle hands lifted her arm off her face. She stirred and tried to open both eyes. Only one would open, and it was too much. Bright morning sun bore into her vision; pain hammered into her head. The ground rocked underneath her, and nausea spread through her belly. She curled into a ball and moaned.

"Is she injured? Is she bleeding?" she heard Sir Remmik demand to know in a tone that was more irritated than solicitous.

Is she dead? Is she rotting? Linsha's thoughts added perversely. Never had she hated that man so much.

"She has a head injury," Leonidas replied. "I can't tell if she's wounded anywhere else."

"Then get her away from Sir Morrec's body. And leave that dagger. I want it for evidence."

Through her misery, the words penetrated her mind like a knife. Sir Morrec's body? Was *he* dead? And what dagger? She tried to remember what happened before her head exploded, but it was so hazy all she could recall was rain and darkness and thunder.

Several people put their hands under her head, shoulders, and knees and carried her to a patch of shade at the side of a tumbled wall. A cloak was laid down for her, and she was left to recover her senses while the new arrivals set to work. Like an appointed guardian, Leonidas brought her water and placed himself beside her.

Linsha lay still and mustered her strength. Slowly she turned her mind away from the light and the noise and concentrated on the keening throb in her head. She did not have enough strength or mystic talent to heal the damage to her skull completely, but she could use the magic power within her to ease the pain and settle the sickening queasiness and the lightheaded dizziness of shock.

The pain gradually receded, and as it loosened its iron grip on her mind, a few memories slowly filtered into place. She now knew who she was and where she was. Only the details of the night in the storm remained maddeningly vague.

Linsha slowly sat up, grunting with pain. She could not yet open one eye, but now her questing fingers found a gash and a massive swelling above her right eye. Blood caked over her eyelid and the side of her face. She sighed and slumped on the cloak, too weak to try to clean her face. Her clothes were wet and clammy. Her auburn curls lay flat, plastered down by blood and mud. An odd acrid taste lingered in her mouth.

"I am pleased you are still alive," the young centaur said hesitantly.

She glanced up at his earnest face. She could not think properly, could not put patterns together. Memory, imagination, and reality went back and forth and made no clear sense. Yes, she remembered riding out of Iyesta's lair with Sir Morrec and the escort, but what happened after that? Why was Leonidas here? She rubbed her arms and finally formulated an answer. "Thank you."

She said nothing more, only sat and stared and tried to think. As she watched the activity around her, the words spoken in her twilight sleep came back to her. *It wasn't the storm that killed them.* She sat up a little straighter and grew more alert.

Sir Remmik sat on a horse about ten paces away, supervising the removal of the bodies. *The bodies.* Oh, gods, no. Linsha's thoughts clutched at that painful reality. A squad of eight Knights had brought a wagon and some litters. Silently, they laid out the bodies of their fallen comrades, wrapped them in canvas, and laid them gently in the wagon. The rigidity of the body that usually occurred right after death had already begun to recede in the heat of the new day, making their job somewhat easier.

Linsha watched this process for several minutes until they came to the last body. When they turned him over, her vision blurred and her head sank to her knees. It was Sir Morrec.

The old Knight lay sprawled on his stomach, his sword near his hand, and his uniform still soaked with rain. The hilt of a dagger protruded from his back.

"Get that dagger out and give it to me," ordered Sir Remmik. "I want all of you to witness where it was found."

Silently, and without looking at Linsha, a Knight pulled the dagger out of the dead man's back and handed it to Sir Remmik. He wrapped it in a piece of cloth and put it carefully in a saddlebag, while the Knights wrapped Sir Morrec and placed him atop the pile of bodies.

"Now, if you're finished, Sir Hugh, you will place Rose Knight Majere under arrest and escort her back to the Citadel. She is to be placed in the cells until her trial."

Leonidas stamped a hoof hard on the ground. "What?" he cried. "On trial? For what?"

Sir Remmik at least had the decency to look pained. "I intend to charge her with murder and treason. At the very least she should be imprisoned for deriliction of duty."

The other Knights looked astounded. Only Linsha, still sitting on the ground, bowed her head. She was not surprised. In Remmik's place, she would have done the same. She had recognized the dagger the moment Sir Hugh pulled it from the commander's body, and her heart sank to her knees. Surely it wasn't possible that she had killed Sir Morrec. She stared down at her

95

hands and saw the rain had washed them clean. There was no blood to incriminate her, and the blood on her clothes was her own. But, unbidden came an image to her mind of a black, faceless figure moving toward her with a sword. *Could it have been?*

Linsha shut her thoughts off. She could not remember what had happened clearly enough to prove her innocence. Probably nothing would prove her innocence to Sir Remmik's mind, but she felt too sick and befuddled to argue with him at this moment.

The same could not be said for the buckskin centaur. He barged forward, full of zeal, and pushed up against Sir Remmik's horse. "Did you take a close look at this scene? Your Knights were attacked! Don't you want to know who did this? Don't you want to start looking for the culprits? It's obvious the Lady Knight was attacked, too. Their attacker probably took her dagger and killed Sir Morrec. There are no other bodies here. Don't you find that suspicious? Why waste your time on punishing your own Knights?"

The new commander of the Solamnic Knights leveled a disdainful glare on the centaur. "I do not consider it a waste to uphold the honor and justice of the Order. A grave crime has been committed here, and I will not allow the culprit to escape punishment. Not this time. We will conduct our own investigation. Now back off. Sir Hugh, do your duty."

The younger Knight stared at his commander, then looked doubtfully at the Rose Knight. The reluctance was plain on his face as he climbed down from the wagon and moved to obey.

Linsha forestalled him by tottering to her feet. She wanted to stand alone and walk to the wagon, but the ground developed a nasty wave, rocking and heaving beneath her feet. She would have fallen if Leonidas hadn't hurried to her side and caught her arm. Sick and shivering in her wet clothes, she leaned against his warm side and tried not to pass out again.

Leonidas exchanged a look with the second centaur and tilted his head toward the west, the direction of Iyesta's lair. The other centaur indicated his understanding with a brief nod and left. No one tried to stop him.

"If the commander will allow me," Leonidas said, his disapproval still radiating in his eyes, "I will carry his prisoner back to the Citadel. She cannot yet walk unaided."

Sir Remmik paused, torn between the desire to drag her back on foot or the need to make her sit on the wagon with the bodies. Finally common sense prevailed. It was obvious she could not make it as far as the Citadel on her own feet.

"Do I have your word you will not try to carry her off?" he growled. "If you try, I will have my Knights shoot you."

Leonidas touched his left shoulder with his right hand in the salute of the centaur militia. "My word."

"If you insist," Remmik said. "Take a place behind the wagon." He wheeled his horse away from the centaur to face the other Knights. "Mount up!"

While the Knights mounted and formed a column behind the wagon, Leonidas helped Linsha onto his back. She clutched the mane on his withers and tried not to let her head sink onto his shoulder

"Thank you," she said quietly. "You are an unexpected ally."

The centaur readjusted his bow and quiver across his back so they did not interfere with Linsha's face. "You could have pressed charges against me for shooting at you," he said equally as quietly. "Uncle expected you to. But you didn't. I owe you. Besides, this is a travesty. It is obvious you were attacked."

"But I don't remember," she murmured, her voice dangerously close to tears. "What if I did kill Sir Morrec? The storm was so . . ." Her words trailed off.

"I can't believe you would do such a thing," he said forcefully. "You are too experienced to make a mistake like that."

"You give me much credit."

"Why doesn't your commander?"

"He wants me to be guilty."

The buckskin was so surprised by her remark that he could not think of anything to say. He suddenly noticed the Solamnics were waiting for him and hurried into place, his expression thunderous.

At Sir Remmik's command, the procession began the slow, sad ride back through the Missing City. Linsha paid little attention at first. She still felt groggy and queasy, and all she could think about was lying down again. Even in a cell. At least a cell would be dark and quiet.

But after a while, Leonidas, worried about her silence, whispered, "Have you noticed?"

She lifted her head, opened her eyes, and looked around, getting ready to say, "Noticed what?" Then the truth hit her and surprise nearly knocked her off the centaur's back. The procession was nearing the Artisans' District where many new houses and shops had been built in the manner of Gal Tra'kalas. The phantom images of the elven town had always been lively here with busy streets, populated homes, and lovely gardens. Now those images were gone, totally erased. There was nothing. No elf, no building, no animal, no flower left of Gal Tra'kalas. As far as Linsha could see there were only the real buildings of wood and stone and mortar.

"What happened?"

The centaur waved his hands. "We don't know. We found it this way when we came out after the storm. It's as if that tempest blew the Missing City away. It is truly missing now."

"What did Iyesta say?"

"I don't know. I haven't seen her. Uncle took us out as soon as the storm blew over to help where we could." He grimaced. "The city is in a shambles. The harbor is worse. It was struck by wind and waves. The docks are gone, most of the ships are sunk, and the waves washed out many of the buildings in the first row along the waterfront. The Legion is down there now trying to find survivors."

Linsha noted a faint overtone of disapproval in the one omission he made. "And where are the Solamnics?"

"Some of them are here. The rest are in their Citadel."

Angry now, and deeply worried, Linsha forced herself to concentrate on the city around her. Without its ghostly sister city, the houses and buildings looked strangely naked. The people who moved about the streets seemed confused and disconcerted.

Leonidas was right. The town was in a shambles. The wind and rain had pounded the buildings. The stone edifices had fared better than those made of wood, but everywhere Linsha looked she saw roofs ripped off, walls collapsed, trees felled, debris blown in heaps against fences, and shutters and awnings torn from their supports. Lightning had struck several places, starting fires despite the torrential rains, while the rains had eroded the roads, washed out gardens, and left pools of muddy water lying in every depression. When the Solamnics passed the open air market,

Linsha saw not a single stall or awning had been left standing. Merchants and tradesmen milled around the marketplace trying to sort through the mess.

In fact, the closer she looked, the more people Linsha recognized who were outside trying to help clean up the aftermath of the storm and help those who were injured. She looked everywhere for a familiar Solamnic face and saw none. Only the Knights with her had apparently come out into the city.

Linsha felt her face grow hot. Surely Sir Remmik wouldn't be that thickheaded. She turned her head and saw Sir Hugh riding behind her. "Where are the other Knights?" she asked, her voice intentionally unaggressive.

Sir Hugh was a well-made man, compact, muscular and erect. He had newly reached the rank of Knight of the Sword and was still learning its fit. He glanced at the others around him before he answered. They didn't look any more pleased than he to his answer. "They are in the Citadel. Sir Remmik called an emergency and ordered everyone in."

"You mean he did not allow anyone out to help in the city? Leonidas says the harbor district was badly damaged. *The Legion* is there!"

"We know," another Knight said quietly. He said nothing more, but Linsha could see his jaw grinding.

"And all of you went along with him?" Linsha could hear her voice rising in angry disbelief, but in truth she could not fault their actions. Most of the Knights in the circle were young and deeply loyal to Sir Remmik. Many respected him to the point of awe, for they only saw his authority and his ability to organize a fighting unit. Very few on the receiving of his ire and dislike stayed long in the Missing City. Linsha had been the exception because of her rank.

"He is the commander now," Hugh pointed out. "The Measure states we must obey him when the safety of the unit is at stake."

"And the Oath you took swore you to sacrifice all for the sake of honor!" Linsha nearly shouted. "What honor is there in hiding behind a castle door?"

"Silence!" Sir Remmik's voice boomed over her question. "You are charged with crimes against the Order. You have lost all right to question the validity of honor."

"Lost all right!" she shouted back, totally outraged, and the sudden outburst nearly made her black out again. She stopped, took a deep breath, and went on. "It is my duty to defend my honor and the honor of our unit. You want to throw me in the cells, then do it. I will defend myself in council. But you have no right to shut up these Knights behind your fancy walls when the people of the city need their help!"

A few murmurs of agreement echoed her last words.

Sir Remmik's veneer cracked. It had been a long and harrowing night for him, and his usual cool demeanor had been stretched too far. He wrenched his horse around and, drawing his sword, charged down on the centaur and Linsha. Leonidas leaped back, whipped his bow off his back, and had an arrow nocked in the time it took Sir Remmik to urge his horse forward. The two stood there, breathing heavily, their weapons trained on each other.

"She may be your prisoner," said Leonidas, "but she is my rider and in my protection. I could shoot you before you could twitch that blade."

"And my Knights will kill you," Sir Remmik snarled.

Linsha glanced sideways and saw the truth of that. Every Knight behind them had their bows lined up on the centaur and herself. She muttered a curse under her breath.

People in the streets stared at the strange actions of the Solamnic Knights and quickly moved out of arrow range.

"Sir Remmik," she said in a calming tone of voice. "I will be silent. Please put your sword down. You have accused me, but there is no justice in an execution without a trial. You were not present at the attack and you have no eyewitness. If you kill me without proving your accusations against me, *you* could be charged with dishonor and murder."

The argument, as Linsha hoped, struck home. Sir Remmik's belief in the justice of the Order would not allow him to kill another Knight until a sentence of execution had been handed down. He made a visible effort to bring himself under control and lower his weapon.

When the Knight commander's blade dropped, Leonidas lowered his bow and returned the arrow to the quiver. The Knights, too, lowered their weapons and a silent sigh of relief fluttered through the ranks. Without speaking, they continued the procession through the battered streets.

They took a more northerly route through the district and passed through the city wall north of the Citadel. It wasn't until they reached the hill where the fortress reared above the bluffs and sand dunes that Linsha caught her first glimpse of the storm damage to Mirage. Her eyes grew wide. Leonidas's description of the ruined waterfront hardly began to convey the widespread destruction caused by wind and waves and storm surge. The great storm had battered the streets of the Missing City, but it had leveled the first two rows of buildings along the harbor and sunk every ship at anchor in the water. The two piers had vanished, and the docks where the goods were unloaded from the freighters were so many piles of scrap wood mingled with the remains of ships and the floating debris of warehouses, taverns, and shops.

Linsha noticed many people down along the waterfront working among the heaps of flotsam and broken buildings. It angered her anew to know none of those people trying to help were Knights of Solamnia. Sir Morrec's soul would be having fits of rage. She bit her tongue to stay quiet for fear of angering Sir Remmik all over again. Surely some of the other Knights would recognize the flagrant breach of service to one's community and try to convince their new commander to relax his stance.

The escort reached the gates of the Citadel to the mournful call of a horn blowing a dirge for the dead Knights from the high parapet. The entire garrison had turned out to meet the wagon, and they stood silently watching as the dead were carried into the fortress.

Leonidas stopped at the first gate, forcing the Knights behind him to stop as well. Ignoring them, he helped Linsha to the ground.

"Make sure Iyesta knows, please?" she asked, her green eyes boring into his.

"I will tell the Legion what is happening, as well. You have friends who will not allow this."

She nodded once and stepped back, allowing him to pass, relieved that her earlier assessment of his abilities were proving to be true. Under his gangly exterior was an intelligent and determined young centaur.

Turning his back to the Citadel, Leonidas cantered down the hill and sped away westward.

Linsha took a deep breath and strode into the castle. A few minutes later she was taken to the cells beneath the gatehouse. The new prison level had been recently completed and consisted only of six small rooms carved out of the bedrock and joined by a single corridor. The newest prisoner was placed in the smallest, darkest cell available, and since there was no one else in the prison level at the moment, there were several to choose from.

At that moment, Linsha would not have cared if an entire tribe of kender was in there with her. When the cell door clanged shut, she sank to the hard shelf that passed for a bed, rolled over onto her back, and fell into a deep sleep.

Varia's flight

9

S hortly after the meeting ended in the courtyard of Iycsta's lair, Varia stepped out of her hiding place and slid quietly away on the evening breeze. No one noticed her go but the two metallic dragons on guard who had grown very uneasy and wary.

The owl sensed the coming of the storm when she was halfway back to the Citadel. She had planned to meet Linsha in her room, so when she felt the wind pick up and her feathers detected the abrupt change in the pressure of the air, she hurried to the Citadel to take shelter from the coming storm and wait for Linsha.

While the storm raged, the owl paced back and forth on her perch, her "ear" feathers rigid on her head, her entire body extended to its full length. Tremendous claps of thunder rocked the fortress that made her flap her wings and screech in pain.

Where was Linsha? she asked herself again and again. Why hasn't Linsha come back?

Lightning flared through the cracks in the shutter then went out, and this time the thunder followed a few seconds later. The rain eased from a torrential downpour to a steady fall, and the wind dropped to merely blustery. The storm was moving east, away from the Missing City toward the Silvanesti Forest and the open ocean beyond.

Varia sat on her perch and drooped. She felt utterly drained and exhausted. She decided to take a nap while she waited for Linsha. Surely the Lady Knight would be back soon. She pulled her head and body into a warm, compact ball and slept.

When the owl woke, the light of a clear dawn shone through the window slit and voices rang in the inner ward. Her first thought was of Linsha, and when Varia saw her friend had not yet come into the room, she tugged open the shutter, stepped to the sill, and flew out over the castle.

She immediately saw the noise in the ward was made by Knights preparing to leave, not by those newly arrived as she hoped. Tilting her head down, Varia listened carefully to their shouts and orders. To her dismay, she caught the name Sir Morrec and the words, "in the street" and "all dead." Sir Remmik strode out of the main hall and mounted a horse saddled and ready for him. A single centaur stood impatiently by the gatehouse waiting for the Knights.

Varia followed the Solamnics out of the castle at a casual distance. They all were accustomed to seeing her fly about, but this morning she wanted to be discreet. Her eyes followed them along the road while she wheeled slowly through the rain-washed breeze. Then her eyes lifted to the skyline of the Missing City and she let out a squawk.

Instead of the familiar translucent images of towers, buildings, and graceful walls overlaying a more solid copy, Varia saw only the real buildings and beyond them where the citizens of the Missing City had not built, the ruins of Gal Tra'kalas lay exposed like the crumbling bones of an ancient grave. The mirage was gone and in its place was a disheveled, storm-battered city, looking undressed and vulnerable and very much in need of help.

Varia stared across the city rooftops, expecting to see the dragons out, lending their strength to the rescue effort, but she did not see any of them. Something about that deeply disturbed the already worried owl. This absence was not like Iyesta and the others. They were very conscientious about the city and its inhabitants. Unless an emergency or dire threat had arisen, they would have been out to help clean out the rubble and find survivors. Maybe one of them was with Linsha and Sir Morrec.

But that hope was shattered when the Knights rode into a section of the ancient city where the weathered ruins were all that remained. From her height above the muddy plains Varia saw another centaur and the bodies on the ground. Linsha's auburn curls were easy to indentify even from the air.

Varia's shrill screech of dismay shivered on the morning breeze. She flew to an old scrub holly growing in the slight shelter of a shattered chimney. It was the only cover near the scene she could find. She wanted to fly straight to the bodies, but although she recognized the young horseman who brought Linsha back to the Citadel several days ago, she did not know him and she did not want to risk exposing herself. It was safer to let them think she was only a pet.

Grief stricken, she scanned the bodies and looked for any sign of life. The corpses remained ominously still, and the flies had begun to gather. She remained silent and motionless, virtually invisible in her shaded hiding place. She watched the Knights arrive and examine the bodies.

All at once her "ears" popped upright, and she stretched forward on her talons. Linsha moved. She was alive! Varia wanted to sing with delight.

Then her joy turned to rage. That vile man. Sir Remmik, that self-centered, close-minded, despot who had created his own private army and now had control of it. Just once Varia wished she could change into an eagle and fly out to tear that man's eyes from his skull. How dare he accuse Linsha.

Trembling, she watched the Knights load their dead onto a wagon and prepare to leave. Her estimation of the leggy, young centaur rose higher when he offered to carry Linsha back to the castle.

She trailed the Knights and their prisoner back to the Citadel. There was no chance to talk to Linsha or even signal her in some way, and the owl could only watch in frustrated silence as the Lady Knight was hurried away to the prison cells under the castle. She knew Sir Remmik's personality well enough to guess what he was trying to do. Without some firm evidence, Linsha would find it very difficult to fight his charges. She would need help.

The sound of the door closing behind Linsha had barely died before Varia shot out of her watching place and flew like a hawk toward the distant lair of the great brass. Iyesta had to know about this. Iyesta would help.

When she arrived at the dragon's lair, Varia winged into the courtyard where the great double doors led into the throne room. Two of the three brass triplets usually stood on either side of the doors, but this morning there were no dragons, neither brass nor gold nor silver, and the great bronze doors hung open to an empty throne room. A large group of city people, militia, and Iyesta's own guards had gathered to talk to Iyesta. They milled around in confusion, their voices raised in loud questions no one could answer and orders no one could hear. It was total chaos.

Varia spotted several acquaintances and friends of Linsha's, considered them, and set them aside. They did not have the authority to deal with Sir Remmik and the Solamnics nor any knowledge of the massacre. She needed the dragon.

Plagued by uncertainty, she sat in a tree and waited to see if the buckskin centaur would appear. It wasn't long before she saw him galloping up the road to the palace. He had wasted no time getting there. She watched as the look on his face changed from fiery determination to surprise and dismay when he saw the crowd milling about the courtyard and no sign of the dragons. He finally spotted an older centaur he knew and hurried over. The two began a heated conversation.

Good. Let the word spread. Sir Morrec was admired in the City, and his murder would not go over well in some circles. A cry would go up for justice, the assassins would be found, and Linsha would be freed.

Or would she? What if the assassins weren't found? Linsha's first trial had taken weeks to put together and eventually fell apart. But that was in Sancrist, the seat of Solamnic power. This was a distant outpost on the edge of the world. What if Sir Remmik rushed a trial through a makeshift council before the real killers were discovered? The Missing City was a long way from Sancrist, and Solamnic law allowed a Knight of Sir Remmik's rank to convene a council in times of need. Sir Remmik would have no qualms declaring an emergency after a massacre of Knights and the chaos caused by the monstrous storm of the night before. He could have Linsha condemned and hanged before anyone knew what happened.

Varia launched herself out of the tree. She needed Iyesta, and she needed the brass now. Only the dragonlord could demand that Sir Remmik make a proper investigation of the killing. She would just have to go look for Iyesta herself. Maybe during her search she would be lucky and find a band of murderous-looking brigands who were fleeing the Missing City after ambushing a troop of Solamnic Knights. Bigger coincidences happened.

The owl began her search on the west side of the city where she remembered Iyesta had one entrance to the labyrinth. She made methodical sweeps east and west, then north and south from the beaches and bluffs of the coast to Scorpion Wadi, from the devastated harbor to Sinking Wells, over the Citadel and beyond to the fields and grasslands that lay between Mirage and the Silvanesti Forest. She flew over the village of Mem-Thon where the tribespeople struggled to rebuild their homes damaged by the storm, and still there was no indication of any metallic dragon, gold, silver, or brass.

At last, weary and wing-sore, Varia risked the evening wind off the sea and flew across the water back toward Mirage. After the night's storm, the day's weather had been delightfully warm and pleasant, and now the sun, setting across the vast southern continent, lit the waters ahead of her with a golden path.

Because of the sun in her eyes, she did not see at first the distant ship, moving slowly along the coastline where the land rose in high bluffs at the water's edge. She had nearly passed by it, when a sail flapped loose and fluttered down the mast. The motion of the sail caught the edge of the owl's broad vision. She swiveled her head sideways and saw the dark ship slip through the shadows cast by the bluffs. She almost disregarded it—ships were not rare in the south Courrain Ocean—until the ship made the turn around a headland and sailed into a small bay.

Varia followed it out of curiosity. The bay was uninhabited, but it was sometimes used as an anchoring site for ships wishing to stop for the night. There could be ships there in need of assistance after the storm.

The sun dipped below the horizon, and its light drained from the land. Varia's sight, good in daylight, improved in the dusky evening. She had no trouble seeing the fleet of ships anchored in the bay.

She slowed her flight in surprise. No one in this region had that many ships. There had to be nearly sixty of various lengths, most of them long, swift oceangoing vessels with oars and sails. They did not have the black coloration of ships belonging to the Knights of Neraka, and they flew no flags, so whose were they?

Varia caught a wind current and rode it toward shore to give any observers the impression that she was a mere owl out looking for an evening meal. As she passed over the ships, she carefully studied all she could see.

Those ships had suffered damage from the storm. Some had lost masts, some listed at their anchors, and two had been towed to shore for repairs. If the fleet had been at sea when the storm struck, it was logical to assume some ships had been scattered, some had sunk, and perhaps some were limping to another shore. But damaged as the fleet was, Varia recognized an armed force when she saw one. Thunder had his army to the west and now this fleet approached Mirage from the east. It was easy to assume they were not coming to open trade negotiations. Was there a connection between the blue and this force?

It would be several days, Varia reasoned, before the fleet made its repairs and reassembled itself. She supposed it was possible the ships would not move on the Missing City, but she did not want to take that chance.

The moment Varia flew over land and the twilight hid her from view, she turned west toward Mirage and flew as fast as her wings would carry her. Her heart beat like a hummingbird's. Those ships! She had to warn Linsha. The woman's premonition of danger had been all too valid. First the storm, the ambush, and now this.

The Solamnic Jail

10

Linsha had been injured before. In her chosen way of life, there were always aching muscles, bumps, bruises, cuts, and scrapes. There had been that incident in Palanthas when the thief broke her arm, the attack in the Crystal Valley that left her battered and bruised, and of course, the duel with Ian Durne in Sanction that nearly killed her. She was familiar with pain. But never had she experienced anything so miserable and painful as this head injury. If she wanted to put words to it, she could have described it as a hangover brought on by dwarf spirts, complicated by a punch between the eyes and a vise clamped around her temples.

After the first hour or so, she woke shivering in her damp clothes and lay in a half-doze. Her head still hurt abominably in a persistent thudding ache that refused to ease off or even change. Linsha tried to move, to warm her muscles, and found it was not worth the effort. She had no strength left in her limbs, and any muscle that moved did so stiffly and with complaint.

She finally gave up and lay still again. Sleep came and went in fitful starts. When she was awake and aware, she could convince herself that she had done nothing to hurt Sir Morrec. Her conscious mind had no recollection of the attack beyond a few vague images of rain and struggling figures. It wasn't until she slept that her mind slipped into evil dreams and the agony of uncertainty brought images out of the depths of her injured brain, bits of memory, visions lit by brilliant light, and dark faceless figures that attacked her with swords only to vanish into impenetrable darkness.

After a long while, heavy footsteps on the stone floor disturbed her restless sleep and the grate of a key in the lock brought her fully awake. She opened one eye to see Sir Remmik glowering down at her. Two guards stood stolidly behind him; a scribe stood close by with a quill and paper in his hand. Linsha did not try to move.

"Majere," Sir Remmik said. "You are awake. Good. I have come to hear your report on the events of last evening."

Linsha felt surly with misery. "You should have asked me before you accused me in front of half the circle."

He lifted a narrow eyebrow. "A slight exaggeration. And you were hardly in any condition to give a coherent report. Now you have had time to sleep, to gather your thoughts. Tell us what happened."

Linsha glared at the scribe's hand and his pen poised to repeat her words. Tell us what happened, she thought bitterly. If only it were that easy. "We left Iyesta's council at sunset. We were caught in the storm. We were ambushed." She said it in short, stark sentences. "Did you get all that?"

Sir Remmik pursed his lips. "I see. You are not going to cooperate. Very well." He turned to go.

"No," she said hoarsely. She held out a hand to him.

"You don't understand. I wouldn't kill Sir Morrec. I just don't remember what happened."

The Solamnic commander gave her a sharp nod. "Of course. Your injuries are worse than I thought. I will have a healer come look at you." He turned on his heel and was gone as quickly as he came. The key turned in the lock; the footsteps echoed quietly down the corridor.

Linsha stared at the door for a long time wondering if that whole exchange had been another dream. Eventually, she dozed again.

The key turned in the lock once again, and this time Sir Hugh walked silently into the cell. He stared down at the sleeping woman for a moment. Although he had never told her, he deeply admired Lady Linsha for her courage and her abilities. He could not believe now that these charges made against her were true. But if there was no basis for the charge, why did the commander put her under arrest? Time would make things clear, he hoped, and meanwhile there was no reason why she should die of chills or lung infection. He laid a warm blanket over her and made his way out.

When Varia returned to Mirage, night had drawn its pall over the city. Torches burned along the wrecked waterfront where rescue efforts had turned to a hunt for the dead and a cleanup. She scanned the area carefully in the hope of seeing a dragon but was disappointed. The streets and skies were still ominously empty of their presence.

Gliding on silent wings, Varia circled the Citadel and, hoping against hope that Linsha would be in her room, swooped down and entered the narrow window in the officer's quarters. Linsha's room was dark and empty, and there were no signs of the Lady Knight having been there since the day before.

Varia hooted in dismay. She had to talk to Linsha. How was she going to get into the cells? They were located in a level below ground under the tower of the front gate in the inner ward. They had been built to be inaccessible by any means but a single stairs that led from the guardroom. No windows, no convenient skylight, nothing that would allow an eighteen inch bird to slip unseen into a prison cell to talk with a prisoner. And she doubted the guards would be accommodating enough to take Linsha's pet owl down there and let it out again.

Perhaps the guards would bring Linsha out for some reason, and she could snatch a quick word with her friend. As an idea, it was better than nothing.

The owl left the empty room, made her way silently around the keep, and swooped noiselessly up to a roost on the guard tower she had used before. In the past, she had made a point of choosing several well-positioned roosts around the Citadel that afforded her excellent views of the wards, the walls, and the buildings and allowed her to hear much of what went on. The Knights in the garrison made no complaint of the owl because she helped keep the rodent population down and owls were believed to be good luck. Varia took full advantage of this open-minded opinion.

She pushed herself into the black shadows of the roofline and waited. She knew she could not be seen, and in a little while, anyone who might have noticed her fly into that spot would probably forget she was there. From this perch she could hear men talk on the parapet above the gate and anyone speaking just outside the guardroom. From here, she might learn what was happening with Linsha. The hour had already passed that Sir Remmik usually made his rounds, and the man was nothing but punctual, so she would have to wait for the changing of the guards at midnight. Perhaps then she would hear some news, or if luck was with her, the guard room would be empty for a moment and she could slip down the stairs to the cells. Although that would be horribly risky, she wanted to try. Somehow she had to warn Linsha of the approaching fleet.

The wards and the gates remained quiet for several hours. The guards paced their beat and stood their posts and said nothing to one another. They seemed very tense to the watching owl, as if they knew something was wrong and did not know what to do about it. The gates to both walls remained firmly shut and no one left the castle. The city outside the walls remained something separate and apart, something that could pose a danger to the well-being of the garrison. No matter that torches flared along the ruined waterfront, or a few scattered fires burned in the neighborhoods, or the Legion and the militia were helping the bewildered and stricken citizens, or Iyesta's guards were holding a massive, frantic search for the brass dragon and her companions. The Knights of Solamnia were safely secured behind their walls and all was well with them.

At midnight a small bell rang from the inner gate. The door of the main hall opened and light from within spilled out into the dark yard. Sir Remmik walked out to stand on the step and watch. Varia hissed at the sight of the man. Then she quieted and listened. Men had come out of the guardroom while others marched up to

the walls. The changing of the guard was under way.
She watched carefully while the squad below her
marched toward the main keep to report to the new
commander. As soon as they were halfway across the
ward, she dropped from her hiding place and floated
silently toward the door of the guardroom.

"Someone get that blasted owl," she heard Sir
Remmik say. Immediately, she stooped to the left away
from the door as if she were chasing a mouse across the
stone pavings.

Fortunately, no one moved to obey his order. The
other Knights stood and watched as she pounced on
something small and carried it back up to her roost.

Varia pushed back into the safety of shadows again
and tossed the horse turd out of her talon to the gutter.
Her feelings turned fiery hot. If her thoughts could
have been made real, Sir Remmik would have been
skinned alive and staked to an ant hill in the middle of
the desert.

"Sir Hugh, I want you to make sure that owl is
driven out of here. We do not need pets in this garrison.
Kill it if you have to." Sir Remmik shouted to the officer of the guard loudly enough so everyone could hear
him.

There was a soft but collective gasp from all the
watching men.

"Yes, sir," Sir Hugh replied. Then he made a friend
of one small intelligent owl by adding, "But the owl is
no danger to us. In truth she kills her share of rats and
mice that eat our corn."

"Get a terrier. We do not need that owl flying
around here. Once the accused is condemned, we will
erase everything of hers from this castle. The owl goes,
or it will be destroyed."

Varia sensed there were a number of "buts" on the

lips of those watching, yet they stood without speaking. Most of the Knights in the circle had learned to respect Sir Remmik, and Varia suspected it would take some time before they found the courage to stand up to him.

She watched and waited to see if any of the guards took the commander at his word and came to drive her out. Thankfully no one did. They changed the guards and went about their business. Eventually Sir Remmik went back inside. The door closed behind him, shutting in the yellow light.

Fifteen minutes passed while the castle settled back into its late night routine. Most of the Knights retired to bed. Hunger grumbled in Varia's belly. She had flown all day and eaten nothing. Perhaps she should slip down to the stable for a meal. Obviously hunting on the castle grounds would not be a good idea for a while. She stepped on the edge of the roof, spread her wings, and just as she was about to take flight, two men walked out of the guardroom and stood in the shadows of the tower. Varia hurriedly moved back out of sight.

"Lady Linsha just awoke. She is asking for a meal. Has the healer seen to her? Is she allowed food?"

"Sir Johand had the healer check her earlier," replied the second. "The Lady Knight sustained a concussion and will be uncomfortable for a few days, but she'll recover. Sir Remmik ordered only bread and water for her. She is allowed no meals."

Varia recognized the two speakers immediately. Sir Hugh, the officer of the watch this night, and Sir Pieter, one of the younger Knights. She craned down to better hear their soft voices.

"Sir, I don't understand this," said the younger voice. Sir Pieter. "Sir Remmik is the only Knight with ranking to sit on a council. Besides the Lady Linsha. How can he arrange a trial council so quickly? He hasn't even called for an investigation first. Why is he so certain Lady Linsha killed Sir Morrec?"

Varia heard Sir Hugh sigh in the darkness. "I don't know how or why he does this. We all know he dislikes her, but he is rushing this too fast."

"And why does he keep us in the castle? It is our duty to help the city. I heard the dragons are still missing. Is anyone trying to find them? And the city! Did you see? The images are gone. The stablehands told me everyone thinks the disappearance is a bad omen. They said the whole city is in an uproar."

Sir Hugh put out a hand to stop the flood of words. As officer of the guard, he knew this young man was not the only Knight in the castle with questions on his mind. The problem was there were no answers yet. "Look, we cannot know what to do until we have more answers. That will take time."

"Lady Linsha will have no more time after tomorrow if Sir Remmik has his way," Sir Pieter said.

"We will see what tomorrow brings," Sir Hugh said, trying to sound calm and authoritative, which he certainly did not feel. "In the meantime, the cook should have the food ready for the nightwatch in the guardroom. I have asked him to add a little extra for the prisoner. If you will fetch it from the kitchen, you may take some food down to her."

Sir Pieter saluted and hurried away to collect the food for the nightwatch. Varia stared after him, then she looked down and saw Sir Hugh looking directly at her.

"Your mistress is in serious trouble," he said to her surprise. "You should stay out of the castle until this is over."

She leaned further over the edge and winked one eye at him. He stared up in surprise, but she gave him no more time to wonder. She spread her wings and flew over the castle wall and into the night.

At least Linsha has a few supporters in the Citadel, Varia thought. And she would need them. Sir Remmik had already set up a council for trial. He certainly wasted no time. He would push this through while the circle was still confused and in an uproar about the city and the storm. By Chislev who would return, what would the Solamnics do if that invasion fleet hove into view?

Varia felt desperate now. Linsha was running out of time. For that matter, Mirage could be running out of time. With the city in an uproar, the Knights of Solamnia playing aloof, and the dragons missing, who would stand up to an invasion force?

She decided to make one more visit to Iyesta's lair. If the dragon was still missing, she would have to devise a new plan.

Like an arrow, the small raptor flew the distance to the lair of the dragonlord and found it little changed from the morning, in spite of the hour. The huge doors were still open, the lair was still empty, and the courtyard was still crowded with people who wished to talk to Iyesta or who were planning search parties to find her.

Torches burned in sconces and in the hands of people who had come from the city, and their flickering yellow light illuminated the tension and worry that was on everyone's faces. Varia flew slowly overhead, wondering what to do. Without Iyesta to intercede, there was little hope for Linsha.

Unless . . . Varia spotted a group of three people she knew were Legionnaires. If there was any group in the city willing to help Linsha it might be the Legion of Steel. She would have preferred to talk to Falaius himself, but the other man Linsha often talked to, Lanther, was there. Varia did not entirely trust Lanther. She did not know him well, and his aura, when she tried to see it, was faint and difficult to read. The last time Linsha befriended a man with an aura like that, she had paid dearly for it. But Linsha had told Varia of Lanther's past, and she had watched the way the man treated Linsha. He had a mind of depth and a wary personality hardened by years of warfare and struggle, which could explain his aura, and he had always given Linsha nothing but respect and friendship. He might be worth a try.

She winged to Lanther and landed gently on his shoulder, her talons gripping his tunic softly. To his credit, he did not leap up or shout in surprise. He simply turned and stared eye to eye with the owl on his shoulder.

"Good evening," he said with some curiosity. "What are you doing here?"

Varia knew Lanther had no knowledge of her ability to talk, yet she appreciated a human who talked to animals as if they could respond.

"I need to talk to you about Linsha," she whispered in his ear.

Lanther started at the owl's dry, raspy voice. He glanced at his companions and forced a grin. "Excuse me while I put this owl back in the brush. It seems to be lost." He walked a short way into an empty patch of shadow near a tree and offered his arm to Varia.

She stepped delicately onto his forearm. "Thank you. Linsha has said she could count on you. She said you were unflappable."

"You almost changed that. I did not realize owls could talk."

"I am different," Varia replied. "I have come to ask

you for help. You have heard of the ambush on the Knights of Solamnia during the storm last night?"

His expression folded into sadness. "Yes. I heard they were all killed."

"All but Linsha. She was found still alive, but Sir Remmik has arrested her. He is convinced she killed Sir Morrec. He plans to bring her before a council of his arranging and have her convicted. If she is found guilty, by their law she can be hanged. It is a very dishonorable death for a Solamnic Knight."

While the owl talked, the Legionnaire's face slowly solidified into a mask of stone. "Will the other Knights try to help her?"

Varia ruffled her feathers in her own frustration. "I don't think they will. They like her well enough, but Sir Remmik has most of them believing in his authority and he will not give them time to think or act."

He nodded. "I will look into this. We will do what we can."

"Has anyone found Iyesta yet?"

"No. The centaurs have looked everywhere they know to look. The golds and the silvers are also gone. This is very strange."

"I have looked as well," Varia said. "What I found is not good. There is a fleet of strange ships in a small bay perhaps twenty miles from here. I think it is an invasion force. Could you also have the Legion look into it? The city will need to be warned."

Lanther looked down at her, his dark blue eyes lost in shadow. "A fleet. That's strange. Have you told anyone else?"

She clicked her beak. "No. I talk to no one but Linsha."

"And me."

"This once. I risk much for her."

"I will see you are not disappointed in your choice."

She hooted softly in thanks and flew from his arm into the tree. She sidled down a branch into the depths of the limbs and leaves and watched him return to his companions. She was gratified that he had not questioned Linsha's innocence, but she wasn't certain he would do anything with her information. He was talking to the others about something, though. The three men looked deep in conversation. Soon, one man left the group at a brisk walk and hurried out of the courtyard. Lanther and the other man talked for a moment longer, then both left together, their faces determined.

Varia watched them go, her hopes pinned on one man's friendship to a woman of another order. She had done all she could in Mirage. It was time to consider one other ally. She dreaded the journey to find him. She would have to fly over Sable's swamp at the risk of meeting the great black or some other horrible denizen of her foul home. It was that or cross the mountains of Blöde, and Varia knew there was slim chance she could make it over the mountains in time—if at all. Iyesta said Lord Bight was busy with some Solamnic plan, but she needed Crucible, and she hoped that for the sake of Iyesta and Linsha, the big bronze might come south to help. If Lanther and the Legion could just delay Linsha's trial, there might be time for her to fly to Sanction and bring Crucible back. If the Legion and the militia could hold off any attack by the strange fleet, there might be a city for her to come back to. It all depended on timing.

Varia snatched a rat just outside the dragon's courtyard and had a quick meal. She was tired after a day of flying, and her wings were weary, but there were many miles between Mirage and Sanction, and Linsha was counting on her.

She finished quickly and sprang aloft into the darkness. It would be safer to fly at night. She could rest at sunrise. Until then, she could put miles behind her and be that much closer to Sanction.

After the Storm

Midyear's Day came and went almost unheeded in the Missing City. Those few who did think of it usually did so when they saw a battered remnant of the garlands and banners hung on the streets of Little Three Points where the festival would have been held, or the flooded race grounds where the horses would have raced that day, or a special bit of finery that would have been worn. Most people, though, thought only of loss and grief and stunned confusion.

The hardest part for many people was the bizarre feeling of unfamiliarity in their own community. The images of Gal Tra'kalas had been irritating, confusing, interesting, and amusing all in their turn, but the phantom city had been a part of the life in the real city for as long as the inhabitants had been there, and its disappearance left a wrenching hole. Nothing looked the same. The streets were emptier, the grounds looked a little shabbier, and there was nothing to hide the almost overwhelming destruction of the great storm. The Storm of 38 it would be called forever in Mirage. The year the Missing City became truly lost.

126

The following day came in warm and windy, and the city slowly dried out. Because of the efforts of the townspeople, the Legion, and Iyesta's militia, almost all the dead had been accounted for and the injured had been tended to. The debris in the harbor was being cleared, as was the ruined waterfront. Plans were already underway to replace the docks. Sadly, the city's small fishing fleet would be harder to replace. Only two fishing boats survived, and those were found among the wreckage and flotsam on the beach where they had been flung after their anchor chains snapped. The others were sunk, and their crews gradually washed ashore in ones and twos at the changing of the tides.

Across the four quarters, the sound of hammers and saws filled the streets. While people sorted through the damage and salvaged what could be saved or reused, others hauled the trash and debris out of the city to be burned, and many more began the laborious task of rebuilding. The dead were quickly buried in a mass grave on a hill overlooking the city. In the open market, a few vendors opened their stalls and sold food or whatever could be found to sell. Mirage slowly resumed a semblance of its normal activity.

Only one other thing truly hung like a pall over the peoples' reviving spirits. The missing dragons. Iyesta and her companions had not yet returned to Mirage from wherever they had gone, and people were growing worried. Could it be possible, they wondered, that Iyesta had abandoned her realm and left for some unknown destination? Maybe she had gone back to the Dragon Isles. Maybe she was hunting Thunder. Maybe the disappearance of Gal Tra'kalas and the dragons were linked. The speculations ran rampant.

A few people thought of Linsha and her friendship with the big brass, and they came to the Citadel to ask if they could talk to the Rose Knight. Word of the massacre had flown around the city, and many people grieved the death of Sir Morrec, but few knew of the charges against Linsha. They were sent away at Sir Remmik's orders, who said only that Linsha was unavailable.

The head of the Legion in Mirage, Falaius Taneek, came to the Citadel to talk to Sir Remmik about Linsha, the assassination, and the Solamnics' reluctance to help. His Order was stretched thin, and he wanted the help of the Solamnics. He left after a short while, his swarthy face suffused with anger.

Sir Remmik paid little attention to the Legionnaire's ire or to the pleas from the city for help, information, or anything the Solamnics would be willing to give. To him, there was only the Circle. They had dead to bury and a trial to complete. The Citadel itself had sustained some damage from lightning and wind and would need to be repaired. After these duties had been completed, then he would consider the Legion's request for help.

The new Solamnic commander debated with himself about holding Linsha's trial that day, then he changed his mind. The seven dead Knights had to be buried—and fairly quickly due to the summer heat. He wanted them interred properly and with the honor befitting their stations. A proper burial with all its pomp and ceremony for a fallen commander and his escort would not allow for a trial in the same day. Nor did Sir Remmik want to besmirch the memory of the fallen with any thought of the one responsible for their deaths. Linsha's trial was postponed for a day.

The Knights dug a grave in the field behind the Citadel. The six Knights of the escort, their bodies cleaned and dressed in mail and uniform, were laid side by side. Sir Morrec had a grave of his own just a pace away. After the rituals of burial had been completed, the two graves were covered with stones and heaped with earth to form a single mound. Seven spears were placed upright on the grave, and a single Knight sang a dirge for the dead.

As soon as the burial was completed, the Knights returned to the castle and went about their duties. Sir Remmik returned to the commander's office and thought for a long while about justice, law, and the organization of a council legal enough to judge the charges against a Rose Knight. He would have to justify his actions in a report to the Grand Master in Sanction. He decided to put the trial off one more day. The extra time could be put to good use questioning others in the Citadel who might know reasons why the accused would do such a terrible thing. There was no question in his mind that this killing had been a murder. He just couldn't understand why she would risk it. Sir Morrec had been more than tolerant of her aberrant behavior. Maybe he had come to learn something about her that she could not allow to be revealed. Maybe he just got in the way of some plot she was hatching. Remmik had to find out and prove it conclusively to the circle and the city. He was not going to allow this woman to evade punishment this time. By the symbol of the crown he wore, he would rid the order of this troublemaker once and for all.

The morning of the 25th of Corij came hot and breezy and dry enough to evaporate the last puddles in the streets of the Missing City. Outside the headquarters of the Legion of Steel, not far from the waterfront, Falaius Taneek tilted his head back and watched his workers repair the roof of their two-story building.

"Have the scouts reported back yet?" he asked the dark-haired man beside him.

Lanther barely shook his head. "I expect them back any time."

"Do you believe this rumor?"

"I have no reason to distrust my informant."

"If you're right, this city could be in serious trouble."

Lanther grunted. "What about the Solamnics?"

"They are still busy with their own affairs," Falaius replied. "I have tried to talk to Sir Remmik, but he is singleminded to say the least."

"Is there nothing we can do? I cannot believe she is responsible for this death."

"We cannot interfere in Solamnic affairs."

"He will do his best to dishonor her," Lanther warned.

"I know."

"It means execution."

"I know."

"Could we get her out?" Lanther whispered.

Falaius did not look around or react in any obvious way. He continued to stare at the roof. "As commander of this cell I am not permitted to authorize such a flagrant infringement of Solamnic jurisdiction."

"Unless, of course, you don't know about it."

"If something is done without my knowledge, I cannot voice an opinion on it."

Lanther understood. He nodded to the plainsman and took his leave to collect his latest disguise. He could not attend the council to learn of Linsha's fate, but he had a way to get into the Solamnics' stable to hear the news from the grooms. They would know almost as soon as the verdict was passed. In the meanwhile, he would wait for the scouts he had sent along the coast and take care of a few details of his own.

Footsteps echoed down the stairs leading to the subterranean prison level. Linsha lifted her head from the bed. This sounded more official than the guard bringing her tray of bread and water. This time there was more than one and she could not hear them talking, which meant this was probably the official council guard who would escort her to the trial. Finally.

Linsha lay back for a moment and waited for them. It had been four days since Sir Remmik had arrested her, and she had been expecting this moment since the first day. She was almost surprised he had taken this long to try her. She closed her eyes. By turning her head slightly she could hear the guards walk down the short corridor and come to a stop by her cell door. She did not make it easier for them by opening her eyes.

One Knight cleared his throat. "Rose Knight Linsha Majere, you are ordered to attend a council of your fellow Knights to determine your guilt or innocence in the charges brought against you by Knight Commander Sir Jamis uth Remmik."

Good. He sound slightly embarrassed. She cracked open her good eye, the one that was not black and blue and still swollen. "What?"

The Knight in charge repeated the order. Two other men stood to either side of him. All of them were Knights of the Crown. None of them looked satisfied with their orders.

Well, too bad. Linsha was in no mood to be accommodating. She was dirty, hungry, and thirsty; her head still hurt, her uniform was filthy, and her anger had been building for four days. She swung her feet around off the slab of a bed and stood up.

"May I have a moment to return to my barracks to clean up and change my uniform?" She was still in the formal uniform she had worn to the meeting with Iyetsa, and now it was fit only to burn. The amount of water they had given her had not been enough to slake her thirst let alone clean herself or her uniform.

The leader shook his head. "Sir Remmik ordered us to bring you now."

"Stupid bastard," Linsha said with venom, not clarifying if she meant the commander or the Knight. She shoved the man out of her way and bulled past the other two out of the cell, down the corridor, and up the stairs. She strode through the guardroom past the surprised guards while her three escorts tried to catch up.

"Lady Linsha!" one of the Knights called. "You do not need to be in such a hurry."

Linsha made a suggestion that caused the man to blush. She continued outside, her jaw clenched, her hands balled into fists. Daylight hit her like an invisible force. Although the late afternoon sun had fallen beyond the walls, the days in near darkness and the swelling of one eye had weakened her eyesight. She blinked a few times before she could see where the council was to be held, then she headed there without wavering toward the water trough, the barracks, or the kitchen. A small crowd of Knights stood outside the open doors of the main keep, silently watching as she approached.

She knew now why Sir Remmik would not give her time to make herself presentable. He wanted her to look disheveled, dirty, and something less than the other Knights. Well, his petty inconsideration would not work. She was Linsha Majere, the daughter of

Krynn's greatest sorcerer, the granddaughter of heroes. She was the first woman to attain the rank of Knight of the Rose, and by the gods, she was not going to grovel at the foot of a makeshift council.

The Knights quietly moved aside as she and her hurrying guards went to the doors. They kept their expressions blank, she saw, but at least there was no open hostility or condemnation on their faces.

A quiet hush enveloped her as she entered the hall. The furniture in the large room had been carefully arranged to resemble the council room in Castle uth Wistan in Gunthar where the Solamnic council usually heard such important cases. All but three trestle tables had been stacked against the walls. One table rested on a dais nearly three feet above the floor and overlooked a four foot square, or dock, marked off by a crudely built barricade. A huge Solamnic flag hung on the wall behind. Two other tables sat left and right of the dais. Four of the highest-ranking Knights in the circle sat on the council, two at each table. As senior Knight, Sir Remmik took the seat of the council judge on the dais. The remaining Knights who were not on duty sat on benches before the tables. They, too, watched quietly as she paused at the door then strode to the dais.

Sir Remmik frowned down at Linsha's guard and pointed a stern finger to the dock.

For a moment she hesitated. Her skills in hand to hand combat far exceeded those of the three Knights beside her. She could incapacitate all of them, and they knew it. But as she looked at the four men who sat to either side of Sir Remmik, her heart sank. The Knight Commander had chosen his council carefully and well, picking the four Knights who most exemplified his ideal of the unbending, law-abiding, unimaginative Knight. They also happened to be four who firmly believed in Sir Remmik's precepts and would not dream of questioning his word.

Linsha decided not to start her trial by antagonizing the council. She allowed the three guards to walk with her to the dock and stand behind her as she stepped inside.

Sir Remmik wasted no time. He listed the charges against Linsha so everyone knew exactly why she was on trial: murder, conspiracy, and treason. Then he launched into a long-winded explanation of her alleged motives, the events of the night of the storm as he saw them, and the evidence he had found to back up his charges.

Linsha's skin grew hot and her eyes widened as she listened. Her head began to pound with tension. This wasn't right! While her memory was still fuzzy on the attack in the storm, four days of rest and quiet had helped clear her mind and restore most of her memories. She knew their group had been ambushed, Sir Morrec had been murdered with her dagger, and she had been left alive for some unknown reason while the rest of the escort had been massacred. In every fiber of her body, she knew she would not knowingly kill Sir Morrec. He had been one of her few reasons to stay in the Missing City.

Still, in the corners of her mind where the pain still shadowed more memories of the attack, lurked that insideous uncertainty. She *had* struck out at someone, some figure she thought was an enemy. What enemy? Who had attacked them and why? Why wouldn't someone investigate that? She desperately wanted to know the truth. If she had killed Sir Morrec by accident, then the Measure provided other penances to pay and ways that she could make up for the tragedy. But because she was still alive, Sir Remmik assumed murder and conspiracy, and that was all he wanted to know.

Her hands clenched into fists. The whole trial was so maddeningly vague. Would no one else see that? Would no one else stand up for her? Surely not everyone in the circle believed this trial was fair.

Nevertheless, as Sir Remmik picked up her dagger and described to everyone who had not been there exactly how Linsha had been found knocked unconscious over the body of the man she had just allegedly killed, a murmur of voices rumbled in the ranks behind her.

Linsha gritted her teeth. She was not allowed to dispute the charges until the judge finished the case against her, but by that time she had a feeling Sir Remmik would be hammering the nails down on her coffin. His belief in the law would not allow him to lie outright or manufacture evidence. All he had to do was cleverly twist everything she had said and done in the past few months into a sordid conspiracy to kill Sir Morrec and discredit the position of the Knights of Solamnia in the Missing City, and because of his reputation and rank, everyone would believe it. Her reputation was already marred by the previous charges against her, and she had not been in the Missing City long enough to overcome Sir Remmik's dislike of her. One hundred years would probably not be long enough.

Was there no one from the city to argue her case? She glanced around at the people behind her. All she saw were the faces of Solamnic Knights. There were no civilians, no representatives of the dragonlord, no members of the Legion. Was it possible Sir Remmik had closed the council to anyone who might be able to help her? Linsha felt the truth like a cold ache in the pit of her stomach.

"Does the defendant have anything to say in her defense?" Remmik said. Her hands gripped the board in front of her.

"Est Sularas Oth Mithas," she said firmly, her eyes pinned on Sir Remmik's stiff face. "My honor is my life. I have lived that oath for nearly twenty years and not once have I ever broken my oath or regretted keeping it. By my honor as a Knight of the Rose, I admired and respected Sir Morrec. I would not kill him. I did not plan the ambush or tip off those who did. I have always had the best interest of the Circle in mind."

"Lies are easy when you are confronted with the truth," Sir Remmik interrupted.

"The truth is easy when you have nothing to fear from it," she retorted. "Can you say the same? This council has only heard your version of this killing. It was a pretty tale, but I see you did not bother to corroborate any of it with Iyesta, or the Legion, or anyone in the city."

The senior Knight looked down at her with ice in his eyes, secure in his mind about her guilt. "Iyesta has not yet returned from wherever she took herself, and this council is no business of the Legion's."

Linsha leaned forward, the fear for herself suddenly lost in flood of worry. "Iyesta is not back yet? There has been no word?"

"No," one of the other Knights answered. "People are beginning to think the dragonlord has left for good."

"That's impossible. Iyesta would never leave this realm willing—" Linsha broke off there, reconsidering the possibilities. A troubling thought occurred to her. Iyesta might not leave the Missing City willingly, but what about unwillingly? Had something forced her to leave without a word to any of her loyal followers? Had the golds and silvers gone with her? What about the eggs under the city? The questions fell into Linsha's mind like boulders crashing down a slope. She needed answers. Would Purestian, the brass guarding the eggs know what happened to Iyesta? Worst of all, would Thunder know?

"The dragonlord has more important things to do than be in town when you are brought before the council," Sir Remmik said. He had never had a good relationship with Iyesta, only a mutual dislike.

Linsha slammed her fists on the rail and said with all her pent up frustration and anger behind it, "Why are you so convinced I killed Sir Morrec? Why do you do him such disservice as to even imagine that one of his officers would kill him? Why do you not investigate this more thoroughly? I never wanted him dead! Look at the results! Do you seriously think I'd want *you* in command?"

She regretted those words the moment she uttered them.

Sir Remmik's elegant silver brows lifted. "Were you planning to take over control of the circle yourself?" he said in a cool, insinuating voice. "Did these *unknown* attackers exceed their orders and leave you too incapacitated to complete your coup? When were you planning to assassinate me?"

Right now would be good, Linsha's rebellious mind thought.

More hushed talking filled the spaces behind her. Linsha could feel the Knights' stares on her back, and she guessed what they were thinking. Without another voice to defend her, no one would listen to her. They would believe their Senior Knight, the Knight who had handpicked most of them, trained them, cared for their needs, and gave them the best billet south of Solace. All of them seemed ready to take his word at face value. No one wanted to investigate who would ambush the Knight Commander of the Solamnic Circle, or why. No one showed any real curiosity about the odd storm that obliterated Gal Tra'kalas, the disappearance of Iyesta, or even the rumors about Thunder. They shoved those matters aside, obeyed their orders, and kept to their insular world behind the walls of the Citadel. Linsha felt ashamed for them.

Sir Remmik leaned back in his tall chair. "Sir Knights, it is time for your judgment. Is the Knight before you guilty of the transgression of murder and conspiracy?"

"Sir Remmik, one moment," came a voice from the audience. Sir Hugh stood and looked around as if he was hoping for some support. "Sir, I feel I must protest the manner in which this council has been called. It is too soon. The accused has not been allowed time to organize a defense, and the ambush of our men has not been properly investigated. I call for a postponement of the verdict to allow for these to be done."

"Paladine bless you to the third generation," Linsha whispered.

"I regret any misconceptions you may have, Sir Hugh, but I assure you, this Knight's offenses have been fully investigated."

"Like Chaos's chausses they were," said Linsha acidly.

Sir Remmik ignored her. "As for its hasty convening, I had reason to hurry this along. I have received word this noon that a large fleet of ships has been seen sailing this way. They have not been identified, nor do they look friendly. In case they mean to attack Mirage, we must be prepared. We do not need to drag out this council or have it dangling over our heads. Let us dispose of the traitor in our midst and move on to plan our defense."

A dead silence met his pronouncement.

Linsha could only stare in disbelief. A fleet of approaching ships. Ye gods. It had to be true. Sir Remmik would not make up a tale like that, but to use it as an excuse to shove her into an execution was intolerable.

Of course, no one else appeared to think so. The onlookers began talking excitedly among themselves, and only Sir Hugh had the decency to look angry as he sat down.

The council members went through the motions of talking among themselves and all too quickly reached a verdict.

"Guilty," they all said in turn.

Linsha felt too numb to react. Her anger drained away like water in a shattered barrel.

Sir Remmik banged on the table for silence. "In accordance with the Measure, the law of the Solamnic High Council recommends execution in the case of murder of a superior officer. Therefore it is the decision of this council that Linsha Majere shall be stripped of her rank and hung on the gallows until dead." He stood up and saluted the Solamnic flag. "So let it be done before noon tomorrow. This council is over."

Linsha's three guards took her arms and quickly tied her hands behind her back. She did not try to fight them. This was not the time or the place to try an escape, nor was she prepared to make the effort. Her mind was reeling. The world shifted beneath her feet. When she had walked into this hall, she had been a Rose Knight and these young guards had not dared do this to her. Now she was nothing to them. She was dishonored and was to be hanged like a common brigand for a crime she had not even imagined, without any hope of time to clear her name.

Her guards took her arms, pulling her roughly, and led her out to go back to the tower guardroom. When she stepped outside, she scanned the walls and towers for any sight of Varia. She wanted to tell the owl what had happened, what was going to happen, but she saw no sign of the the bird.

A shove to the middle of her back sent her staggering. "Keep moving," snarled one of the guards. Because her hands were tied behind her back, she lost her balance and fell to her knees.

The three Crown Knights moved in. They shoved her and buffeted her, inflicting pain and indignation while staying just short of an actual beating. If any other Knights watched the assault, they made no move to interfere.

Except one.

"Enough!" A voice cut through the afternoon heat. Sir Hugh's compact form broke into the middle of the group and shoved the three younger men aside. "Where is your honor?" he said in a low, furious voice. He pulled Linsha to her feet. "You are excused. Report to your duty officer."

"But, sir, the prisoner—" one tried to say.

"I will take her to the cells." His voice was flat and brooked no argument. Chagrined, the three hastily saluted and left Sir Hugh with Linsha.

Linsha found herself gasping for air. She ached in every part of her body. The Knights' roughness had not been brutal, but it had aggravated the injury on her head and the other bruises on her body.

Sir Hugh caught her elbow to hold her steady. "I'm sorry," he said in a low voice as they walked toward the guard tower.

She forced a faint smile past the pain in her face. "It's a relief to know someone is willing to stand up for the honor of this Circle."

He grimaced. "We have not stood strong enough this day."

Linsha swallowed hard. Her mind felt disconnected and dizzy; she was having trouble focusing on the castle around her. "Have you seen my owl?"

"Not since Sir Remmik ordered her to be driven off. I think she left on her own accord." He remembered the creamy round eye circles framing the dark eyes that had looked down on him from the roof and winked. "She seemed to know."

Linsha bowed her head to hide the sudden glitter of tears in her eyes. "If she comes back, tell her what happened. She will understand."

He said nothing else until he had escorted her down to the cells. Slowly he opened the heavy door and stood fidgeting with the key. "Sir Remmik has ordered a gallows to be built just outside the castle. Apparently, he intends to use you as an example."

"An example of what?" She sank to the bed slab. "Is it true there is a fleet of ships out there?"

"A messenger from the Legion came around noon today with a message for the commander. If that was the news, Sir Remmik did not tell us until the council."

"In his own good time," Lunsha muttered. "Will you untie me?"

A spasm of anger passed over Hugh's strong features. "Sir Remmik ordered the officers of the watch to keep you tied so you do not try to escape. He wants to chain you as well, but it seems chains for the prison cells have not yet been made."

"Lucky me," she muttered. A thought came to her, and she had to blink fast to keep back the lingering tears. "I know you're on duty tonight," she said hurriedly. "Please let me write a letter to my parents. My father must know the truth."

Sir Hugh locked the cell door behind him and said softly through the bars in the small window. "I will bring you paper tonight, and I will see your letter is sent." He turned on his heel and left her alone in the damp darkness.

Linsha stared at the glow of faint light from the lamp left burning at the foot of the stairs. Her hands felt numb from the ropes around her wrists. Slowly she took a deep breath and forced her tears away. Self-pity was weakness. Tears were a waste of time. She still had about eighteen hours until the hanging. Anything could change in that length of time. With her self-pity, she added her fear and all thoughts of the feeling of a rope around her neck, the fall, the crushing force at her throat. She balled these together and locked them out of her mind. She had to concentrate on other matters, such as easing the pain in her head, calming her breathing, and focusing on escape. She would not go easily to that rushed sentence without knowing the truth.

She lay down on the slab on her side. Her fingers moved clumsily but they could move, and she put them to work on the knots of her bindings. Beneath her filthy tunic, the two dragon scales on their chain slipped down to rest against her breast. Their shape and feel gave her comfort and strengthened her resolve. Iyesta needed help, and Linsha was not going to let the overlord down.

12

An hour before sunset, a ragged-looking figure in a broad-brimmed hat walked up the road to the Solamnic stables. He was leading two horses. The grooms, who had seen him before, welcomed him and the horses he led.

" 'Ere two of yours," he said with a lopsided grin. "Figured it might be worth a bit to git 'em back."

The grooms were quite willing to give the old beggar a few coppers for returning the animals, since one of the bedraggled looking horses was Sir Morrec's own mount. Four of the horses from the escort had found their way back, and now two more had been returned. The only ones still missing were Linsha's desert horse and a gelding.

"I found them out in the Rough," the beggar said, meaning the edge of the grasslands north of the city.

While the stablehands groomed and fed the horses, they were not loath to chat with the old man who sat on the edge of a water trough and listened to their chatter. He quickly learned what he needed, and after a while, he nodded his thanks and limped down the hill toward Mirage.

143

Eight hours after Sir Hugh left Linsha in her cell, she collapsed back on the wall by the slab bed and nearly gave in to the despair that pounded against her resolve. Less than ten hours left and she was no closer to freeing her hands than she was hours ago. She had managed to squeeze her arms around her legs so her hands were in front of her, but her arms were aching, her wrists were rubbed bloody, her hands were so swollen she could not move them, and the knots remained stubbornly tied. The rope, made from the tough hemp grown in the marshes along the Blood Bay, was barely frayed from the constant rubbing she had tried on the edge of the slab bed.

Linsha closed her eyes, ignoring the pain, and tried to rest for a minute or two. She must have slept a little, for the next thing she knew, an unexpected noise jerked her awake. She peered muzzily at the door of the cell and saw it swing open. Sir Hugh and another Knight she couldn't see well walked into the cell. Maybe Sir Hugh had finally remembered that paper he promised.

Linsha forced herself to sit upright. "Water," she croaked.

"Untie her," the strange Knight demanded. He shifted slightly behind Sir Hugh, and Linsha saw the faint glint of a short sword in his hand. Her eyes flew to his face. He wore the daily work tunic of the Solamnic Knights and a light cloak, but even in the dim light she would have recognized those features anywhere.

Sir Hugh approached her, the planes of his face wary and tense. He looked at her wrists and the rope, winced, then shook his head. "You'll have to cut it," he said.

The other Knight swiftly slid the blade of a dagger between Linsha's wrists and cut the ropes. She gasped as the ropes fell away and the blood throbbed through her wrists and fingers.

Sir Hugh backed away from the Knight.

The strange Knight turned swiftly, the short sword raised to strike.

Linsha moved quickly, too. She threw herself on the Knight's arm, deflecting the weapon from its intended victim. "Don't kill him," she demanded. "It's not his doing."

Sir Hugh had not moved to evade the Knight or fight back. He held up his hands in a gesture of conciliation. "Take her and go. The guards on the walls will soon grow suspicious if they do not see the sentries posted at the inner gate."

"Bring the others down here," the strange Knight called up the corridor.

Footsteps hurried down the stairs and four Solamnics appeared, carrying a fifth. Two of the Knights uncermoniously dumped the recumbent man on the slab, shoved their two companions into the cell, and blocked the doorway with their swords.

"You," the stranger said, pointed to a Knight closest in size to Linsha. "Give her your tunic."

Linsha pulled hers off with clumsy fingers and put the man's plainer and cleaner tunic on. Her three rescuers backed out of the door, opening a way for her to leave the small stone penal cell.

She turned once and said to Sir Hugh, "Thank you. Your willingness to believe in the possibility of my innocence is not misplaced."

He watched her with shadowed eyes and said nothing.

The stranger ushered her out and, after locking the cell door behind her, led the small group up the stairs and through the guardroom. This late at night, only the Knights on duty were awake, so the room in the tower was nearly empty. Two men who had not fared so well when the intruders entered, lay close to the door. They were quickly moved out of sight from casual view.

"They're not dead," the leader reassured Linsha when he saw the look of pained dismay on her face.

At the door, he held her back and placed a light helm over her head to hide her tell-tale curls. "We brought an extra man with us," he explained. "So four arrived and four will leave."

Linsha settled the helm carefully over her bruised face. "The man you had to carry down?" It wasn't much of guess.

"Yes, but he is a gift to your circle."

One of the other "Knights" chuckled. "He's a spy from the Knights of Neraka we caught a few days ago. Sent by Beryl. We thought your Knights should have him."

In the brighter light from the oil lamps around the room, Linsha finally recognized the other two men as well. Legionnaires, all three of them. "Lanther," she said to the leader, "Why are you doing this? Does Falaius know?"

"He didn't want to know. Something about Solamnic jurisdiction." The tall Legionnaire opened the door wide so the light spilled out into the darkness. "We're not out of here yet," he cautioned the others, "so keep quiet and move fast."

Linsha picked up a light cloak from a hook on the wall and threw it over her shoulders to help disguise her shape. "How did you get in here?" she asked softly.

"We told the gate warden we had messages for the Senior Knight from the elves outside Silvanesti. We have delivered our message, and we are leaving. Now."

As he said the word, he stepped out the door and strode to a post where four horses stood hitched. Linsha came behind without hesitation, followed closely behind by the other two. Silently, with stern purpose, they mounted and rode through the outer ward to the castle's main gate. A small postern door had been placed on the right side of the stout iron bound gates. It had already been closed and locked again for the night, but a sentry came quickly at their approach.

"You're not staying the night?" he said in some surprise. "It is a long way back to Silvanesti without rest."

"Our commander told us to return as quickly as possible," Lanther said, adding just the right amount of world-weary disgust in his tone.

The sentry shrugged. Holding his torch in one hand, he began to turn the lock in the postern door.

Linsha glanced surreptitiously around the outer ward. From her position near the main gate, she could see the stony ramparts of the inner wall and through the tower gateway into the inner ward. A block of light shone in the darkness at the base of the gate tower and went out as quickly. Linsha stiffened. Someone had just walked into the guardroom.

Lanther and the two Legionnaires had not noticed, for their attention was fixed on the sentry, who was taking an inordinate amount of time unlocking the postern. Any moment the unconscious Knights in the guardroom would be discovered, or Sir Hugh and his men would give an alarm.

Linsha strained to listen, her body taut as a bowstring. Her horse, sensing her tension, tossed his head and sidled nervously into the horse beside him, who jumped forward into Lanther's mount. In that brief moment of jostling horses, Lanther glanced back, and Linsha caught his eye and jerked her head toward the inner tower.

In that moment the click of the lock came loud and very welcome. The sentry began to pull the gate open. A distant, muffled shout sounded from the inner ward. The sentry paused, the gate half-open. Lanther snatched the moment of surprise. With a muffled oath, he wrenched the gate open and kicked his horse into a full canter, knocking the sentry aside as he went by.

Shouts echoed from wall to wall; a horn blew an alarm from the inner keep. Linsha knew all too well the skill of the archers who manned the high parapets and the tower vantage points. Like a plainsman, she ducked low over her restive horse's neck and sent him leaping through the gate after Lanther. The other two men followed suit. Spread out in a line, the four riders spurred their horses out from the shadow of the great wall and down the road into the dark, out of range of the powerful Solamnic bows.

Linsha heard the sharp snap of several bows and the thrum of speeding arrows, but the shafts missed the last horse by several lengths. The surprise had been complete enough that the four escapees were out of range before the archers could find their targets. Linsha lifted her head into the wind and grinned in pure relief.

Out of the corner of her eye, she saw a silhouette, a ghastly shape on the hillside, showing black against the stars—the gallows, nearly complete and waiting for morning. It could continue to wait, Linsha thought. Let Sir Remmik find some other use for it. She was away.

Hogan Bight, Lord Governor of the port city of Sanction, stalked down the long corridor toward his suite of rooms. He walked the gait of a man pushed beyond endurance, and at every step, he slapped his thigh with his gauntlet in the manner of someone whose mind was on matters both infuriating and far distant. His eyes straight ahead, he paid no attention to the bodyguards who worriedly followed him along the marble-tiled floor.

For a day that had begun in such promise and hope, yesterday had ended in despair. Sanction should have been free by this time. It should have been celebrating. Instead, the inhabitants of the city were burying their dead, treating their wounded, and wondering what had happened. The victory they had planned for so long was snatched out of their hands, and there wasn't a thing Lord Bight, the Solamnic Knights, or the townspeople had been able to do about it. The plan had failed.

Lord Bight still was not certain how it had failed. The Knights of Neraka had been routed! They fled the battlefield in a state of total panic. But something—or someone—had turned them back, and only by the grace of the moats of lava and the fury of the defenders of Sanction had they been thrown back at the very walls of the city.

Now everything was as it was before. The siege still continued; the enemy still camped at the gates. He still needed the Solamnics to bring men and supplies.

Lord Bight cracked a glove against his thigh again. Gods, how he hated the Knights of Neraka. This was his city. He had rebuilt it almost from the ground up. He had given Sanction his devotion, his wisdom, his time, and his strength. Yet the Knights were determined to get it back, and they were crumbling it out of his grasp a little bit every day.

Yawning, he reached his apartment and slammed the door in the faces of his guards. Let them stand their posts out there tonight. Just let an intruder or assassin dare enter his room. He would welcome something to vent his rage upon. Striding into the front room, he stopped, his arms akimbo.

"Out!" he bellowed.

His two servants bowed once and cleared the rooms. They knew better than to argue when their lord was in this mood.

Lord Bight found himself alone at last. He stretched to work some of the stiffness out of his aching muscles, then one by one he shed his bloody, smoke-stained garments and kicked them in a pile. He would give anything for a swim in the bay, but it was too late—or too early—for that. It would be dawn soon and he would be needed in the city. He would have to settle for a bath in the garden bath house.

Something banged against one of the leaded windows.

Instantly alert, Lord Bight snatched his long dagger and placed himself out of sight of the window. The noise came again—a muffled thumping followed by an owl's shrill call of distress.

Lord Bight leaped for the window, a curse on his tongue. The dagger clanged to the floor. He yanked open the leaded frame and threw out his arms to catch the bedraggled bird that flopped through the casement. He recognized the owl immediately, for she had been in this room before.

"Varia!" he said in astonishment. "What are you doing here? Where is Linsha?"

The owl tried to stand upright and failed. Her leg and one wing were bloody and torn; her body was so thin he could feel her bones beneath the feathers. She looked up at him, her dark eyes huge.

"We need Crucible," she rasped.

he four riders reached the base of the hill, and the three Legionnaires continued to urge their horses along the road toward Mirage and the Legion headquarters. Only Linsha turned her horse to the right on the path she often took to Iyesta's lair.

Lanther almost missed her departure. He glanced back to be sure everyone had survived unscathed and saw the tail of Linsha's horse disappearing into the darkness of another path. Reining his mount to a stop, he waved on the other two, wheeled his horse around, and galloped after her.

He rode hard, pushing his mount on the uneven, night-dark trail, and caught up with her near the crumbling foundations where the road crossed the remains of the old city wall.

"Where are you going in such a hurry?" he yelled over the pounding hooves.

A look of irritation flashed over Linsha's face. Although she was deeply indebted to Lanther and his men and greatly relieved that she was free, she had hoped to slip away in the darkness for just an hour or two without curious eyes and questions she could not answer.

"I'm going to Iyesta's lair," she said tersely.

"She's not there. She has not been seen since the storm."

"I know. But I can't believe she has left. I want to go look around."

"Now?" he sounded surprised and dubious. "Wouldn't daylight be better?"

Daylight wouldn't matter where she wanted to go, but she didn't want to tell him that. Instead she slowed her horse to a trot and said as patiently as she could, "Sir Remmik will have the circle out in arms looking for me before too long. He won't let this go."

"We have a few hiding places you can use."

"I know. I accept your hospitality. I just have to do this first."

He heard the urgency in her voice and accepted her decision. "Fair enough. I'll go with you. The militia is camped all over the grounds, keeping watch on the dragonlord's lair and treasure until she returns."

Linsha felt a pang of uneasiness. "Shouldn't they be out preparing the city's defenses? I heard there is a strange fleet near the city."

"We've heard that as well, and we have scouts out to watch for its approach. The militia is doing what it can."

She frowned. He certainly sounded casual about all of this. Everything she had heard in the Citadel had sounded dire. Was it possible Sir Remmik had exaggerated the situation to help grease her conviction through the council? She desperately wanted to believe this gathering disaster was being inflated out of proportion—that Iyesta had left on business of her own and would soon return, that the fleet was not hostile and would pass Mirage by, that Thunder was playing at overlord and would stay on his side of the river, and that the storm damage would be easily repaired and the Missing City would return to normal. But things rarely turned out so neatly. What she really wanted was facts, hard fresh news from a source she could rely on. She wanted Varia. Where was the owl?

She made no more comment but held her words until they reached the dragon's lair. She had to admit the militia was vigilant in protecting Iyesta's lair. Sentries stopped them in three different places before they reached the courtyard in front of the throne room.

A dense darkness filled the old ruins, for no torches or campfires were allowed to burn, and the pale moon had already set an hour before. The crowd of people hoping to see Iyesta had given up and returned to their homes, leaving the dragon's guards and the militia to keep their fretful vigil.

Linsha halted her horse and glanced around to get her bearings. She could already see the lair was empty; however, there were one or two other places she wanted to check that might not have been carefully examined.

"Stay and do not move," spoke a voice at Linsha's right. "There are a dozen weapons aimed at you right now."

Linsha raised her hands to show they were empty. Lanther did likewise.

"Mariana?" she called softly. "I know your voice."

"Lady Linsha?" The reply was immediate and filled with surprise. "We thought you—" The words broke off as if the speaker reassessed the possibilities. "Lower your weapons," she ordered her silent guards. "I will talk to them."

A form, lean and lithe, took shape out of the night and came to stand by Linsha's stirrup. Mariana Brownstem was a friend, as well as a half-elf and a captain of the dragonlord's militia. She gave Linsha a feral grin. "If Lanther is with you, then I am guessing the Solamnics have lost their prey."

"For now," Linsha replied.

"I am pleased. I did not understand their desire to destroy their best Knight."

"It depends on how you interpret 'Best Knight.'"

"You are welcome to stay here. The Solamnics would not dare to probe too deeply into militia territory."

The words clashed in Linsha's mind. Militia territory. Solamnic jurisdiction. Legion domain. Each group had its own territory and influence that it jealously defended to the detriment of cooperation, allied effort, and possibly the safety of the city. Time would tell if the three groups could find a way to work together without Iyesta. In the meantime, she supposed she should be grateful that the Legion and Iyesta's militia liked her well enough to offer her sanctuary from her own Order.

"Thank you. What I'd like to do now is look around the grounds."

Mariana pursed her lips. She knew well Linsha's skill at gathering information. "Do you know something about Iyesta's departure?"

"No more than you. I just want to satisfy my own curiosity."

The half-elf scanned the eastern sky where a blue-white star was glimmering on the horizon. "It will be dawn soon. If you will wait for daylight, I will escort you."

Linsha knew she had little choice now. Of course, it was very possible more people knew about the labyrinth under the city, yet Iyesta had deliberately told her only she and the dragons knew of the eggs. If she

155

had an escort following her everywhere she went, she would not be able to visit the egg chamber. That would have to wait for later when she could go alone.

There was nothing else for it. Dismounting, she followed Mariana to a lightless camp in the shelter of the courtyard wall. A sentry led the horses away. Lanther threw down a blanket and stretched out on his back to rest. While Mariana treated the raw wounds on her wrists, Linsha recounted the trial and Sir Remmik's verdict.

"What will he do now?" Mariana asked.

"If he doesn't recapture me, and I can't find a way to clear my name, he will have me blacklisted from the Order. I will become an exile and a target for every Solamnic Knight who wishes to remove a blight from the good reputation of the Order." Linsha heard herself and recognized the bitterness creeping into her voice. She thought this would never happen again. The ugly business with the Clandestine Circle in Sanction had been bad enough. She had been blacklisted for several months while she tried to convince the Solamnic High Council that Lord Bight was better left alive and the Clandestine officers had overstepped their authority. The Council finally reinstated her pending the outcome of the trial and cleared her record when the case against her fell apart. Sadly, she did not think that was going to happen this time, unless she found the culprits and presented them, their bloody weapons, and their signed confessions to Sir Remmik.

"Unless, of course, the entire garrison is wiped out," Lanther commented from his blanket.

Linsha had to wrench her thoughts back to what he had just said. "What?"

The Legionnaire put his hands behind his head. "If the entire Solamnic garrison is wiped out by some disaster, you won't have to worry about the blacklist," he pointed out.

Linsha wasn't amused. "I don't want my reputation cleared that way." She rubbed her eyes. The excitement of the escape had worn off, and she felt like something the cat left on the stoop.

"Just a thought."

"I've been through this before," she explained. "I will regain my rank again." She said it with more hope than conviction.

Mariana's pale oval face turned toward her in surprise. "Again? Do the Solamnics make a habit of blacklisting you?"

Lanther made a hard, scornful sound. "Forget them. Join the Legion. We will take you any time you say the word."

Linsha leaned back against the warm stone wall without answering and let her eyes slide closed. While she admired the Legion and respected their work, the Solamnic Order was her heart and soul and had been in her blood since she was old enough to hear the tales of Sturm Brightblade and her uncles, Sturm and Tanis, who died in the service of the Order. She was not yet ready to turn her back on the Knighthood no matter how often it tried to get rid of her.

Someone pressed a cup into her hand. Without opening her eyes, she inhaled the rich fruity fragrance of a red wine vinted in Mirage and drank it to the dregs. Her cloak was pulled warmly about her shoulders. Lethargy stole over her, warm and langorous and heavy with sleep.

But true sleep came only fitfully and was beset by bad dreams and visions that appeared and vanished with irritating abruptness. Pictures formed in her mind—her family; her brother, Ulin, standing on a strange-looking promontory and staring at the sky; her aunts, Laura and Dezra, standing at the top of the stairs of the Inn of the Last Home; her father, Palin, and her mother, Usha, saying nothing and looking grim. These images would glow with perfect clarity like flashes of lightning and then be gone.

Worst of all were the visions of the wind and the storm and the ambush. She could see the pounding rain, the slick, drenched ground, the ruins, and scattered glimpses of the Knights as they struggled with their foes. She saw Sir Morrec try to rally his men with his call. The black, indistinct figure lunged at her, and she saw again the blade sink into his chest. Then she saw the second man who stalked her. In one brief and brilliant illumination of memory, she saw the form who leaped out of the darkness and swung at her head with a short, heavy club. Something about him seemed familiar. His stance or the way he moved or something about his build—Linsha did not know, and her dreams did not give her clarification. They only teased her with hints of memory filled in with gleanings from her imagination.

She had only dozed there for two short hours when Mariana shook her out of the strange dreamworld. She came out of it slowly like a drunk out of a stupor, and when she pulled herself upright and forced her eyes to open on a new morning, she felt more exhausted than she had before her rest. The dreams faded away.

"Sorry to wake you so soon." The half-elf looked down at her with sympathy. In the clear light of morning a quirk of her dual heritage was revealed. Mariana had one blue eye and one green eye as clear as gems. Come," she said. "We must get you out of sight."

Linsha accepted her hand and allowed herself to be pulled to her feet. Pain shot through her neck and arms from the uncomfortable position she had kept the past few hours. Groaning, she stretched her tight and weary muscles. This had been a very difficult six days. She would have given anything for some of her grandmother's tarbean tea and a huge plate of eggs and ham from the Inn's kitchen. Instead, Mariana handed her a steaming cup of Khurish kefre strong enough to strip the hair from hides. She tasted it and grimaced, then dumped the contents down her throat. It flowed down hot and powerful and jolted her tired body awake.

"If you feel as terrible as you look," the captain suggested, "perhaps we should get you a healer. The bruises on your face have turned a charming shade of green."

"Thank you," Linsha said with a weak grin. "Any more of that kefre and I'll need a healer. Where is Lanther?" She pointed to the empty space on the ground where his blanket had been.

"He left a while ago. He said he would be back to get you, so look around while you can."

She considered asking if she could investigate on her own, then promptly answered herself. No. There were too many guards and militia around the palace grounds who considered this their territory. They would not favor someone else poking around the place to look for evidence of their missing dragonlord—at least not without their help. Perhaps later, if she did not find anything of significance here—and she really did not expect to—she could slip away and try to find the entrance to the labyrinth where the water weird guarded the stairs. Iyesta had said the brass dragon scale would allow her to enter the passages safely.

She took a deep breath. The morning was fresh and cool with a sharp breeze from the sea. No clouds marred the perfect sky. It was a beautiful day to do anything but evade capture and explore an underground labyrinth.

She picked up two lanterns from a pile of gear and lit them with tiny flames from the cooking fire.

"I'll not leave yet," she said to Mariana and handed her a lantern. "Let's go this way."

The two women walked out of the courtyard and made their way across the wide ruins to one of the lushly overgrown gardens. Several other militia and guardsmen joined them until they had a group of eight striding along behind them.

"Do you know of a series of passages under the palace grounds?" Linsha asked.

Mariana nodded. "Iyesta did not like anyone to go down there because she kept her treasure in the large chamber under her throne room, but most of us know about it."

"Has anyone gone down there recently?"

The half-elf grew thoughtful. "I know a group of the dragon's guards went downstairs through the throne room entrance to be sure the treasure was intact. We feared Iyesta might have taken her treasure and left for good."

"She didn't."

"No. Nothing was touched and there was no sign of her." Mariana looked around curiously at the path they took. She was a tall, well-balanced warrior who was fiercely loyal to the dragonlord and the militia, and someone who took her job very seriously. She had made it her business to know every inch of the grounds of the palace, yet she knew of no reason why Linsha would bring her to this particular area. "What do you know about the passages?" she demanded.

"That they are much more extensive than mere passages under this palace," Linsha said.

She slowed down along a narrow path and scanned the crumbling, ancient buildings around her, looking for the one she remembered. Then she saw it, its doorway nearly lost in a mass of vines and flowering creepers. She led the way inside and found the steep stairs that led downward. The others followed silently.

The light swiftly faded behind them, and the damp, cool darkness took over. Linsha held her lantern high and found the right passage that led downward into the labyrinth.

The half-elf chuckled mirthlessly at the stone walls around her. "I did not know that entrance was here. I wonder what other entrances she had hidden around."

Linsha was about to reply when she noticed something slightly different. She stopped so fast, the captain behind her bumped into her back and jogged the lantern in her hand, sending shadows jigging madly over the walls. Fearfully, Linsha pushed the lamp into Mariana's hand and strode forward several paces where she could be away from the smoke and smell of the burning lantern. She sniffed the dank air slowly and deliberately, and she caught it again—a faint smell that had not been there the few days ago when she came this way with Iyesta.

"Mariana, leave the lamps and come here," she insisted.

The half-elf heard the tone in her voice and did not argue. When she reached Linsha, she started to say something then she, too, found the taint in the air. Her brow lowered to a worried frown. From her elf-blood she had inherited stronger senses, including a more powerful sense of smell. She knew immediately from which direction the smell emanated, and with Linsha beside her, she hurried along the passage. The rest of the group followed close on their heels. The tunnel here was high and wide and skillfully built, full of moving air, echoes, and a sense of space.

"I don't know where this leads," Linsha said.

"I don't either," was Mariana's only reply.

They said nothing more for nearly a quarter of an hour as they walked through the dark passages of Iyesta's lair and followed a smell that grew stronger with every passing minute. Even the soldiers of the guard and the militia had caught the smell and murmured worriedly among themselves.

All too soon the stench became heavy and pervasive. Linsha and Mariana covered their noses with their sleeves and pressed on in the thick darkness.

Something small and multilegged skittered out of the light, its claws making hard scratching noises on the stone. The two women exchanged glances. They both recognized the creature in the brief glimpse they had before it disappeared—a large carrion beetle. And where there was one, there were usually more.

Linsha held the lantern overhead. There was a mutual gasp. More beetles clung to the wall and the ceiling of the passage, their oblong bodies iridescent with a sickly greenish light reflected from the lantern. So replete were they that they did not move as the group passed by them with lanterns.

"I believe we're near the throne room," Mariana said quietly. "There are supposed to be more large chambers under there connected by passages large enough even for Iyesta."

"Did anyone notice this smell when they went down to check Iyesta's hoard?"

The half-elf's voice was muffled through the cloth of her sleeve. The reek was so strong now that her eyes were watering. "I don't believe so. That was three days ago. They would have investigated this."

Just ahead, at the farthest edge of the light, they saw the passage come to an end in a high-arched doorway.

Beetles clung to the doorframe and scuttled across the floor. The blackness beyond was impenetrable, and out of the void came a stench so foul that the searchers could hardly draw breath.

Fighting off fear and sickness, Linsha, Mariana, and the soldiers groped forward into the dreadful opening. The walls and ceiling around them vanished into a vast space that echoed with their footsteps and the sound of uncountable insects scrabbling and chewing and chittering in the darkness.

Linsha raised the lantern again. The feeble lantern light spread a small pool of pale light across the great floor. It was not nearly bright enough to light the entire cavern, but it was enough to show them the end of their search. Her hand flew to the dragon scales on the chain under her shirt. Mariana gave a cry of despair.

They had found Iyesta.

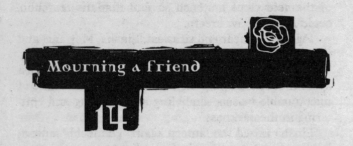

She lay sprawled across the floor of the abandoned stone chamber, a great hulking carcass that stretched almost from wall to wall. They knew it was she by the size of the corpse and by the piles of brass scales that heaped on the floor where the carrion beetles had chewed them loose to get at the flesh beneath. Withered and tattered skin hung over the skeleton like a ragged blanket. Bone shone through the rents and gaps in the half-devoured flesh. It was difficult to tell how long she had been dead, for the beetles had been hard at work and through the gaping holes and tears in the skin, the searchers could see the corpse writhe with the gorging insect bodies.

"Paladine preserve us!" Mariana moaned. "What did this to her?"

Huddled around the two small lanterns, the group made its slow way around the corpse toward the head. What they found dismayed them all.

"Oh, gods," Linsha murmured for everyone.

The long, supple neck lay collapsed on the stone floor, mostly eaten away by the beetles, but where the head should have been was nothing but a dried pool of blood.

"Someone took her head," breathed Mariana. "Who would do that?"

"Another dragon," Linsha said flatly.

"Thunder?" gasped one of the soldiers.

The captain shook her head in disbelief. "How would a dragon have gotten in here? We've doubled the guards on this palace since Iyesta's disappearance."

"Since her disappearance," Linsha repeated. "What about the night of the storm? All this time we've worried for her and looked for her, she's been dead below our feet." She whirled around, glaring at the tiny pool of light thrown from the lanterns. "We need more light. We must learn what happened here. Who killed her? Who took her head?"

Mariana readily agreed. "You three. Go back the way we came. Bring torches and all the help you can find. Tell anyone who comes down here to wear a mask. You three—" she turned to the next set of soldiers— "take word to the city elders, the Legion, and the Solamnic fortress that Iyesta is dead. I'm sure you are smart enough to leave Lady Linsha's name out of your report. Now, you two—" she spoke to the remaining soldiers— "there is another entrance over there, large enough for a dragon. Get torches and see if that corridor leads to the treasure vault. The way should be shorter than the way we came."

The guards and the militia soldiers were quite willing to obey, anything to get out of that chamber of reeking death. They took one of the lanterns and departed to their tasks, leaving Linsha and Mariana alone in the darkness that rustled and clicked with the sounds of thousands of carrion beetles.

Linsha stifled a shudder. This was so unbelievable.

How could Iyesta be dead? She was vibrantly alive and well and . . . invincible! . . . only six days ago. What had happened to her?

Linsha heard an odd, stifled sound and turned to see Mariana wipe tears from her eyes. Her strong shoulders were shaking. Linsha felt like weeping herself, but not here, not yet.

She strode around the corpse to the opposite side to examine it from a different angle and to allow the half-elf a measure of time to grieve alone. She lifted the lantern and began a careful and gruesome examination of the corpse under the feeble light. There wasn't much to see. Except for the missing head, the dragon's body was fairly intact despite the beetles. She had not been blasted or burned with sorcery or seared with another dragon's breath weapon. It looked to Linsha as if the dragon had walked into the chamber and dropped dead in her tracks. A few hours ago, Linsha would have said that was impossible. Of all the possible clues or evidence Linsha had hoped to find down here, a dead dragon had never occurred to her.

A sickening thought suddenly struck her like a blow to the ribs. The dragon eggs. Iyesta had trusted them to her. What if they, too, had been destroyed? And what of the guardian, Purestian? For that matter, Linsha's thoughts bolted up another path, where were the gold and silver dragons who had befriended Iyesta and stayed in her realm to serve her? Anger, grief, and blinded frustration swarmed into her heart like giant wasps stinging her to tears. She shook her head savagely.

The fact that Iyesta's head was missing and the body withered pointed a finger to Thunder. Linsha could not believe that any one of the monsterous dragon overlords would have slipped into the Missing City unnoticed, killed Iyesta, taken her head, drained her magical energy, and left. Those dragons would have erupted into the city like comet, blasting death and destruction. They would have fought the brass for the thrill of the kill and, after taking her head, they would have burned Mirage to the ground.

No, this killing was done in secret by an assassin who did not wish to be found or even suspected until he was long gone. It was something Thunder would do. The big blue could not fight Iyesta face to face and hope to win. His move would be a surprise, in the dark, in a tight cramped place where Iyesta could not use her wings or size to the best advantage. The great storm had come from the west, so it passed over his realm first. He could have followed the storm to use it as a shield and a diversion as it raged over the Missing City. He might have lured Iyesta down here, and killed her, and taken her head to add to his totem of skulls. Linsha hoped she was wrong.

Voices echoed up the corridor, drawing Linsha's dark thoughts back to the present. She and Mariana walked to the arched doorway and waited for the approaching company. Neither of them could find words to say. There would be much to do and much to discuss with the leaders of the city, but Linsha could not participate as long as she was wanted by the Solamnic Order, and Mariana knew she would have to hand over the investigation of this tragedy to her superiors—not that she truly minded. Until the torches came to flood the cavern with light and the people came to crowd around the corpse and mourn, they had the darkness and the dead to themselves. They used the time to say goodbye in their own hearts to the dragon they both loved and respected.

An hour later Linsha walked out of the tunnels into the hot sunshine and blessedly fresh air. She dropped the Solamnic cloak in the nearest dark hole she could find and stripped off her outer tunic. If only she could change the rest of her clothes so easily and take a long bath. She knew she reeked of death and decay. She could still smell it on everything.

Lanther waited for her in the courtyard, his rugged face grim. "I heard the news," he said. "The city elders have sent out criers to spread the word."

"How are people taking it?" Linsha asked wearily. She sat down on a stone bench and put her head in her hands.

"Not well. Most are terrified and appalled. First the storm, then the murder of the Solamnic Knights, now the death of Iyesta. The mayor is running around in a panic. Falaius is badly shaken. I have never seen him look so old." He looked closely at her hunched shoulders and pale face. "Is it that bad?" he asked softly.

She glanced up at him, her green eyes shimmering with unshed tears. "It is beyond bad. Iyesta is nothing but a withered, beetle-chewed hulk. I could not even tell how she died, Lanther. It was horrible! And I don't . . . I don't know how to avenge her."

The Legionnaire came to put an arm around her shoulders, caught a whiff of her clothes, and changed his solicitous gesture to a pat before he moved upwind. "I've seen patrols of Knights out in the city this morning searching for you. We need to get you out of sight. And Falaius wants to talk to you."

"Could you get some clothes, too?" Linsha asked, a faint spark back in her red-rimmed eyes.

"Absolutely." He thrust a bundle into her arms. "I've already taken care of that."

She untied the bundle, and for the first time in days,

she laughed when she saw the bright colors and flimsy fabrics of the clothes he had brought. "A courtesan? Whose bits did you steal?"

"Borrowed. They're Callista's. She said the last thing the Solamnics would expect you to wear is a veil and courtesan pants."

She held up the flimsy, baggy pants and the tight corset favored by many of the courtesans in the city. She had to agree it would be a good disguise. As a thirty-six-year-old Knight with sword callouses on her hands, she was hardly courtesan material. With a wry smile, she ducked into a nearby building and changed into the outfit.

When she came out, Lanther gave her such a slow appraisal from head to slippered foot that her cheeks burned. "You missed your calling, Lady Knight," he said.

Linsha adjusted the bright gold veil over her curls and across her mouth and nose so only her eyes were showing. "I hardly think so," she replied tartly. "Now, how am I supposed to get to your headquarters? I can't ride in this . . . this . . . " She waved wordlessly at the pants.

Lanther's eyebrow rose to herald the quirky expression that often passed for a smile. He snapped his fingers. From around the open gateway of the wall came two men carrying a covered sedan chair with gauze curtains. Lanther pulled open a curtain and beckoned her inside.

Trying to look demure, Linsha stepped inside and sat down on the cushioned seat. The chair swayed and rose as the men lifted it and set off at a bumpy trot. Linsha gripped the armrests of the chair in alarm. The conveyance jerked and swung like an obstinant colt. After a while, seeing the chair remained upright, she relaxed a little and tried to enjoy the novelty. She flicked open the curtain just enough to see the city streets.

"Comfortable?" Lanther's voice called from the outside.

"I'd rather walk," she admitted.

"Not yet, my lady." His voice suddenly took on a quiet note of caution. "A patrol of Knights is approaching as I speak."

She pulled the curtains closed and leaned back in her chair, trying to look relaxed. The curtains were thin enough to reveal the outline of a person within and opaque enough to hide the details. With luck, the Knights would see only a woman inside and not bother to examine the chair's occupant more closely.

Especially since she had none of the jewelry, perfume, nail decorations, or face paints the real courtsesans preferred. Only smudges of dirt and a pervading smell of rot and decay.

"Halt!" ordered a male voice.

Linsha felt her heart beat faster. It was Sir Hugh, and the man was nothing less than thorough. Would he recognize Lanther's face or her profile through the gauzy fabric?

"Yes, my lord," whined a second voice. Linsha started. Did that nasally, obsequious voice belong to the Legionnaire?

"Where are you going with that chair?"

"My master sent me to escort this lady to a place unknown to his wife." He made an obscene gesture even Linsha could see through the curtains. "If you get my meaning, Sir Knight."

Linsha held her breath. She could make out Sir Hugh's outline through the curtain, and she could see he was staring intently at her. She leaned forward and blew a kiss at him.

"Let's get moving," Sir Hugh snapped. Without a backward glance, he reined his horse away and led his patrol up the street toward the North Quarter.

Linsha let her breath out in a sigh. For just a moment she thought he had recognized her . . . but, no; surely he would have spoken. She opened her mouth to say something to Lanther when a long horn blast came singing on the wind and stopped her words in her throat. The sound was picked up by another horn and another until the city rang with the clarion warning. In every street people stopped in their tracks and stared fearfully toward the sea.

"The signal is given," Lanther said. "The ships have been sighted."

Muttering an oath, Linsha thrust aside the curtain and swung her legs around to hop out.

Lanther's hand clamped around her ankle. "Where do you think you are going?"

Linsha froze. In those seven simple words she heard a steely edge of command that would not tolerate even the thought of disobedience. She had never heard that tone coming from him before, and it startled her enough to make her pause.

He made use of her hesitation to push her feet back in the chair and pull the curtains closed. "Stay in the chair. There are Solamnics just up the road. These men will take you to our safe house."

"I want to know—"

He cut her off. "I know you do. I will find out what I can."

The horns had finally stopped blowing, and an eerie silence held its breath in the city. The morning sun beamed clear and hot over Mirage, but everyone felt the chillness of the shadow of fear. There were no more dragons to protect the people, no more ghostly images to fill the streets and act as a mirror to hide behind. The dragonlord they had counted on for so many years was dead, and the city council was in a panic. A fearful storm had left buildings damaged, people dead, and the militia scattered. Now a strange fleet of ships drew near, and no one knew what to do about it. Iyesta would have flown over the ships and driven them off if they so much as showed a weapon, but by some hideous stroke Iyesta had become a withered, beetled-chewed hulk, and there was no one left to take command of her realm.

Linsha heard hoofbeats galloping toward them, and she looked back the way she and Lanther had come to see a patrol of centaurs cantering fast toward the center of the city. Their faces looked grim, and their hides were dark with sweat. They raced past without a glance, intent on their mission. Linsha guessed what that meant. The militia, scattered and distracted though it was, was making an attempt to regroup and plan their defense. She knew the Legion would be doing the same. Only Sir Remmik knew what the Solamnics would do.

With everything in mind, Linsha damped down her arguments, bolstered her patience, and nodded to Lanther. She would do as he ordered because it was the wisest thing to do. As a wanted criminal, there was little she could do to help at this moment. If the people on the approaching ships proved to be enemies and a fight ensued, she would come out and do what she could defend this city. Meanwhile, she would bide her time and look for an opportunity to return to the labyrinth and reassure herself that Iyesta's precious hoard of eggs was safe.

Lanther spoke to the two men carrying the sedan chair then hurried away. The chair began to move again, slowly wending its way through increasing numbers of people in the streets. The population of Mirage, on the treacherous edge of shock and panic, was moving again. Some people grabbed whatever weapons they could find and hurried down to the waterfront to join the defenses that were being hurriedly thrown together. Others hastily packed a few belongings and made their way west or north to get out of the city. Visitors and traveling merchants also gathered their goods and hurried to leave a city that might be plunged in the midst of war at any moment. Older people, poorer people, and those with nowhere to go simply did what they could to prepare for what might come and retreated into the shelter of their homes.

Linsha watched the activity in the streets through the slit in the curtain and felt her heart go out to the people of the Missing City. She had lived in a city under constant seige and had seen firsthand what panic could do. But where Sanction had a powerful lord governor, city walls, a moat of lava, a ring of volcanoes, and high mountains to help defend it, the Missing City had nothing. Parts of the city wall were still in ruins, the dragonlord was dead, and the lands beyond the city were mostly treeless, rolling, and easy to move across. There were no barriers to attack any longer. There was only the militia, the Legion, and the Solamnic Knights.

The Legion safe house proved to be a small house on the southwestern side of the city just outside the Garden Gate, a newly repaired city gate in a large section of replaced wall. The house sat in an unobtrusive little neighborhood on a low hill overlooking the city, not far from the sea and only a short walk from several farms where olives, grapes, and wheat were grown and sheep grazed on the scattered meadows. Linsha did not like its isolation or its distance from the center of the city and the waterfront, but it had the advantage of being at the opposite end of the city from the Solamnic Citadel.

She found the two-storied house already occupied by a staff of three older Legionnaires whose duty it was to care for any person the Legion decided should be kept safely out of sight for a while. In an Order where many of the members were deserters from either the Solamnic or Nerakan forces or had performed some task that angered a powerful enemy, the safe house was often in use.

After several good-natured jibes about her courtesan dress, the three Legionnaires brought Linsha a basin and water for a simple washing and some used clothing in good repair to replace the flimsy pants and the gold embroidered corset and belt. She gratefully accepted their offerings and used a chunk of scented soap to wash her hair and as much of her body as she could reach with a wet cloth. She carefully piled Callista's clothing aside to be returned to the courtesan with her thanks, and maybe a bottle of scent to ensure future goodwill. Callista, the girl who entertained the captain of the small city watch (among others), was one of Linsha's favorite and most active informers.

When she finished bathing, she pulled the clean clothes that smelled delightfully of herbs from their storage. There was a plain linen shirt, a short-sleeved over tunic dyed a rust brown, and soft leather pants. These clothes were much more to Linsha's liking. All she needed now was a sword, a dagger, and the slim stiletto she liked to carry in her boot.

She paused for a moment over the dragon scales and let the slender gold chain flow through her fingers. The bronze and the brass scales lay cupped in her palm like shining pools of metal. Iyesta and Crucible. These two dragons had befriended her, saved her life, and meant more to her than most humans. She could hardly bear the truth that Iyesta was dead. A great longing welled up in her to see Crucible again. Years ago, she had been cradled in his great legs, sheltered by his wings, and given the freedom to pour out every trouble in her heart to a caring ear. True, she had thought it had been a dream at the time, but later she had come to know Crucible and that feeling of friendship and comfort had never faded. She would give almost anything, short of life itself, to see him come winging down from the north to share her grief for Iyesta and to help her fight this growing chain of disasters. He would help her find the eggs, and he would know what to do about them if they had been abandoned.

She sighed sadly and hung the chain back around her neck. Until she could find Varia, she had no way to send a message to Crucible, and even if she managed to get word to him, she knew he probably would not come. He had pledged his loyalty to Lord Bight, and he would almost certainly be helping with the defense of Sanction.

That thought led to another that had concerned her since she fled the Citadel. Where *was* Varia? The owl was more intelligent than many humans and had the advantage of being able to hide in small places and listen. She surely would have known about Linsha's arrest and the trial. So where had she gone? Why hadn't she stayed? Sir Hugo said Sir Remmik had ordered her to be driven out or killed, but Linsha could not believe the Knights would do that, let alone be successful at it. Varia was fast and cunning, and she was a good-luck symbol to the Citadel. She would not allow the Knights to drive her off if she did not want to go. The puzzle confused Linsha and worried her. She needed Varia now more than ever, and the owl's absence was one more trouble to plague her mind.

Clean and clothed, Linsha went to the tiny kitchen in the house to talk to the Legionnaires. They fixed her a light meal and brought her cool fruit juice to drink, but they did not know what was happening in the city or at the waterfront. The isolation that gave them anonymity also made it hard to keep up on the latest events. Lanther would be coming soon, they promised—and Falaius, if he could make it.

Linsha had to be content with that. She asked for

weapons, but all they could give her was an old dagger with rust on the blade. She shoved it in her belt. It was better than nothing. She paced in the house and tried to help in the small vegetable garden in back to distract her mind. She helped feed the chickens and fix food for the evening meal, and all the time she could only see ships in her imagination and hordes of warriors flooding to shore to burn and kill.

By the time evening came and the sun was settling into the west, Linsha was ready to slip out of the house and into the coming dark and find out for herself what was going on, in spite of the Knights' patrols. Before she could find an excuse to absent herself, though, Lanther appeared at the door, his rugged visage lined with exhaustion and concern. He sank down in a chair at the small dining table and gladly took a mug of ale offered by one of caretakers. Linsha and the three Legionnaires sat down at the table with him, their expressions anxious.

"The ships are out there," he said without preamble. "About sixty-five by rough count. They are anchored in staggered rows around the bay, cutting off the harbor. Nothing can get past them."

"Who are they?" Linsha asked. "Have they made any demands yet?"

"We don't know who they are. I've never seen ships quite like them. They're lean and fast-looking and rigged for the open sea. They fly no colors and have sent no delegations. There have been no demands, no requests, nothing. The ships just sit out there like they are waiting for something. We can see men onboard, and they are busy working on something, but we can't tell what they are doing."

"Has anyone tried to make contact with them?" one of the three inquired.

Lanther sighed and rubbed a hand over his eyes. "Oh, yes. The mayor sent an envoy out with a small escort to greet the strangers. They were all shot at close range by arrows and their boat set alight. None survived."

"So what is everyone doing?" Linsha said impatiently.

Lanther began to tick off on his fingers. "Falaius has been named temporary lord governor because Iyesta is gone, and he and the Legion were here first. For now, he is in charge of the defense of city. The mayor was so distraught over the murder of his delegation that he has resigned and is packing to leave. The city council and the city watch declared martial law and turned over their authority to Falauis. The commanders of the militia and the dragon's guard spent a good part of the day arguing with the Legion and the city council about who should be in charge, and the dragon's guard finally decided they would stay at Iyesta's lair and guard the premises. I'm not sure from whom."

He sounded disgusted, but Linsha was pleased to hear the dragon's guard would still be watching the lair. That meant no one would make unauthorized visits into the tunnels to desecrate Iyesta's body, steal the scales, or worse, find the eggs.

She refilled his cup with the golden ale and pushed a plate of oat cakes to him. "What did the militia do?"

"They fell in line. Finally. Dockett, the general of the militia, is a wise man who saw the wisdom of bowing to the inevitable." He drank his ale then relaxed and grinned at his audience. "Falaius offered him the position of second in command. They have groups scattered all along the western borders of the city where they were keeping watch for Thunder and long-range patrols that need to be called in, and the general told Falaius that he had more men under muster in the city. Falaius is also a wise man. Our meager one hundred is hardly a match."

Linsha crossed her arms. There was one group Lanther seemed to be leaving out, and she had a feeling she knew why. "What about the Solamnics?"

"They returned to their citadel, locked the gates, and will not come out. We sent a messenger up there to invite them to our council, but Sir Remmik refused. He claims his Knights are not ready to commit themselves. He said, and I quote 'The true course in conducting military operations is to make no—' "

"—movement until the preparations are complete," Linsha finished for him. "It is one of his favorite quotes. It's from an old military manual in the Solamnic Castle at Uth Wistan. It's a load of manure coming from him. He couldn't have that citadel more prepared."

"Maybe *he* is the one who is not prepared."

Linsha's eyebrows rose. She had not considered this view. Could it be possible that the man who organized, trained, and supplied a superb circle could not decisively lead it into battle? She thought back over the bits of information she knew about him and the few records she had seen, and she realized she had never heard him associated with a war, a battle, or a skirmish of any kind. He was trained to fight, but perhaps he never had. That explained some things about him. Solamnic leaders led by reputation, rank, and skill—of which Sir Remmik certainly had plenty—but they were also chosen by the Knights in the circle. How much longer, Linsha wondered, would the Knights of the Mirage circle put up with Sir Remmik's inflexible inactivity? It would hardly do their reputations any good to be known as the circle who hid in their shiny new castle while the town around them fought to defend itself. She grinned. If she hadn't already been put in the penal cells for murder, she'd probably be in there now for insubordination and disobeying a superior officer.

"So what is going on now?" asked another Legionnaire.

"Falaius and General Dockett are reorganizing their forces," he said with a yawn. He added to Linsha, "Falaius sends his regrets. He hopes you are comfortable for now."

She nodded to the other Legionnaires so as not to hurt their feelings. "For the moment. But I will not hide here if the city is attacked."

"I know. You would be a formidable ally if you were in command of the Citadel," said Lanther. He rose to go and gave Linsha a mock salute. "Tomorrow, Lady Knight, if you choose, I will bring you weapons and armor and make a Legionnaire out of you."

She returned his salute. "I don't suppose you have seen my horse."

He checked and said with a snap of his fingers, "No, but I have seen your owl. She was the one who told me about your trial and how you were imprisoned in the fortress."

The others looked at him astonished.

"She told you?" Linsha exclaimed. "She *never* talks to anyone else."

"You have an owl that talks?" said one of the three.

"She must have believed it was important to tell someone who could help you," Lanther said, ignoring the question.

"Where is she now?" Linsha asked.

He lifted his shoulders in a slight shrug. "I don't know. She left me, and I have not seen her since."

Linsha swallowed her disappointment as she said goodbye to Lanther. Varia did know about the trial and was worried enough to risk her safety to talk to Lanther. After that, she must have left, as she was no longer at the Citadel, the lair, or any of her other favorite perching spots. Perhaps she had finally decided to leave her companion. Linsha was still not certain why Varia chose to stay with her, so it should be no surprise if the owl grew tired of her and left to seek quieter or less dangerous surroundings. But her absence saddened Linsha more than she expected. With her heart heavy and her head aching with too many unshed tears, Linsha bid goodnight to the caretakers and sought solace in sleep.

Five hours after midnight, just before the rising of the sun, Linsha awoke to a crack of thunder. It was so loud it boomed over the city, shaking people awake and echoing among the towers. Linsha bolted upright in her bed. She could hear the other people in the house calling to one another in consternation. Surely this was just a common thunderstorm, not another storm like the one six nights ago. To be sure, Linsha pulled her tunic on over her shirt and padded barefoot outside to look at the sky.

The three Legionnaires joined her, and together they looked upward. Linsha felt a chill crept down her skin. There were no clouds. The sky was clear and filled with stars. Only a pale apricot glow on the eastern horizon heralded the coming of day.

Another peal of thunder cracked across the city.

A hand grabbed Linsha's arm, and its owner pointed wordlessly down toward the center of the city.

Thunder had come.

The great blue dragon hung over the city like a monsterous bird of prey, his wings outstretched to catch the rising heat from the fires that burned beneath. Lightning cracked from his jaws and struck a warehouse in the Port District, adding another fire to the growing inferno. The sound of thunder rolled over the streets and buildings. The dawn was calm with no wind yet from the sea, so the smoke from the fires rose in columns and slowly spread out in an ever-increasing canopy, blotting out the stars and casting a pall over the light of the coming sun.

"He's going to burn the entire city!" one of the caretakers cried.

"I don't think so," Linsha said, staring spellbound at the city below. "What good is a scorched ruin? Look! He's started fires in each district. I think he's trying to distract the city's defenders."

They watched, appalled, while Thunder circled over the Missing City. Light from the fires glowed on his belly and under his wings, illuminating his shape in golden hues. He seemed satisfied with his handiwork, for he contented himself with spreading the paralyzing dragonfear among the people below and using his lightning breath weapon only to destroy the few brave attempts the militia made to stand up to him.

Linsha shook herself free of her dread and shock. She bolted into the house and grabbed her boots and the dagger. She would have to get a sword somewhere and some armor or a shield. Running outside again, she shouted, "Do you have horses here?"

The Legionnaires barely looked at her, so mortified were they by the burning fires in the city. "Lanther said to keep you here until he called for you."

Linsha drew herself up to her full height and snarled, "Listen. You are members of his Order. I am not. I am a Knight of the Rose, and my place is down there."

One of the Legionnaires silently pointed to a small barn beyond the garden.

Linsha followed his gesture to the stone outbuilding and found a small desert-bred horse within. The gelding tossed his head nervously when Linsha entered and would not hold still to be bridled. Linsha knew he sensed the dragon, but she did not have time to cajole him. She clamped his upper lip in a vise-like grip and shoved the bit between his teeth. She decided not to bother with a saddle. Springing bareback onto the horse, she kicked it out of the barn and down the road toward the city.

In the dimness the road was unfamiliar and treacherous. People were out in the streets, in front of their homes, or standing on the flat rooftops to see what was happening. Others already knew and frantically grabbed for any transportation they could find to flee the dragon and the fires. Someone ran in front of Linsha's horse and tried to snatch at the bridle. Linsha rammed her heels into the terrified horse's sides and forced the animal past the man and his flailing arms.

Shouts and screams filled the night, dogs barked, and a few fire bells rang frantically in the distance for help that could not come.

When she passed the city wall and entered the Garden Gate, she saw the guards trying desperately to push the people back from the gates. Someone had managed to get it unbolted, and a mob of panicked citizens pushed frantically to get out. Linsha worked her way to a small messenger's gate where a militia soldier recognized her and let her in. She kicked her horse into a canter again and pressed on toward the center of the city.

The closer Linsha drew to the more inhabited districts the worse the chaos became. People crowded the roads, some trying to escape, some trying to reach the fires to help put them out before they spread out of control; some simply ran in a blind panic. Smoke settled among the houses and buildings, intensifying the darkness. The acrid air became difficult to breathe. It stung her lungs and nose, and its thick fumes brought tears to her eyes. She slowed her horse to a trot while she scanned the buildings, houses, and streets for some landmark that looked familiar in the lurid glow of the distant fires.

Linsha was well among the larger homes in the Garden District before she realized where she was and how to find her way to the Legion headquarters. Turning her mount east on a wide, open avenue she was about to urge it into a canter again, when she heard the recognizable sound of wind rushing over large and leathery wings. At the same instant a massive, paralyzing fear swept over her that was so horrendous, she threw her hands up to her head and screamed.

The horse went mad. It swerved to escape the hideous creature, and Linsha lost her balance. Her body slid off the horse's slick back and fell hard on the stone-paved road. Pain lanced through her back and the half-healed injuries in her head. She curled into a ball and vomited on the paving. The dragon slid overhead, his massive body a half-seen nightmare in the clouds of smoke. He weaved his horned head from side to side while he stared down at the city beneath him. His malevolent eyes glowed red with his pleasure. He flapped his wings once and swept over Linsha's place without seeing the Rose Knight curled on the ground. A heartbeat later, he had moved over another part of the city, and the worst of the dragonfear faded behind him.

Linsha lay still and panted. The aftertaste of sickness tainted her tongue. Her head pounded. Her back and shoulders protested the slightest move.

People ran by her. A few ran over her. She hurt so much she could not move. She could only breathe and lie still and hope no one tripped and fell on her. After a while she felt strong enough to draw her energy within her heart to ease her pain and convince her muscles to move. Her concentration gradually increased and the warm, healing power flowed through her. She accepted the fact long ago that she did not and never would have the skill for or the love of sorcery like her father and her brother, but thank the absent gods she had inherited enough of her father's talent to bolster her own few skills. Under the gentle ministrations of her healing magic, the pain eased and her back muscles loosened and relaxed.

In time, she was able to sit up without the world spinning. She took several calming breaths and climbed to her feet. Her body felt sluggish, and her head was still heavy with pain, but the ground stayed where it was supposed to, and her stomach made no more nasty heaves. All she could do was ignore the discomfort and move on. She had to find Falaius and the Legion. They would not be hiding in a castle. They would be doing what needed to be done. She gritted her teeth and began to walk in the direction of the Port District.

The sun had lifted above the horizon and changed the deep night beneath the roof of smoke and dust to a sickly pallor, adding a yellowish patina to the city. With the dawn came the freshening wind from the sea. The rising breeze stirred the smoke and sent it swirling through the streets. It tattered the canopy of fumes, carrying shreds inland toward the plains. It also stirred the fires in the burning buildings.

Missing City was built mostly of stone, but there were enough trees, wooden rafters, furniture, thatch roofing, hay barns, shutters, and other burnable things that a fire could make good headway through the homes, shops, and warehouses of the city. Once it took hold, a fire was very difficult to control. Would Thunder value the city enough to stop one of his fires if it blew out of control?

Linsha tore a strip from her linen shirt and tied it over her nose and mouth. She forced her feet to move forward one after the other, and she found that the more she moved, the easier the movement became. Her bruised muscles and battered joints warmed to the effort. She headed toward the Mayor's Hall in the center of the city with the plan to go on to Mirage and the Legion Headquarters if she could find no one there. More people crowded past her, their panic making them blind and thoughtless to everything but escape. She had to shove and beat her way through several mobs that streamed around her, threatening to carry her with them like floodwaters.

She grabbed one man who bled from several minor wounds to his head and shouted at him for information. From his uniform and weapons she took him for a soldier of the city watch, but he shook her off, threw his sword to the ground, and fled. Linsha picked up the sword. Short bladed and evenly balanced, it sat in her hand comfortably and gave her a small feeling of relief to be holding a weapon again. She pressed on deeper into the city.

Not far from the row of guild houses marking the edge of the Port District, Linsha was forced to stop to catch her breath. She leaned against a stone wall, the linen strip clamped over her mouth, and tried to catch some clean air from a gust that swept in from the sea. She knew where she was now, and it seemed to be the right way, but she sensed a large fire somewhere ahead of her. When the sea gust died, the smoke poured back over the streets, thick and hot and suffocating. She could hear a babble of voices strident with fear and anger and determination.

Then she heard something else—the clatter of hooves. They came from behind her, sharp and staccato, and something about them sounded familiar. She stood upright in time to see a centaur materialize out of the pall of smoke.

"Leonidas!" she yelled, leaping in his path.

The young stallion's hooves slid on the slick paving stones in his effort to stop. He yanked his javelin out of her way and barely managed to keep his footing without banging into the stone wall.

"Lady Linsha!" he bellowed, swinging around to face her. "Do not do that to me!" And in the next breath, "What are you doing here?"

"What are you doing here?" she countered. "Shouldn't you be at the city defenses?" The centaur, she noticed, was sweating profusely and grimy with smoke and dirt.

He gave his equine body a shake, sending a cloud of dust and hair into the smoky air. "I was. But I have to find the Legion. Caphiathus sent me to tell Falaius. There are armed warriors marching on the city. From the west." He spoke rapidly, in short bursts between gasps of air.

Linsha's eyes closed, borne down by despair. A menacing fleet in the harbor, a dragon overhead, and now warriors approaching the city. There was not much point in hoping the massed troops were the forces of some ally coming to the rescue them. The city had no allies anywhere near.

"Can you tell whose troops they are?" she asked.

The centaur jigged sideways impatiently and said, "They carry blue flags with gold lightning bolts emblazoned on the centers. My uncle says they are the army of the dragonlord Thunder." He cast a nervous eye skyward. "Lady, if you are in a hurry to go somewhere, don't let me keep you."

"Leonidas, I am going the same place you are, and I would really appreciate a ride," Linsha replied.

A gust of wind sent a cloud of smoke billowing over them.

"He's coming around again!" Leonidas cried.

"Down!" Linsha bellowed. "Get down!" To force her point, she grabbed Leonidas's mane and threw all her weight backward to haul him off balance.

Taken by surprise by her unorthodox movement, he staggered sideways. Normally surefooted, he could have easily scrambled back to his feet, but the form of the dragon darkened the sky overhead and the dragon-induced terror spread before his shadow like a palpable wave. Leonidas collapsed to the ground, his human torso wrapped around Linsha's, his horse body sprawled on the earth.

The ungainly position saved his life. Had he been upright and moving when the blue soared overhead, he would have been a target too tempting for the dragon to resist. Flattened on the ground, Thunder did not see him or Linsha through the swirls of smoke and ash. With a lazy flap of his massive wings, the dragon passed on to find other victims.

The dragonfear faded, leaving a sick taste in Linsha's mouth. She raised her head and felt the pain come thundering back into her skull. Her head was taking a serious beating these days. Groaning, she lay back and waited for the centaur to move.

Leonidas heard her groan and, mortified, unwound his arms from her body and scrambled upright. "Lady!" he gasped, his brown eyes wide with embarrassment and shame. "Forgive me. I hurt you. The dragonfear . . . I didn't . . ." His voice faltered to a stop.

She offered him a feeble grin from her place in the dirt. "It wasn't you. Without you, I might have been caught moving in the open. There is no one, not even my inestimable brother the dragonmage, who is immune to dragonfear."

Leonidas helped her up and, because he liked and respected her, allowed his fear and his bruised dignity to be soothed. He carefully helped her onto his back and moved out in a gentle trot toward the city center.

"The last we heard, Falaius set up a temporary headquarters at the city hall where he could stay in touch with the watch, the militia, and the Legion," he told Linsha. "Uncle said to look for him there."

Linsha sat quietly on his back for a few minutes then smiled. "Leonidas, it's all right. Just because my head hurts, it won't crack. You can go faster."

The centaur cast a worried look back at her, but he took her at her word and shifted his trot into a fast canter.

In less time than Linsha had taken to reach the edge of the Garden District, Leonidas carried her through the streets to the town square where most of the city offices and guild halls were located. They found the buildings and the square itself untouched by the dragon. In the shade of an ancient yew on the green, they found Falaius surrounded by a circle of heavily armed Legionnaires while he issued orders. The spot around the Legion commander was the only quiet place in the square. The rest of the open space was a scene of disorder and uproar as people ran heedlessly by, teams of horses pulled wagons loaded with families and belongings or merchants' wares along streets already overcrowded with pedestrians and pack animals. Soldiers tried to form ranks to march out, while members of the beleaguered city watch tried to keep some sort of order.

"Lord Falaius!" Leonidas shouted over the raised voices of other messengers who were also trying to reach the new city commander to pass on messages of the utmost importance. He pushed through the crowd right up to the ring of armed Legionnaires and shouted again. "I bring word from Caphiathus!"

His words reached Falaius, and with a gesture to his bodyguards, the commander waved the centaur into the circle.

Linsha stayed where she was on the centaur's warm back, and as they approached the big Plainsman, she wondered for the first time what her reception would be. She was an exiled Knight accused of murder, a representative of an order that was doing precious little to help. As far as she knew, only Lanther knew the details of her trial and escape, and Lanther was not there. She hadn't had time to talk to Falaius.

But she needn't have worried. The Legion commander greeted her with a weary grin and welcomed both of them into the circle of officers.

"Lady Linsha, you are not unexpected," the Plainsman said. "Although you may wish you had stayed in the Citadel's dungeon. You would probably be safer there."

She grimaced at the memory of the framework she had seen in the starlight. "No, sir, I'd probably be swinging on the gibbet by now. Lord Remmik wouldn't let a small thing like a dragon distract him from his duty."

"Then where is he now?" one of the militia officers snapped. "Where are the Knights of Solamnia? Why won't they come forth and help us?"

"Lord Remmik probably feels he is doing his duty by staying in the castle." Falaius replied. "He is keeping his beloved garrison safe."

An astute observation, Linsha thought, from a man who would find Sir Remmik's way of thinking totally foreign. Falaius had been commander of the Legion cell in the Missing City since its founding, and while he worked hard to keep his members safe, not once had he considered sequestering them "safely" in a fortress. That was not the way of the Legion.

She felt Leonidas shift from hoof to hoof and realized she had distracted the commander long enough. "Don't be polite," she told the centaur. "Tell him."

Falaius turned to the centaur. "Forgive me. What is the news from Caphiathus?"

The young stallion stiffened to attention. "Several large troops have been seen approaching the city from the west. They are flying the colors of the blue dragon."

A sharp outburst of curses and exclamations broke from the officers around the commander, but while Falaius remained quiet, his weathered face sagged and seemed to grow more haggard.

Then there was time for nothing more.

The blue dragon Thunder appeared suddenly out of the smoke and ash and settled his great bulk in the space of the square. Screaming in terror, people tried to get out of his way but there was not much warning and not much space between the buildings. Several dozen men, women, and children were crushed beneath his great weight, and many more were brought down by the sweeping of his massive tail. Without warning he belched a great gout of lightning that burst like a fireball in the top of the ancient yew tree.

The tree exploded, sending deadly splinters into the nearby warriors. What was left of the grand tree burst into flame.

The blast blew Linsha off the centaur and sent the buckskin staggering backward. Something slammed into her, and once again Linsha found herself on her back, aching and breathless. She felt her heart drumming with the terror of the dragon, but stronger still was a frantic concern for Leonidas and Falaius. She forced open her eyes and saw the burning tree. Voices screamed and wailed around her.

"People of the Missing City!" Thunder bellowed in his granite voice. "Surrender to me now, or I will unleash the fury of my armies!"

A heavy weight pinned Linsha to the ground. She managed to raise her head in spite of the pain it cost her and saw a body in the uniform of the city watch facedown across her stomach and hips, effectively weighing her down. The head was turned away from her, so she could not see who it was, and something warm and wet seemed to be soaking into her clothes. She stirred to try to get him off her, but his body had the heavy, collapsed feel of a corpse. Tilting her head further, she looked at the dragon crouched over the bloody square, his hideous horned head weaving back and forth. She felt his gaze sweep the green, and she remembered the look in his eyes when he saw her for the first time on Iyesta's back. She had an urgent desire not be seen by the monster. Her head dropped back to the grass, and she tried to press her body down into the earth beneath the dead man.

"In the name of our Dragonlord Iyesta," she heard Falaius shout, "we will never surrender this city to her murderer!"

The commander's voice rang rich and deep as a bell across the sounds of terror in the square. The dragon lifted his head. His wings rose and spread like a blue shroud.

"You heard him, General," Thunder said. "You may release your men."

Surprised, Linsha looked up again. She saw someone she hadn't noticed before—a figure seated on the dragon's back between the wings. A man, perhaps. His skin was blue and a mask of gold hid his features. He carried only a great round shield and a huge ram's horn. A man. Thunder allowed a man to ride him. Linsha could hardly take in the significance.

At the dragon's words, the warrior lifted the horn to his lips and blew a great blast of sound that soared over the city. Twice he blew the horn, and at the end of the second blast Linsha heard a reply echoing from the bay.

Thunder's wings swept down and the dragon sprang into the smoke-poisoned air, carrying his passenger with him. He paid no more attention to the ruin in the square. Rising above the buildings, he angled eastward and flew over the harbor.

"We're in for it now," Linsha muttered to the dead man on her hips.

17

As the dragonfear passed, a heavy silence settled on the square. Everyone who still lived drew a breath, then the quiet disappeared into a cacaphony of screams, shouts, cries for help, and groans of the wounded.

Falaius strode among the prostrate officers of his command and urged those who still lived to get to their feet. "War is coming!" he shouted. "Go to your posts!"

Most clambered to their feet and obeyed. Considering the force of the explosion that shattered the tree, surprisingly few men were dead or too badly wounded to move.

Linsha pulled her arm free and rolled the watchman's body off her stomach. She found the source of the wetness on her tunic. A large splinter from the yew had impaled the man's chest, and much of his life's blood had leaked out of the massive hole.

The smell of blood clogged Linsha's nose. Dizzy and sick, she tore off her overtunic and laid it over the dead man's face. Her linen shirt and pants were stained with blood as well, but unlike some barbarian races, she did

195

not believe in running into battle naked. What she needed now was armor—chain mail, a breastplate, anything.

A groan in a voice light and frightened hit her senses like a bucket of cold water. Leonidas!

She found the centaur sprawled on the grass, his body pricked red by a dozen large splinters. He groaned again, more irritably this time, and struggled to an upright position.

"Hold still," Linsha ordered. Using her dagger and a deft hand, she removed the splinters from his side and withers while he pulled out a few out of his chest.

His teeth clenched, he pulled out the last sliver of wood from his arm and tossed it aside. "I suppose I should be glad it was merely splinters and not the whole tree."

Linsha shot a glance at the dead man who had fallen on her. Before she could say anything, Falaius approached, his seamed face reddened with rage and iron determination. "Go back to the centaurs, Leonidas. Tell them what happened. Tell your uncle I will send reinforcements if I can. But he must hold out on his own for a while."

"Where do you want me?" Linsha asked.

The Plainsman looked at her pale face and the blood spots on her tunic. "Are you wounded?"

She shook her head then wished she hadn't. This was one headache that would not fade anytime soon. "The blood is someone else's."

"Then if you are able to fight, I would be pleased to have you come with me. I could use an able lieutenant."

An expression of disappointment passed over Leonidas's face, but he bowed to the commander and the Lady Knight. "Fight well," he said to Linsha, "and we will celebrate our victory together in the streets of the city."

On impulse, she took his hand, pulled him down until she could reach his face, and kissed his cheek in both blessing and farewell.

He bowed again, turned on his heels, and cantered away to the outskirts of the city. His light form quickly disappeared in the gloom of the smoke.

Linsha went the opposite direction toward the harbor and the city gate. She followed Falaius and what men he could gather of both the Legion and the militia to reinforce the defenders already in place.

Not far from the Mayor's Hall they passed a burning tannery—one of the many fires Thunder had started. Instead of staying to fight it, Falaius called the fire-fighters off the site and told them to join his force.

"Let it burn," he ordered. "The smoke and flames will hamper the enemy as much as it hampers us."

At the Legion Gate in the city wall, Falaius climbed the guard tower with Linsha and two other officers to view what lay ahead. The sight shook them all to silence. In the thirty minutes or so it had taken the Legionnaires to regroup and reach the wall, the harbor had come alive with small dark boats. Like so many carrion beetles, the boats clustered around the larger ships, then made their way to the ruined docks and the beaches where they disgorged their cargo of armed warriors and returned to the ships for more. Already the first wave of invaders was marching into the storm-damaged streets of Mirage and meeting the first resistence, while the second wave disembarked and formed their ranks on the little crescent beach near the foot of the hill where the Citadel sat.

"What are those?" a Legionnaire gasped.

Falaius was quiet for a moment, then he spoke in a voice filled with dismay. "They are Brutes."

"Brutes!" another man cried. "They can't be. I don't see any Dark Knights. Don't those things fight only for the Dark Knights?"

"Apparently not."

Brutes, Linsha thought. The gods help us. The Brutes were known to the people of Anaslon as ferocious fighters who had fought as slaves or mercenaries for the Knights of Takhisis during the Chaos War. After the war and the decimation of the Knightly orders, the Brutes had faded into the background, showing up every once in a while as shock troops for a Dark Knight offensive or as mercenaries for a war lord with enough money to afford them. No one knew where they came from or who they really were, and never in anyone's memory had so many Brutes arrived together to invade a city in Ansalon.

"Did Thunder organize this?" Linsha said in amazement. She thought she knew the huge blue from Iyesta's stories and from tales she heard from Thunder's realm. Never would she have imagined that the hungry, malevolent, territorial blue would have the imagination, the audacity, the courage, and the funds to arrange, plan, and set in motion a massive invasion of Iyesta's realm. Apparently, she'd been wrong. Not only had Thunder organized his own mercenary forces, he had also hired the Brutes, found a way to slay Iyesta, and devised a two-pronged attack that caught the city in a vise-like trap. She would never have believed it if she hadn't seen the evidence landing on the beaches and setting fires to the few merchant ships trapped in the harbor. How in the name of the gods were they going to fight an enemy force this big? She scanned the sky over Mirage to find Thunder, but for the moment he was out of sight.

"You might as well wait, Iyesta," Linsha said to herself. "It appears we might be joining you soon."

If Falaius had similar thoughts or regrets, he did not show them. He left a detachment behind to strengthen the guard on the gates, then he led the remainder of his forces toward the Legion headquarters. They heard the sounds of battle even before they reached the white, stuccoed building that served as home to the Legion cell.

Falaius moved into a jog, his fist clenched around the hilt of his great sword. He glanced down once at Linsha by his side and noticed for the first time she carried only a short sword and a rusty dagger. They were moving down a street parallel to the street in front the headquarters, and as the troop moved closer to the building, the commander jabbed his weapon toward the back door.

"There are weapons and armor within," he shouted to Linsha over the uproar of fighting in the streets ahead. "Get what you need. We will meet you around front."

From the shouts and clash of weapons, the battle was in the Legion's front yard. Waving her thanks, Linsha dashed across the weedy yard behind the Legion house and barged in the back door.

Someone nearly nailed her to the door. She heard the peculiar twang of a crossbow and felt a swish of air by her neck as a bolt slammed into the wood of the door. "Don't do that!" she cried, her voice furious. "I'm with Falaius!"

Distracted though she was by the battle out front, a part of her mind made note that for the second time in a few short days someone had just missed her with a crossbow. If only her luck would hold for the rest of the day!

"Lady Linsha?" cried an incredulous voice. "What are you doing here?"

"Just passing through," she replied dryly. "I need weapons."

The Legionnaire with the crossbow was a young man who had recently arrived from Port Balifor. Linsha knew him only vaguely. He pointed to a door in the hallway behind him and without apology, he retrieved his bolt and began to crank his crossbow into firing position.

Linsha hurried. Although most of the Legionnaires had already drawn their weapons and armor in preparation for the expected invasion, there was still enough left to give Linsha a choice. Swords of several lengths, axes, battle stars, helmets, shields, breastplates, greaves, crossbows, spears, lances, and heaps of chain mail lay in haphazard piles. She did not take the time to pick and choose. Her own armor, made and measured specially for her, lay in her room in the Citadel but might as well have been a thousand miles away. All she wanted was a corselet of chain mail, a shield, a better dagger, and a helmet. She found them all in less than two minutes, threw on the corselet and the helmet, and for good measure, stuck a battle star in her belt. The Knights of Solamnia had trained her well, and now she was as ready as she ever would be to face the enemy.

From outside came the sounds of intense fighting. Those few Legionnaires still in the building dashed outside to join their commander. There wasn't much sense staying to guard the interior of a building if the enemy was at your front door. Linsha swiftly followed across the covered porch and into the street crowded with fighting men and women and the towering forms of the attacking Brutes.

While she was tall for a woman, most of these warriors stood at least seven feet tall, with long arms and a reach that far outstripped hers. As graceful as elves, they were also as muscular as humans, and they fought nearly naked to show off their powerful limbs. They painted their skin blue and plaited their long hair with feathers. For weapons they carried both a short sword and a long sword, and many of them scorned shields.

The Legionnaires and Iyestas's militia fought with everything they had. Teeth bared, their faces white with fear or red with rage, they hacked and slashed and punched. Sword to abdomen, shield to head, blade to throat, axe to knees. They thrust and danced away and came back roaring. They fought with the courage and tenacity of people defending their homes. The Brutes who faced them fought with equal ferocity. They were the invaders, the seekers of slaves, the plunderers, and the gods knew what else, and they fought with the fury of men who loved war.

Although Linsha had been trained with every weapon available to the Knights of Solamnia, she was intelligent enough to realize that as a woman, she had certain disadvantages in a pitched battle against men. Those disadvantages became even more pronounced when she faced the Brutes. In the first five minutes of vicious fighting, she realized she could not beat these blue barbarians sword to sword. She would have to use her agility, her superb balance, and her sense of timing. Dropping her cumbersome shield, she used her sword and battle star in a primitive dance of thrust and hack and stab. Weaving and swaying, she wove her way around her opponant's swords until she could make a quick killing thrust and slide out of the way. It was a dangerous dance that left her trembling, pale, and gasping for air, but she fought on, keeping the big form of Falaius in the corner of her vision.

Despite their courage the Legionnaires and the militia were falling back. The second wave of Brutes had arrived, and they swept through the waterfront and the roads closest to the water, overwhelming the roadblocks and pushing the defenders inexorably back toward the city wall. The Legion had to abandon its headquarters, and soon the entire street fell to the marauders. Refugees fled toward the inner city.

Falaius had fought enough battles to know when to retreat. The streets of Mirage were swiftly filling with Brutes, and there was nowhere the outnumbered Legion and its allies could regroup. They would have to fall back on the city gates. He knew all too well that the wall itself was not a final defense. There were gaps in the ancient stonework and places on the north side of the city where entire sections of it had vanished over the centuries, but the gates were strong and the wall would give his fighters a chance to recover their breath.

"Fall back!" he bellowed. "Fall back to the gates!"

The word passed from group to group. Slowly but steadily the defenders disengaged from the fighting, grabbed what wounded they could, and retreated to the towering walls of the Legion Gate. Unconcerned, the Brutes let them go.

Falaius, Linsha, and several Legionnaires were the last to enter the gates. They staggered inside and watched as the gates were swung shut and barred. Linsha listened to the solid thud as the gates closed and the bar fell into place, and she closed her eyes sadly. It seemed to her the final knell for the Knights of Solamnia had been sounded. Even if they wanted to, they could no longer fight their way into the city to help the Legion. They would have to stay within their Citadel or find a way to escape north and join the forces of the militia.

Weary to the bone, Linsha wiped her sword blade clean and pushed it back into the scabbard. A young girl with a pitcher of water offered her a ladle. She drank two full ladles and dumped a third over her head before she regretfully passed it on to someone else. Her head hurt abominably and the soreness returned to her back, yet she felt too tired to do anything about it. She just wanted to lie down and sleep. She cast a look at the sky, hoping it would be dark soon, and was dismayed to see the day had barely passed midafternoon.

"Lord Falaius!" called a sentry from the wall. "Come see this. The Knights are about to join in the battle whether they like it or not."

Linsha was ahead of Falaius and shot up the stone steps to the battlements like a catapult. She pushed into a crenel and stared out at the fortress on the hill above Mirage. It looked so invulnerable on top of its hill, its defenses strong and its pennants flying defiantly above the towers.

She could see another large group of Brutes had climbed the road to the Citadel and were standing out of arrow range while they looked over the castle.

"Do these Brutes know siege tactics?" Linsha asked the Legion commander as he came to stand beside her.

"Unfortunately, yes."

Other people crowded up onto the walkway that looked out over Mirage, the harbor, and the distant hill. They watched as the Brutes began to spread out across the practice fields and around the crown of the hill to surround the Citadel. They saw the raiders break into the outbuildings and set fire to the stable—although Linsha knew from Sir Remmik's constant training that the horses had already been released or removed to the safety of the bailey. They spotted the dark showers of arrows that fell from the walls and the larger missiles that were flung from the high towers, forcing the Brutes to keep their distance.

"They have enough supplies and weapons to hole up in there for months," Linsha heard someone remark.

"That's all well enough for them, but it doesn't help us much," another voice grumbled.

"It won't help them much either if Thunder—"

A shadow dark and prophetic swept over their heads, and the wind of the dragon's passing choked the words in Linsha's throat.

Wordlessly the observers on the wall watched the huge blue sweep over the harbor and make a lazy circle above the Solamnic Citadel.

Linsha's throat went dry. The Citadel had been her home for over a year. While the Missing City wasn't the best assignment she'd ever had, she had grown to appreciate the castle's amenities and its strengths, and she had come to know many of the Knights and servants who worked within its walls. She even liked a few of them. Neither they nor the fortress deserved what was about to happen next.

Falaius rubbed a hand over his sweating face. "Does Remmik have defenses against dragons?"

Linsha did not take her eyes off the fortress or the dragon. She simply gave a dry laugh that held no humor. "He had one of our sorcerer Knights concoct some spells to protect the walls and the gate. Those might hold since they are a few years old. But magic has been failing all over Ansalon. The Knights have nothing new, and no weapons that will fight a wyrm that big."

"What was Remmik thinking to build a fortress like that?"

"When he designed it, he never imagined that Iyesta would be dead or that magic would be so unpredictable," Linsha said.

She didn't know why she was trying to defend the Solamnic commander. She had often asked the same questions herself. But what Sir Remmik had done was the same thing he had done in other parts of Anasalon—organize a circle, build defenses, and train young Knights into a fighting unit. The only difference here was he had had more authority, more time, and more resources to create his vision of a perfect Solamnic Circle. The problem was he had not taken into account some extraordinary circumstances, and now one of those circumstances was circling overhead and eyeing the fortress with utter malice. Linsha wondered what Sir Remmik was thinking at that moment.

In the blink of an eye, lightning crackled from the dragon's jaws and exploded on the cap of one of the Solamnic gate towers. The boom rolled across the Missing City. A second bolt of lightning from the dragon struck the tower again, and pieces flew off the tall structure. Smoke wafted from the interior. A third strike curled around a stone column, pulverizing mortar and weakening the structure even more. Without waiting to see the results of his breath attack on the first tower, Thunder concentrated three more bolts of lightning on the second gate tower, then he moved around the walls, systematically attacking each tower until the defenders were dead and the stonework was scorched black. Thick clouds of smoke rose from the interior where fires consumed the buildings, the fodder, and the stores.

The massive dragon slowly came to ground in front of the gates and tucked his wings close to his body. The Brutes watched impassively. For one brief moment, Linsha wondered if the dragon was going to allow the survivors of the fortress to surrender, but that fragile hope shriveled a heartbeat later as Thunder swung his blunt, heavy tail into the base of the gate. The two towers guarding the gateway shattered like cheap pottery. They collapsed with a rumble and sent a cloud of dust and mortar billowing over the Citadel.

The big blue roared with pleasure. Using his front legs, he clawed a hole through the wall where the gate had stood and shoved his massive forequarters into the fortress. More towers on the outer wall fell to ruin; more lightning seared the carefully built stonework of the outer wall. Soon he brought down the entire front section of the outer wall and began to concentrate his cruel will on the inner gateway. There seemed to be no sign that the surviving Knights were fighting back.

"Is there any way for them to get out of there?" Falaius said softly.

Linsha had to swallow hard to get enough moisture into her mouth to answer. "I don't know. I heard some time ago that Sir Morrec had talked to Sir Remmik about building an escape tunnel, but if it was ever done, no one told me." She gave a bitter laugh. "It would be like Remmik to have workmen construct a small tunnel from the other end so no one knew about it, then in a crisis he could reveal his planning and forethought and look like a hero once again."

The faint rumble of a distant crash drew them both back to the destruction of the Solamnic Citadel. They watched as Thunder demolished the inner gateway, doing the damage it would take a human siege party weeks to accomplish. Dust, smoke, and ash whirled around his blue hide. Lightning from his powerful jaws smashed into the barracks and the main hall. Like a creature maddened, he roared and stamped and swung his heavy tail into the walls and the towers until they cracked, shattered, and came tumbling down.

In less than twenty minutes, Sir Remmik's pride and joy became little more than a pile of rubble. No building remained standing, no tower stood above the heap of broken masonry. Like a victor swollen with triumph, the blue dragon scraped the mounds of rock and smoldering debris into a large rough platform, then he leaped to the top to survey the Missing City from this new height. The Brutes cheered.

"I guess this makes you the new Solamnic commander," Falaius said. There was no levity in his voice.

Linsha remembered Lanther's words to her only two nights ago, that her sentence would be erased if the entire garrison were wiped out. The entire garrison. Seventy-two men and women. Sir Hugh, young Sir Pieter, all the Knights she had come to know the past year. Perhaps they had let Sir Remmik have his way too often, but they were good men, and she never wanted their blood to buy her freedom.

She turned her head away without answering and slid down the stone until she was sitting with her back to the cool wall. She rested her aching head in her hands. The new Solamnic Commander . . . of a ghost garrison.

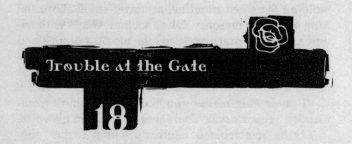

Trouble at the Gate

18

here is Lanther?" Linsha asked. It was a question that had lurked in her mind for some time and only now found a moment to be asked.

Falaius leaned against the stone crenellations of the city wall and gestured vaguely behind him. "I don't know. I sent him to a militia post near the north gate this morning. Not seen him since."

Linsha nodded. If the Legion commander was even half as tired as he looked, then he felt about the same way she did. That brief conversation was all she could manage for now. She closed her eyes again and let her muscles relax. She had rarely felt so sore and listless, not even after that sword duel with the Dark Knight assassin.

"Look at that," Falaius commented softly. "They really want this town."

Linsha forced herself to stir and turn her upper body around so she could see the streets of Mirage below. It had been about three hours since the city defenders had fallen back on the wall and left the outer city to the mercy of the Brutes. So far, the invaders had shown a sort of brutal mercy to the town and the inhabitants who had not escaped. All the buildings and houses were being thoroughly searched, but none had been put to the torch and few had been ransacked. There was no sign of the expected pillaging, drunken riots, or rape and slaughter. The survivors, including the women, were being herded into a guarded pen of sorts on the beach near the waterfront. Only the wounded had been killed outright and hauled to a growing heap of bodies left piled in an empty lot. The bodies of those Brutes killed in the fighting were immediately collected and carried back out to the ships. They were, Linsha noted, nothing if not methodical and thorough.

Meanwhile, workers resumed the repairs to the docks and the unloading of supplies on shore continued without a break. Any fires outside the walls had been put out. In the past few hours only the Solamnic fortress and the Legion headquarters had been stripped and demolished.

The Brutes had made no move on the city wall yet. The man with the blue skin and golden mask had made one appearance—on a horse this time— to the people guarding the Legion Gate. He offered them once again a chance to surrender, and once again Falaius said no. The leader of the Brutes saluted the Legionnaire and promptly ordered archers to guard the gate. Their whole attitude seemed say, "Just wait. We will come when we are ready."

Thunder seemed to be content to let them do what they wished. After destroying the Solamnic Citadel he had settled on the ruins to talk to the leader of the Brutes. Moments later he lifted his great blue bulk into the air and disappeared to the west. He had not been seen or felt since.

Linsha acknowledged Falaius's comment even though she was not sure what he had seen to prompt it, then she pulled off the hot, heavy chain mail and sagged back against the wall. The next attack would come soon enough. She sat patiently, silently suspended between sky and stone, breathing the thick hot air laden with dust and smoke. The heavy afternoon sun soaked into her battered body and dragged her consciousness under. She had fought it for a while, wanting to stay awake in case Falaius needed her. Now, she felt her strength ebb beyond her reach. Her head grew heavy; her eyelids slid closed and locked in place. The world faded away.

In its place a dream took shape that filled her mind like a room fills with smoke. She saw herself standing on a ledge on the side of a great mountain—a mountain she knew all too well. The ledge was empty, and the cave that opened at the ledge's head remained silent and abandoned. She looked up and saw the mountain's peak looming against a brilliant blue sky, then smoke belched from its fiery summit. A black cloud of ash and smoke billowed down the mountain's side toward her. She wanted to run, but she could not move fast enough, and in the blink of an eye she was enveloped by the hot, stinking fumes. Coughing and choking, she reached out to the cave entrance. But he did not come. Another form came instead—a smaller, upright shape that walked slowly out of the darkness and materialized before her startled eyes. Even after all that had passed between them, she felt her traitorous heart lurch at the vision of his roguish good looks and his cool blue eyes. Ian Durne. She thought she had loved him, until he killed her friend and turned his blade against Hogan Bight.

Linsha, you are as beautiful as ever. And just as blind. Do not trust him.

"You are a fine one to be telling me about trust."

Ah, but I always trusted you to do what was right. I knew you better, you see. I knew when the time came you would follow your honor.

"Yet you loved me."

He gave her that grin she remembered so well. *Honor can be a powerful aphrodisiac to those of us who have none.*

As can the allure of the dark rogue, she thought. "What are you doing here, Ian? Who is this I should not trust?"

Look carefully, Green Eyes. There are other rogues in this world besides Dark Knights. He turned back into the smoke and vanished.

"Ian!" she cried into the emptiness, but he was gone, and the loneliness he left behind swept over her with startling intensity.

"Linsha," a different voice said. A hand fell on her shoulder. Tired as she was, she came instantly awake and her reactions responded with the speed of a striking adder. Her left hand clamped on the offending wrist, and her right hand snatched the dagger from her belt. She opened her eyes and looked into the imperturbable brown gaze of the old plainsman. She blinked in surprise; she had expected blue.

His deep-sunk eyes gazed at her steadily, unshook by the dagger inches from his chest. "Remind me just to kick you the next time you are dreaming," he remarked.

She collapsed back to the wall and let her dagger drop. Her heart galloped madly under her breastbone; her breath came in long drawn gulps. "Gods, that *was* a dream." She groaned. "It was too real."

Falaius studied her curiously. The tribes of the Plains of Dust believe in the power of dreams and in

211

the realities revealed in their interpretations. "Who is Ian?" he asked, his voice calm and deliberately soothing.

"He was an assassin sent by the Dark Knights to infiltrate Lord Hogan Bight's inner circle and kill him." She said it as if listing Ian's sins would help her put things back in the right perspective.

"He is dead then. His spirit came to you?"

She hesitated, then said, "It was just a dream. His spirit is gone . . . wherever Dark Knights go when they die."

The older man pursed his lips. "Not necessarily. Our mystics have found that many spirits have not left this world yet. Something appears to be blocking their departure. Perhaps this Ian found a way to come to you. Would he care enough to do that?"

Linsha stared at him. Was he serious? Spirits of the dead still haunting the world? Why? Did that mean her grandmother was still out there somewhere? Was her friend Shanron? That could not be true.

"It was only a dream," she said softly, insistently.

"Are you sure?"

Could it be possible that Ian still cared enough to find her and warn her about someone? But if he had truly come to her, why hadn't he given her a name? Why did he have to be so mysterious? The mere thought made her head swim. No, this was not some spiritual visitation. This was just a dream wrought by her exhaustion and fear. Who else would her imagination pull out of her collection of memories to haunt her at a time like this?

Several messengers arrived just then with urgent news for the commander. He winked once at Linsha and hurried down the stone steps to speak to them.

Feeling irritable, she climbed to her feet and decided to find something to eat. The Brutes beyond the wall did not seen to be in a hurry to kill them, so perhaps she would have time for a quick meal.

"Lady Linsha, " Falaius called her over. "I've received word from Lanther. He is at the North Gate. He is looking for you. He wants you to come if you can."

"Did he say why?"

At the commander's nod, the messenger answered. "He captured two men from Thunder's forces. They told him some things he thought you should hear."

Her eyebrows rose. "He just went out and captured two men in the middle of an attack?"

The messenger shrugged. "You know Lanther."

"That section of the wall and the gate are still holding fast," Falaius said, "but we have received word that portions of the Northern District and the Artisans District have been overrun.The militia is falling back out of the ruins to more defensible positions. Be careful where you go." He walked with her a short way beside the city wall before he said farewell. "You fought well at my back, Rose Knight."

"It was an honor to join you," she replied.

He twisted a grimace into some semblance of a grin and said, "We may not be here tomorrow, so I want to take the opportunity to invite you to join the Legion of Steel."

It was an honor, and Linsha knew it. She flushed at the genuine regard in his voice. "I think," she said slowly, "if I had not grown up on the stories of my uncles and my grandfather's friend, Sturm Brightblade, I would have joined the Legion instead of the Knighthood. I remember Sara Dunstan with fondness."

The Plainsman's dark eyes warmed at old memories. "I remember her, too. The invitation stands ready at any time you want to accept it. We'll waive the apprenticeship."

Linsha thought about the impossibility of their situation and suddenly laughed. "It could be the shortest membership in the history of the Legion."

"Then so be it," he replied. He touched his fingers to his heart in salute, bowed to her, and left to return to his duties.

The city wall on the northeast side of the Missing City was one of two large sections that had been rebuilt. Twenty feet high it stretched from the harbor seawall for nearly four miles around the Port District and well into the Northern District. It reached as far as the old North Gate and its two squat guard towers. For about one hundred yards, the wall extended beyond the North Gate where it came to an end in scaffolding, piles of rock, and heaps of sand for mortar. There was nothing left of the original wall beyond that but scattered stones and the old foundation, but since most of the Northern District had never been rebuilt, no one thought it necessary to rush into rebuilding the walls in that area. The other portion of wall had been rebuilt from the southwestern side defending the Garden District and Iyesta's Lair. The original idea had been to build the two sections of wall around the city and eventually join them on the northwest side, making the rough circle complete. Unfortunately, Thunder had surprised everyone.

When Linsha finally worked her way to the North Gate, she found the defenders there in much the same state as the soldiers at the Legion Gate. They had suffered hard fighting with Thunder's army and had fallen back to the Gate to recover. The worst of the wounded lay in makeshift shelters and were tended by townspeople and healers. Many of the walking wounded had returned to the city for rest and care, but a few sat where they could find shelter and waited for the next attack. Those who were still unhurt stood on the walls and kept watch on the distant enemy.

The forces of the blue dragon had paused all along the line, whether to rest in the heat of the day, regroup for a new onslaught, or pause while Thunder instigated another part of his plan, no one was sure. They were just grateful for the respite.

Lanther saw Linsha first as she came striding along the path that paralleled the wall. He jumped up from his resting place in the shade of an awning and limped to meet her.

They surveyed each other from battered heads, down blood-stained clothes, to dusty boots and finally grinned at each other like two survivors who had found each other against hope.

"You made it," Lanther said. "I knew you would not stay in the safe house. Is that blood yours?"

She glanced down her white linen shirt now smeared and filthy with blood, dirt, soot. "Only some of it." She pointed a finger to the chain mail and the sword slung across her back. "Falaius allowed me into the Legion armory."

"He's a good man," Lanther said, taking her arm. "Come with me. I've got something to show you."

She fell into step beside him and felt his companionship slowly dissolve the ache she still felt from her dream. While she felt no desire for Lanther, she liked his company, and after the disasterous relationship with Ian, that's all she wanted from any man she had met so far. Maybe her heart would thaw one day, but Linsha hoped it would not budge any time soon. Her choice of men had been less than advantageous, and with two of them it had proved almost fatal.

"What's happening in Mirage?" she heard Lanther say, and she had to shake herself to clear her muzzy mind.

Quickly, she told him of the Brutes' landing and how the streets of Mirage were now in their control. She described the fighting in the streets, between the buildings, and beside the city wall, and she told him as best she could of the Legionnaires who had fallen.

When she finished, he rubbed a grimy hand over his eyes like a man who had seen too much that day. "I am glad to hear Falaius is still alive." He paused then went on. "It's similar to here. The militia set up outer defenses beyond the walls, hoping to drive off Thunder's forces, but they're stretched too thin. The enemy has driven us back to the walls. Out there, where there are no walls, they have penetrated the militia's defenses in a number of places. If these Brutes continue their advance into the inner city and the dragon's army pushes through from the north, the city is lost."

"You're not including Thunder," Linsha said. "Except for scaring the population half to death, starting a few fires, and destroying the Citadel, he has been leaving most of the work to the two armies."

"He has been busy nonetheless," said Lanther, escorting her into the ground-floor room of the guard tower on her left.

After the heat of the day's sun, the dim, cool light of the round stone room was a welcome relief. Other people thought so, too, for the room was crowded with injured men and women sitting on the floor or at the tables usually used by the tower guards. A girl from a tavern nearby served ale to the defenders from a barrel donated by her father.

Lanther worked his way through the crowd to a small narrow stair leading down to the lower level. The small room below the tower was mostly used for storage, but tucked away in the darkest space was a set of holding cells.

"Ah," Linsha breathed. "Your prisoners."

"I just wanted you to see them. They are in no position to talk at the moment." His lips pulled back in the dim light to reveal his white teeth like a snarl. "I had to be a little rough on them."

She followed him forward and looked over his shoulder at two men sprawled on rough blankets thrown on the floor. Both men looked battered and bloody, and both wore a makeshift emblem of the blue dragon on their sleeves. One, a rugged-looking plainsman, scrabbled back into the darkest shadow when Lanther approached and huddled there, his breath rasping through his swollen nose and mouth as he stared fearfully at the Legionnaire. The other man did not move. The skin on his face hung slack and his half-opened eyes stared unseeing at the ceiling.

Lanther muttered something under his breath that Linsha could not understand, then louder he said, "That one didn't make it. I'll have to get someone down here to get him out."

He turned and ushered his companion up the stairs before she had a chance to say a word to the other prisoner.

Linsha felt her irritation rise. Surely, he had not dragged her away from the Legion Gate and some much-needed sleep just to get a quick glimpse at a dead man and a battered prisoner. "Why did you want me here, Lanther? What did they tell you?"

He said nothing. Passing by the barmaid, he whisked two cups off her tray and held them out to be filled. Still without a word, he took the brimming cups of ale and led Linsha outside, past a row of sheds and huts left by the wall builders, to a clump of shrub hazel growing in the foundation of an old ruin. He sat carefully on on a fallen pillar and indicated a seat beside him.

"No prying ears out here," he said quietly.

The ale looked so good to Linsha that she would have sat anywhere just for the chance to drink it. She accepted his offering and sat beside him where she could keep a watch on the comings and goings at the distant gate. Far to her right, she could see a burial party hastily burying some of the dead before the summer heat took its toll on the bodies. To her left, she saw a troop of human militia taking advantage of the lull in the fighting to bolster their flimsy defenses with rocks and sand bags. She wondered briefly where the centaurs were and if young Leonidas was faring well enough.

"What do you know about the brass eggs Iyesta was guarding?"

If Lanther had thrown a bucket of ice water on her, Linsha could not have more stunned and surprised. She choked on the ale. "What?"

"I know Iyesta took you somewhere the day the triplets disappeared. Some place that left smudges of dirt on your face and the smell of damp on your clothes."

Linsha glared at him. Good gods, where had this come from? "She took me into Thunder's realm to see him. I told you about that."

"Yes, you did. But I know Chayne and Ringg came back long before you and Iyesta. The dragon took you to another place." He narrowed his eyes and stared at her; his blue eyes gleamed cold like the water at the foot of a glacier.

Linsha felt his gaze bore into her brain to the very back of her skull, and she felt a shiver run up her back.

Fiercely, she closed her thoughts and shuttered her eyes and brought her pulse back under control. He had taken her by surprise but it would not happen again. "Iyesta and I spent some time in her garden talking. She was worried about the triplets and furious at Thunder. She wanted someone to listen."

A flash of speculation tightened the lines around Lanther's eyes, then he smoothly changed his tone. "I'm sorry. I should have approached this from a more discrete direction. Those men we hold told me Thunder is looking for eggs. He has ordered his entire force to search for them as soon as the city falls. This was news to me. I had no idea Iyesta had a nest of eggs around here."

"What makes Thunder think there are eggs?" Linsha countered, but the answer came to her with sickening certainty. The three young brasses. If the giant blue captured and tortured any one of the triplets, or all of them, he could have used his greater, more malevolent power to wrench the knowledge from their minds.

"Dragons have ways of learning things," Lanther said. "The men did not say how Thunder came by this information, only that he had it. Is it true?"

Linsha felt a cold sickness creep through her and settle in her stomach. She took a long swallow of her ale, but it tasted flat on her tongue. Of all the dreadful possibilities to endanger the eggs, it had to be Thunder. She did not doubt Lanther's information. There was no reason that he would make up something like that and several reasons to believe his sources.

"I don't think we need to worry about it," she said, trying to sound casual. "If there is a nest, it is too well hidden for anyone to find."

Lanther rested his elbows on his knees and gazed deep into the golden depths of his ale. "Not if there are

219

enough people looking for it." He stopped and looked at her again. "Just why did you want to go to Iyesta's lair so desperately after we freed you from the Citadel?"

"To look for Iyesta. I found her, too. Remember?"

"Linsha, we cannot let Iyesta's eggs fall into Thunder's control. He will destroy them."

"What about Iyesta's skull? It seems to me we should be more concerned about Thunder collecting dragon skulls. Did you ask those men if he is building a larger totem?"

"Yes, I asked. They did not know. All they would tell me is that Thunder plans to move into Iyesta's lair as soon as it captured."

"Like Chaos he is!" Linsha snapped. She shot to her feet.

Lanther grabbed for her arm. "Where are you going?"

Linsha was too quick for him. She twisted out of his grip and backed away. "To the palace. I can fight as well there as anywhere. I will not let that foul monster use her lair as his own!"

With a speed that belied her aches and exhaustion, she tossed him the empty cup, spun away, and jogged into the last golden streaks of the setting sun toward the palace of the dragonlord.

Lanther made no move to follow. He watched her go, his face impassive, until he could no longer see her in the gathering twilight. Only then did he allow a faint smile to lift his lips.

The Dragonlord's Palace

19

Thunder's forces launched a second attack just before midnight. From the hill of the ruined Citadel came a great horn blast that soared out over the city and, in the quiet of night, was heard from Legion's Gate to Iyesta's palace west of the Garden District. A roar rose up from the enemy surrounding the beleaguered city, and in almost the same movement the Brutes and the mercenaries gathered by Thunder threw themselves forward against the fortifications and walls. Rank after rank pressed forward, their spears and swords gleaming in the light of hundreds of torches. Their trampling feet made the ground tremble.

Grim and angry, the defenders held their ground. Falaius had placed most of his available troops in a line across the Northern District and the Artisans District to block entry into the heart of the city through the missing sections of the walls. During the lull in the fighting that evening, they had built hasty fortifications and barriers, and there the centaurs had placed themselves foremost before the barricades, counting on their size, strength, and speed to help beat back the attackers.

At the Legion Gate, the Brutes revealed they had come prepared for a seige. From the shadows of two buildings they wheeled out two squat catapults. With practiced efficiency, they set up the machines just out of arrow range and began to hurl missiles at the watchtowers. At the same time, another engine of war wheeled up the street and rolled into position outside the big gate. It was shaped like a simple, peaked tent covered with damp cow hides, but inside the wooden framework hung a heavy tree trunk tipped with iron and suspended with ropes. Men inside the framework swung the ram, and the first loud boom echoed through the streets. While the siege engines kept the gate defenders busy, other Brutes stormed the city walls.

Falaius, the Legion, and people from all walks of life fought back with everything they had. Arrows flew in deadly showers into the struggling enemy. Firepots, jugs of lime, and cauldrons of boiling water were hurled over the walls. Older children with axes scrambled back and forth around the archers to cut the ropes of the grapnels that Brutes threw over the wall in an attempt to climb to the battlements. Women carried away the wounded and the dead, collected spent arrows and spears, beat out fires started by fire arrows, and piled up rocks and debris behind the big gate. Everyone who could do something at the walls did their best, but the toll for their courage was high.

Try as they might, the defenders could not keep the ram away from the gate. They killed many Brutes inside the tent structure and scorched the hide covering with burning tar, but there were always more Brutes to fill in the gaps and the ram continued to swing with relentless force. Already cracks appeared in the tough oak timbers and the iron supports were buckled and bent. The hinges creaked with every crash of the heavy tree.

"My lord," a Legionnaire cried to Falaius on the wall. "The Brutes are nearly through. The gates are about to fall."

The city's commander drew a small horn from his belt and sounded three long notes—the signal for retreat.

Boom, the ram crashed against the gate. The oak doors shuddered.

"Go!" shouted Falaius. "Get off the walls! Fall back!"

The Legionnaires obeyed. They grabbed their wounded comrades, herded the women and children off the walls, and drove everyone back to the streets and houses that formed their second line of defense.

Boom. This time the gates shook, and the right half split from ground to peak.

Falaius was the last to the leave the wall. Gripping his sword, he watched the ram swing back and forward into the city gates. The heavy oak barriers splintered into useless firewood. Feeling sad to his bones, the old Plainsman dashed down the steps and raced across the pavings to the house directly across the street. There he lined up his archers and prepared to make the Brutes pay dearly for every man who crossed that threshold.

All around the perimeter of the city, the defenders gave way step by bloody step in the face of the merciless onslaught. The two gates, the Garden Gate in the west wall and the Legion Gate, held out the longest, but they were overwhelmed by the siege engines, and the defenders were forced to retreat into the streets, buildings, and cellars of the city itself. In the Port District and the western edges of the Garden District the fighting in the streets became ferocious. The city dwellers fought for their homes and their families, but their courage and devotion was not enough to overcome the Brutes' superior expertise and hunger for battle. Only the centaurs were the Brutes' equal in skill and weapons, and most of them were too busy fighting among the barricades to the north. House by house, street by street, the defenders were pushed back toward the center of the city.

Shortly after the fall of the western Garden Gate, the mercenaries under the command of the Brute officers slowed their advance when they reached the wealthy neighborhoods in the Garden District. These warriors—thieves, thugs, outlaws, exiles, and sellswords— lacked the discipline of the Brutes. They took one look at the richly furnished homes and lost their momentum in a spree of looting, pillaging, and gluttony. The Brutes who handled the siege engines looked on in disgust.

The battered militia, who had guarded the gate until it burst apart at its hinges, withdrew toward the palace and the wild gardens of Iyesta's lair. Half of their number met with the dragon's guards and established a defensive ring around the palace. The other half melted into the city streets to set up ambushes, build barricades, and recruit more help. Runners were sent to Falaius and messages arrived from other strong points. Linsha and her companions learned the lines of centaurs and militia had grudgingly fallen back all along the northern defenses, but they had fought hard and did not flee in panic. They had abandoned the entire Northern District and most of the Artisans District and were gathering along a line north of the palace to the Little Three Points.

When dawn lifted the veil of darkness the next day, Falaius and the people of the Missing City still retained control of the heart of the city, Little Three Points, large areas of the Garden District and not quite half of the Port District. But there was little cause for celebration. The walls had fallen, the harbor was lost, and many members of the irreplaceable militia and Legion were dead or wounded. There was no hope of aid or godly intervention.

As the sun rose and the heat returned to the land, the fighting in the streets and houses dwindled to an exhausted standstill. Thunder's army settled down to strengthen their grip on their stolen territory while the defenders assessed the damage and looked to a gloomy future.

* * *

At the edge of the dragonlord's gardens where the wild parkland gave way to the homes and streets, Linsha dispatched the last swarthy swordsman that had probed too far into the defenders' lines. Panting, she wiped her sword blade clean and slid it back into the leather scabbard.

"Vermin!" Mariana said vehemently. She dabbed ineffectively at a slash that crossed the back of her right shoulder.

"Sit down," Linsha suggested. "I'll do that."

The wound was not deep, but it was a long laceration and would be very uncomfortable for a few days. Linsha cleaned it as best she could and wrapped a pad made from Mariana's torn shirt around the shoulder.

A chestnut centaur, a runner from Mariana's troop, came to take a look. "Captain, you should go back to the palace and have a healer treat that. It may need stitching."

"Or a poultice to keep the swelling down," Linsha added.

The half-elf grimaced. "Those things are always so noxious. Why, oh why, did the healers' magic have to fail? I thought we were done with primitive medicine."

"At least we have that," said Linsha helping her to her feet.

"All right," Mariana sighed. "I should report to General Dockett anyway. Luewellan, tell your group leader to post guards and let the troop stand down for a few hours. They need rest."

The centaur saluted, gathered the weapons from the dead soldiers, and trotted back to his position.

The half-elf nodded her thanks as Linsha gave her a steadying arm. The two women made their way back toward the palace courtyard to find a proper healer and a meal.

"I never want to see another night like that again," Mariana muttered while they walked. Her normally robust, healthy enthusiasm had dulled to a thin patina under a full day of fear and fighting. Her long braids and uniform were filthy, her skin looked pale, and bluish shadows ringed her eyes.

Linsha knew without looking that she probably looked even worse. She struggled for something to say and found nothing. How could you pin platitudes to a day like yesterday? Or one like today? There was no help in sight. They would have a brief respite, and then the fighting would begin again, tearing away the city's defenses a little bit at a time. Linsha knew she was worn to the bone, bruised, cut, aching, and her energy was nearly gone. But worst of all, her usual reservoir of optimism that had kept her going through many difficult crises was flagging. She could see no solution in sight, nor she could she relieve the biting worry in her mind about the brass eggs. The fighting had been too intense for her to slip away in the night to find the entrance to the labyrinth. She desperately wanted to go into the tunnels and check the eggs, to relieve her mind that they were still in the nest and unharmed, but then what? If they were still there, how safe would they be if Thunder sent his army combing the city for them? Iyesta's safeguards might protect them for a little while, but Linsha doubted they would work for long against a determined blue dragon. Should she risk harming them and move them to some place out of the city? Would Purestian understand the danger and accept her help?

Linsha ground her teeth in frustration. Maybe she should trust Lanther and accept his help. He already suspected the dragon eggs existed, and he seemed quite adamant they be protected.

"Are you all right?" Mariana said beside her.

Linsha gave a lopsided grin and said, "As well as anyone else. Just lost in thought."

The two women arrived in the courtyard and found it a place of barely contained chaos. Rows of wounded lay under the trees where healers worked hard to ease their suffering. Dragon's guards, militia, centaurs, and a few Legionnaires ran back and forth carrying messages from Falaius to General Dockett, restocking supplies, fetching water, collecting weapons, and doing their best to fortify the walls of the old palace. This, Linsha realized, would probably be the place where those who survived would come to make their last stand. The thought grieved her more than she imagined it would.

From a battered table set up under a tree, General Dockett waved for Captain Brownstem to join him.

Linsha helped her friend over to the table. Without asking the militia commander's permission, she eased the half-elf into the single chair and poured a glass of water from a pitcher on the commander's table.

The militia commander took a look at Mariana's shoulder and did not complain. He called for a healer, and while the man carefully cleaned and stitched the worst of the slash, he listened to her report.

Linsha had met the commander only a few times, yet she had only to look at the tightly-knit, well-organized militia under his command to know he was a good leader. The centaurs, too, thought highly of him, which said a good deal for his character and abilities. While the two officers talked, she sat on the ground in the shade and added only a rare comment. She shut out the noise and hubbub around her and concentrated on the tranquil movement of the wind through the tree leaves above her.

She was nearly asleep where she sat when something heavy moved beside her and a familiar voice said, "You're not going to believe what I found."

A charge of fear shot through her. It was Lanther's voice. The eggs! He'd found the eggs. Her eyes flew open, and she stared uncomprehendingly at the man standing in front of her.

"He insisted on seeing you," Lanther said beside her.

She twisted around to look at the Legionnaire then back to stare at the ragged, dusty young man in the blue Solamnic uniform. "Sir Hugh," she whispered.

"Curse me for a draconian," said General Dockett in surprise. "I heard your whole garrison was wiped out."

The Solamnic Knight wiped the sweat on his face and folded his legs to sit on the ground across from Linsha. "Almost," he said, his voice subdued with exhaustion and sadness. "About twenty of us managed to escape."

Linsha held up a finger. "Don't tell me. Let me guess. Sir Remmik had an escape route. Probably a tunnel under the hill. He led you all down there and as soon as it turned dark, he led you out and you fought your way through the lines to the North Gate."

A pale twinkle lit in Hugh's red-rimmed eyes. "You know the man well. We came in through the gap as the Brutes took down the North Gate."

She sighed an exaggerated breath. "I guess that means he is still alive."

"Very much so," Lanther said.

"And the rest?"

Sir Hugh shook his head. "Sir Remmik waited too long to pull them off the walls. The only reason I survived was because I was in the cells at the time. The escape tunnel entered the dungeon at the back of the corridor, and Sir Pieter let me out as the survivors fled."

"The cells?" Lanther asked. "What were you doing in there?"

"Spending some time reflecting on my incompetence as a Knight. I allowed an important prisoner to escape."

Linsha did not appear to hear him. She stared at the tree. "Nearly fifty Knights," she said. "How much we could use them now."

"We're fighting now," said Sir Hugh. "Sir Remmik is coming here to join our forces with the militia."

"Oh?" General Dockett exclaimed. "That's news to me."

"Sorry, sir. I was sent ahead to tell you."

An unexpected feeling of irritation burned through Linsha. Sir Remmik was coming to the palace. Now. He never came to the palace when Iyesta was alive—only now when she was dead and her lair appeared to be the last large stronghold left. Now, when Linsha thought she had some time to rest and recover before the next attack. Why couldn't that man stay away from her?

"Thank you for the warning, Sir Hugh," she snapped.

Snatching up her weapons and helmet, she jumped to her feet and stalked away from the tree.

"Wait a minute," Mariana called. "Where are you going?"

"I'm an escaped prisoner, remember? If I stay here, Sir Remmik will hang me from the nearest tree."

"He wouldn't, would he?" The half-elf turned to the general. "She is with us."

Sir Hugh watched Linsha cross the hot courtyard and answered for him. "He might try. The commander is very unreasonable about her."

Mariana shrugged her shirt back over her shoulder. "Huh," she grunted. "I never thought much of that man before this. Now I'm afraid if I see him I will put a bolt through him. With your permission, sir, I will go back to my company."

General Dockett frowned. "Eat something first. The company will wait."

Lanther, too, watched Linsha leave and made a note of where she turned and entered the gardens. After a moment he climbed to his feet and saluted the general. "I will be back," he said. "And you," he told the Solamnic Knight, "will not mention to Sir Remmik that you saw her here."

Sir Hugh rose to his feet and stared up at the tall Legionnaire. Even at his fullest height, the young man barely reached Lanther's nose. "No," he said mildly. "I won't. I didn't tell him about the courtesan either."

Lanther's weathered face split into a grin. "You're a good man, Hugh."

Leaving the others behind, he limped out of the courtyard and took the path he had seen Linsha follow.

It soon became clear to him, though, that Linsha was no longer on the path. In the wild, heavily overgrown gardens full vines and shrubs, trees and tall grass, it was very easy to lose sight of someone who did not want to be seen.

The Legionnaire paused. There were many questions about Linsha he had not yet found answers for. She was an enigma to him, and he found that fascinating. She knew about the eggs—of that he was certain—and he was also very sure she would try to go find them. The question was when and where. He studied the woods around him for while then walked back the way he had come. He had a thought that perhaps she would not go far from this palace. She kept returning here, and only the Solamnics had driven her away for now. No, she would be back, and when she came he would find her.

In a clump of wild chokecherries, Linsha pressed into the shaded cluster of trunks and watched Lanther walk back to the palace. When she was sure he was out of sight, she slipped out of the trees and moved deeper into the ruins of the palace gardens to the place she remembered where a door led down into the cool, dark tunnels of the labyrinth. At last she had an opportunity to go down to the chamber alone. Her fingers reached for the dragon scales around her neck and gripped them tightly. She could only hope Iyesta had been right and the scales would protect her from the guardians in the dark.

Linsha.

She started violently, nearly slipping on the stone step. The name rang in her head.

Linsha! Where are you?

Her heart gave a great bound. "Varia?" she cried, both delighted and amazed.

She ran back outside to a clearing. She had to answer, but not with her voice. The owl called in her mind, using a telepathic link between the two of them that only seemed to work in times of great need. She had used it once in Sanction to help the owl find her. Now she tried again, concentrating her thoughts into one single plea. *Varia, I am here.*

Relax, relax, she told herself. She knelt in the long grass, closed her eyes, and focused her mind. She shut out the sounds of the insects around her, the feel of the sweat that trickled down her back, the sight of the wind dancing in the trees, until all she could sense was the warm, steady pounding of her heart. As Goldmoon had taught her, she found the energy that radiated from the center of her heart, and she pulled it forth to leash it to her will. The power spread through her body with rejuevenating warmth, driving the pain from her head and arms, strengthening her legs, and filling her with comfort. She stretched out with her mind and sent her answer winging to find the one being so close to her in thought.

Varia, I am here.

Linsha! came the reply. *You are alive! I am coming!* The call was a little louder this time, perhaps a little closer.

Linsha grinned with joy, flung her arms wide, and fell back in the grass. Varia was back, and she was coming. She hadn't deserted her. The owl would help her find the egg chamber. *Varia, I am here. By the palace.*

She lay in the warm grass and felt something tickle her forehead. She swatted at it, thinking it was an insect, but something about that faint sensation on her skin was familiar. She had felt it each time she tried to use her few magic talents the past year or so, and each time the power she so laboriously called forth washed away like a small dam bursting. It was very vexing. Just as times before, her energy flowed out of her and left her lying there weak and empty. This time it didn't matter, though. She had had enough time to answer Varia. The owl knew where she was. All she had to do was wait, and Varia would come.

She stretched out and smiled peacefully at the sky. Her eyes slipped closed. For just a short while she was able to luxuriate in the solace of a quiet hour.

All at once the peace shrivelled in her mind. Terror, cold and sickening, dashed over her. She came fully awake and saw a shadow moving over the trees toward her. Pressed into the grass, she lifted her gaze to the east and saw a blue shape wing ponderously over the palace gardens. The wind of its passing whipped the trees like a storm and sent leaves and dust flying.

Shouts and screams came from the distant palace. Somewhere nearby a horn sounded a belated warning. Linsha realized it was a Solamnic signal. The Knights had arrived just in time to meet the dragon.

She sprang to her feet. What would the dragon do? Was this just another fly-over, or did he plan to fight for Iyesta's lair?

Her answer came almost immediately on the trumpeting notes of the Brutes' horns. They were launching another attack.

Escape into the Labyrinth

20

Linsha drew her sword. She had no idea how close Varia was, but she had to warn the owl of Thunder's arrival. *Varia!*

The name had barely left her thoughts when a single word thundered over the palace grounds. "You!" it rumbled with mingled surprise and malicious pleasure.

Linsha heard a roar of fury and protest. Another dragon? Incredulous, she sprinted along the path toward the palace courtyard. She plunged out of the trees and skidded to a halt, staring at the air above the palace ruins. Thunder curved overhead, his huge body filling her vision. But just to her left, crouched in the road leading to the palace was a big bronze dragon, his head raised to challenge the blue, his wings half-furled.

Linsha gawked as she tried to take it all in. Lanther, Mariana with her arm in a sling, General Dockett, and several others stood bunched in front of the bronze as if they had been talking to him when Thunder arrived. Lanther drew his sword, and he and the others backed hurriedly away.

Armed warriors on the road from the city poured toward the palace, their homemade dragon badges clear in the morning light.

Linsha bit back a curse. There wasn't time to ponder where or how the militia's lines had been pierced, or how or why Crucible was here. She had only a second to accept the obvious and decide what to do.

A bird winged away from the bronze dragon and streaked for her. "Linsha!" The owl hooted and came to circle overhead.

Linsha looked from the owl to the dragons to the approaching enemy to the palace in one sweeping movement. Then she shoved on her helmet to cover her telltale curls and raced for the courtyard gates.

"Varia!" she called. "Tell Crucible to hold off Thunder for five minutes. That's all! Then he's to bolt for Iyesta's throne room."

The owl whistled in reply and wheeled around. As she flew to warn the bronze, Linsha charged into Lanther's group.

"Mariana, the treasure room, the tunnels," she grabbed the half-elf's good arm. "Get everyone down there."

Lanther's eyebrows shot up. "Tunnels? Under the palace?"

"Under the whole city!" Linsha shouted over the uproar of angry dragons.

"Gods," breathed General Dockett at this unforseen possibility. "We could get the rest of the militia out."

A massive bolt of lightning exploded behind them just short of Crucible's side. The thunder was instantaneous. The force of impact sent them staggering.

Linsha clapped her hands to her ringing ears, yet she could still hear Thunder bellow, "Crucible! So the little lapdog returns to crouch at his dead mistress's rotting feet. Your timing is excellent. I am in need of a bronze skull."

Linsha shuddered in fear for her friend. He was large for a bronze and had grown nearly forty feet since she'd last seen him, but even at that size he was only slightly less than half of Thunder's massive bulk. Crucible had participated very little in the bloody Dragon Purge of the previous ten years, choosing to stay out of sight and to kill only those evil dragons who threatened his territory around Sanction. Because of that, he had not attained the huge size of Iyesta, Thunder, or the other greater dragonlords.

To his advantage, he had a powerfully elegant build and the speed to compensate for his smaller size. He also had a breath weapon that could melt rock. A beam of light as hot and intense as the light of a star sheered from his mouth and struck Thunder's underbelly. The white-hot light could not instantly penetrate the dense, protective scales of the blue's belly, but it was hot enough to burn.

The blue roared in pained fury. Before he could turn his ponderous bulk around, Crucible fired a second long beam of light at the approaching foes then arrowed into the air after Thunder.

Through the dust and the tumult, Linsha saw the small body of the owl blown sideways by the gale whipped up by the dragon's wings. She tumbled head over tail feathers and landed hard in the dirt. The Rose Knight sprinted out to scoop her up. She snatched up Varia without stopping, turned on her heel, and bolted for the courtyard.

Mariana, the general, and Lanther were already ahead of her. Like madmen, they ran from group to group, urging everyone off the wall, out of the court-yard, and into the throne room. Already, people were snatching up the wounded and fleeing for the open palace doors.

Linsha hesitated a step when she saw the small group of battered, weary Solamnic Knights looking very confused. They had just arrived and stood in a group around the commander. Sir Remmik was arguing with Lanther.

Hoping the other Knights would not recognize her in her helmet and strange, bloodied clothes, Linsha hurried close to Sir Hugh and hissed, "Get them out of here! We cannot fight a dragon. Live to fight another day."

He glanced down at the owl cradled in her arms, gave her a brief wink, and ordered the Knights into the throne room.

Sir Remmik raised a hand to reprimand the younger Knight when a bolt from Thunder exploded against one side of the massive stone gatepost of the courtyard wall. Chunks of stone and splinters flew outward in a deadly hail. Sir Remmik did not hesitate further. He led the Knights into the throne room and followed the militia and the dragon's guards down the stone steps into Iyesta's splendid treasure chamber.

In barely five minutes the defenders of the palace abandoned the upper levels to Thunder and his forces.

Linsha, Lanther, and General Dockett were the last to leave. They paused in the palace doors and looked out. All of the living had left the courtyard; only the dead remained. Outside the gates they could see the mixed force of Brutes and dragon mercenaries make their way cautiously toward the palace. Crucible's warning bolt had killed the first line of soldiers and thrown the others into fearful dismay. Under control now, they spread out and advanced toward their objective. There was no sign of the two dragons.

"Five minutes," Linsha breathed. "You did tell him five minutes?"

Varia wiggled loose from Linsha's grip, fluffed her feathers back in place, and climbed to Linsha's shoulder. She stared up at the sky.

"Of course, I did," she said. "There they are. They're coming down."

The militia general started in surprise and stared at the owl, but Lanther and Linsha studied the sky. It took the humans' weaker eyes a moment longer to see what the owl spotted. Lanther suddenly pointed upward. Two specks, one bright in the sunlight and one larger, were diving toward the earth. Lightning split the sky around the smaller, brighter speck.

Linsha had a horrible vision of the bronze dragon tumbling out of the sky. In her mind, she saw his body scorched and broken, his wings torn to shreds. Unable to stop himself, he smashed into the ground in a heap of shattered bone and splattered blood. The vision was so real to Linsha that she cried out as Crucible dived toward the palace. He would never stop in time. He was too big. He was going too fast.

At breakneck speed he curved his body and angled his wings just enough to swoop out of his fall and skim to a landing outside the courtyard, leaving the heavier and more ponderous Thunder far behind. The blue roared in rage as he tried to slow his descent so he could land without breaking all four legs and his neck.

But Crucible was not in the palace yet. His speed on landing proved to be more than he anticipated. He landed briefly, bounced, skidded, lost his balance and slid heavily into the undamaged side of the stone gate. Linsha heard something crack.

"Crucible!" she yelled. "This way!"

Before the dazed dragon struggled to his feet, several

quick-thinking Brutes sprang on him with their long, two-handed swords drawn. They slashed at his wings several times before he managed to sear them in half, but the damage was done. Other Brutes swarmed toward Crucible. With a snarl he scrambled over the wreckage of the gate and galloped toward the palace.

Lanther, Linsha, and Docket ran for the stairs to get out of the way of the charging bronze. He thundered into the huge throne room, skidded around at the head of the stairs, and backed carefully down.

One light beam, then a second ate into the stone roof. A crack, sharp and ominous, boomed through the room.

Brutes poured in through the open doors, their courage impressing Linsha. But their courage proved their undoing. A third beam of light from Crucible, as dense and hot as liquid fire, burned away the last support. The great domed roof crashed down in a huge cloud of dust and debris. It buried the warriors in a massive pile of stone, clogging the stairs that led down.

In the darkness of the treasure chamber, the three humans leaned against the wall, coughing on the mortar dust. Linsha heard Crucible breathing heavily and felt her way to his front legs. Elated, she touched him, unsure whether to hug his wide leg or shout her relief to the oppressive darkness.

"What are you doing here?" she cried. "Are you all right? By Paladine, that was incredible."

"Ask that owl of yours," he growled. "And no, I am not all right. We must get out of here. Get lower into the tunnels. It won't take Thunder long to dig out that lot."

Linsha bit back any further questions. She, Lanther, and Dockett followed the dragon out of Iyesta's treasure room to a smaller stone staircase leading deep down into the tunnels of the labyrinth. Although she could not see him, Linsha listened to Crucible's steps and felt the way he moved. He was limping on his right front leg, and his wing did not hang quite right.

At the foot of the stairs, Crucible sent the humans back into the tunnel, then he swiveled his head around and focused his breath weapon on the stone arch and walls above the stairs. This time, instead of cracking, the stone turned fiery orange and yellow and began to drip onto the stairs. Abruptly the entire section of the ceiling collapsed and poured like lava onto the steps. It cooled to the consistency of a thick porridge almost immediately. Crucible melted more rock until the stair was firmly sealed by a plug of cooling granite.

He grunted in satisfaction.

In silence, they walked down the tunnel until they came to the rest of the people huddled in the darkness. At the arrival of the dragon, talking abruptly ceased until there was only the moaning of the wounded echoing through the hollow corridors.

"Now we have a little time. Linsha, would you please tell me what is going on and why are all these people down here? Where is Iyesta? What is Thunder doing here?"

Linsha saw his eyes glowing in the darkness like embers. "Could you give us a little light? We don't see as well as you."

That type of magic was simple for a dragon of Crucible's skills. He muttered a few words in the draconic tongue and formed a bright white light that burned with a steady glow above their heads.

The refugees relaxed a little and began to whisper again among themselves. General Dockett left to check his people. While Mariana and Lanther squatted against the wall and listened, Linsha quickly told

Crucible, and Varia, everything that had happened since the owl left Missing City.

She was describing her rescue from the Citadel when Sir Remmik pushed his way through the crowd, strode up to her, and waved his dagger in her face. He looked disheveled, exhausted, and completely out of his element, which perhaps explained the stupid thing he did next.

"You," he snarled. "I thought that voice sounded familiar. You are still a convicted prisoner of the Solamnic Order. I am placing you under arrest."

Linsha stared at him in surprise. She had forgotten he was down there, too.

Lanther and Mariana sprang to their feet and stood beside her. Suddenly, Sir Remmik found himself facing three angry people, an owl whose eyes were starting to glow a fierce yellow, and a dragon with teeth as big as his hand. His mouth opened, but no words came out.

Lanther spoke instead. "She is no longer your prisoner. She is under the protection of the Legion of Steel."

"And the militia," Mariana added, her hand meaningfully close to her sword.

Crucible was in no mood for diplomacy. He picked up the Solamnic commander by his blue tunic and tossed him over the heads of the other people. Linsha heard a thud and a groan and some muffled oaths, then silence. The crowded people edged back a little more from the dragon. Sir Remmik did not try to approach her again.

Hiding an un-Solamnic smile, Linsha continued with her narrative until she came to that morning and the bronze's arrival. When she finished, Crucible remained silent for a long time. The glow in his slanted eyes turned red then orange and brightened to fiery coals.

At last he stirred and his voice was a rumble in the depths. "Get these people out of here. I want to see Iyesta's body."

"Um . . . " Linsha hesitated. "We can't. I don't know where to send them. I didn't think of this until I saw you. I thought you could lead them out." She lowered her voice. "I was hoping, too, you could help me check on the brass eggs. I haven't been able to get down there."

Crucible regarded her down his long nose. "So she told you about them, did she? Good. Is there anyone in your group with a good memory?"

"My memory is clear enough for directions," Mariana said.

Varia twitched her wings and bobbed on Linsha's shoulder. "I remember the way to the entrance where the water weird lives." The owl had obviously given up her shyness for a while.

Crucible lowered his head until he could look the humans in the face. "That's on the northwest edge of the city beyond the lines of fighting. That might do well enough. They can hide in the Scorpion Wadi for now."

"How will they get past the water weird?" asked Varia. "Iyesta said she is very cranky."

Linsha pulled out the gold chain from under her tunic and carefully detached the brass dragon scale and handed it to the half-elf. "Take this. Iyesta said it would protect me from the guardians of the tunnels. I will go with Crucible."

"I'll go with you," Lanther said. "You may need help with those eggs."

Crucible gave him a shove with his nose that nearly knocked the Legionnaire off his feet. "Who are you? I do not know you."

"He's with the Legion," Linsha said hurriedly. "He is the one who pulled me out of the Citadel."

"Do you trust him?"

Linsha shrugged. He had saved her life. How could she say no? "Yes."

So it was decided. General Dockett and Mariana, with Varia on her shoulder, listened carefully to Crucible's directions for finding the tunnel entrance on the north side of the city ruins. Although the instructions were complicated, both officers seemed confident they could find the way. Especially with the owl to help them.

Linsha said a quiet and regretful goodbye to Varia. "Tonight," she said softly, rubbing the owl's head. "We will talk tonight."

She and Lanther watched as the militia, the dragon's guards, and the remnants of the Solamnic circle trooped past and disappeared into the dense darkness of the labyrinth, taking only some makeshift torches and Linsha's silent prayers with them.

When the last of the wounded and the rear guard shuffled out of sight, Linsha turned down a different tunnel and led Crucible to the chamber that had become Iyesta's tomb.

There was little left of the great brass except for bones, withered skin, and piles of scales that shone like coins in the light of Crucible's white flame. The carrion beetles had finished their feast and abandoned the carcass to the smaller carrion eaters and the final decay of time.

Crucible said little as he walked around the remains of his friend and ally. He studied the bones silently, lost in the depths of his own thoughts.

"I will kill him for this," he snarled.

The cold words rang with the adamant of a vow in the stone chamber. Linsha and Lanther looked at each other.

"If the Missing City is to be ours again, we have to seek a way to destroy the blue," Lanther said. "He found a way to kill Iyesta without a fight, perhaps we could learn what weapon he has and use it against him."

"An excellent idea," growled Crucible.

A frown crossed Linsha's face. As much as she wanted Crucible to stay, he had other responsiblities. Or did he?

"Are you saying you will help us? Why did you come in the first place? What about Sanction? Where is Lord Bight?" Try as she might, she could not keep the worry out of her voice.

The bronze lowered his head between Linsha and Lanther and gently pushed her toward a tunnel entrance, separating the two humans. "We will talk as we go." He led her forward and left Lanther to follow as he wished.

"I see you still wear the scale Lord Bight gave you," Crucible said to Linsha.

"Always. Iyesta gave me one, too, when she told me about the eggs."

"She did well to trust you."

Linsha put out a hand to touch the dragon's shoulder. "Crucible, you are limping. And your wing doesn't look right. Are you hurt?"

"To answer your earlier question, I came because Varia told me Iyesta was missing and you were in trouble. I came to see if I could help. Now I shall have to stay, because I cannot fly."

"What?" Linsha exclaimed, horrified for her friend. A dragon who could not fly became very vulnerable and ran a terrible risk of injury or death from other dragons or even determined humans.

A rumble of anger came from the dragon's chest.

"When I hit the gate I bruised my leg and cracked a bone in my wing. Then those men with the swords slashed the membrane of my left wing. It will heal, but I must give it time. So here I stay."

"But what about Sanction? And—" Her words broke off as she contemplated the scope of this disaster.

"Lord Bight?" The dragon filled in for her. "He is well enough. I would have come sooner, but your Knights in Sanction ran into a problem. They tried to break the siege and failed. Lord Bight had me settle a few things before I left. Then someone tried to assassinate him."

A gasp escaped Linsha before she could stop it. She shouldn't have been surprised. The lord governor had a unit of personal bodyguards to prevent that very thing, and she had risked her career and her life to save him from a Dark Knight assassin.

"He survived," the dragon went on. "Sergeant Hartbrooke took the dart instead."

Linsha searched her memory and found a face of one of the guards she vaguely remembered. She had not served in his squad, but she had seen him several times and noticed him at his post when she went to Sanction a year and a half ago. She remembered he had lost his wife in the plague that struck the city.

"He is dead." It was a statement, not a question.

"He was buried with honor."

"Will Lord Bight be able to handle the siege in Sanction without you?"

He gave a snort that was both resigned and contemptuous. "The Knights of Solamnia are there. They will have to deal with whatever comes their way."

They walked together in quiet companionship for several minutes through the dark, wide tunnels while Lanther trailed behind. Here in this section of the labyrinth, the high, rounded tunnels had been too tight for Iyesta, but Crucible was smaller than the brass dragonlord. By lowering his head and stretching out his long body, he fit through the passages without too much trouble.

After a while, Linsha's weary mind began to sort through the events of the past three days. Something nagged for her attention, something that had been in the back of her mind for some time. She rubbed her eyes and tried to concentrate her thoughts. She was so tired she could hardly stay upright, but somehow she had to think, she had to recall what was wrong. Something about the dragons. The triplets. A certain smell.

She stopped in her tracks so fast Crucible nearly stepped on her. There was a faint odor in the air. She thought it had been a residue of decay from the carcass of Iyesta, but what if the smell was from something else?

"Lanther," she cried out. "You said your prisoners told you Thunder knew about the eggs, and he certainly knew about the tunnels under the palace. Is it possible he also knew the full extent of the labyrinth? Maybe what he was looking for was the egg chamber."

There was a silence from the back, then Lanther said reluctantly, "That may be so. The men I talked to were not very clear."

"Thunder learned about the labyrinth?" Crucible trumpeted. His voice was so loud it echoed back to him from distant tunnels.

Linsha waved at the air around them. "Do you smell that?"

The bronze sprang past her and charged down the tunnel. The small flame of light went with him. Linsha listened to him go.

"Now how do we get there?" Lanther said, coming up beside her.

She took a long breath and let it out unsteadily. "We follow our noses."

Hand in hand so they would not be separated, the two walked carefully through the intense darkness. All too soon the smell filled the tunnels and became a stench. From somewhere not far ahead, they heard a bellow of grief and rage.

Linsha knew then with sick certainty what she would see when she and Lanther reached the end of the tunnel and peered into the huge chamber.

She could not bear it. As they stepped into the great cave, she closed her eyes and leaned on Lanther's shoulder. She had seen enough.

The huge mound of sand sat barren and empty in the warm light of the magic glows on the roof. Behind the mound stood Crucible, his entire body quivering with rage. At his feet lay the withered hulk of the brass mother, Purestian. Carrion beetles gorged on her remains, and her scales lay in heaps around her corpse. Like Iyesta, she lay sprawled as if she had simply fallen down. There was no sign of a battle or a struggle. And like Iyesta, she was missing her head.

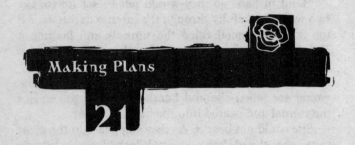

When Crucible, Lanther, and Linsha finally came to the opening by the old pool, Varia flew down to meet them. By that time, the sun had arched over to late afternoon. As they stood at the bottom of the narrow stairs and looked up the stair shaft, they saw the faint glow of golden light gleaming through the cracks in the pool chamber.

Lanther and Linsha looked back at Crucible and knew there was no possibility of a dragon his size passing through that exit. Iyesta had shapeshifted to a woman to get through. Crucible was obviously going to have to do the same or risk bringing tons of sand and rock into the tunnel.

Linsha waited expectantly. This was her chance to see what he might look like as a man. But when the dragon's spell was complete and the glow of magic faded, Linsha stared at the place where she expected to see a man about six feet tall and saw nothing. Her gaze dropped.

In the dragon's place sat an orange-striped barn cat.

Varia chuckled, *Coward.*

Shut up, bird. The cat meowed. Like the owl, he could communicate telepathically when he chose to.

"A cat?" Lanther exclaimed. "Can't he do better than that?"

Linsha laughed for the first time in too long and scooped up the cat in her arms. It was like seeing an old, dear friend. "If he goes out there as a dragon, he will be seen and killed. Thunder would never suspect a dragon would hide as a cat. Besides, bronzes like small, fluffy animals."

"But a barn cat? Why not a tiger? A lion? A griffin for that matter. At least he could fly."

"He's injured," Linsha said reasonably. "He can't fly even in a different shape."

Lanther threw up his hands and stalked up the stairs ahead of them.

Crucible squirmed out of the woman's arms. He fell heavily on his injured leg, but he scurried up the steps and scooted in front of the Legionnaire. Just in time.

The water weird reared out of the pool like a snake out of the grass. Its simple upright form was shaped from water, and like water, its strength was deceptive. Two arms detached from the torso and reached for Lanther's throat.

The Legionnaire gave a yell and went for his sword, but the cat crouched by the water's edge and hissed a furious command.

Immediately, the water weird drew back. It spit water at Lanther, then slipped sulkily beneath the surface of its pool.

"Not bad for a barn cat," Linsha said behind him.

Lanther chuckled, a little shakily, and made a short bow to the orange cat. "My thanks, Crucible."

This time, he waited until the cat went ahead of him up the short stairs to the crack in the ruined stone.

As soon as they were outside in the afternoon sun, a shape detached itself from the meager shade of a nearby outcropping.

"Lady Linsha! Lanther!" called Mariana. The half-elf hurried over. She studied their faces for the answer to her unspoken question and found it in the tension in their faces and the sadness in their eyes. "The eggs are destroyed," she said flatly.

"Not destroyed," Lanther told her. "Gone. Purestian is dead, her skull taken. We believe Thunder is responsible."

"Why take the eggs?" Mariana asked. "Why wouldn't he just smash them?"

Linsha remembered the pride she had heard in Iyesta's voice when she spoke of the eggs, and she shuddered. "I don't know. He's vindictive enough to keep them for himself or use them as a threat against us."

Mariana looked appalled. "Why would he keep them? Can he do anything beyond killing them?"

Lanther sat on a rock to ease his aching leg and looked south toward the city and the dragonlord's lair. The scar on his face looked livid in the sunlight, and his visage was dark with supressed anger. "Maybe. If he had enough power."

"Which he could get if he increases his skull totem," Linsha said fiercely. "Any more skulls just add to the power. I don't think he has a bronze skull yet."

Mariana glanced around and behind them. "Where is Crucible? Did he not come back with you?"

"He is here." Linsha pointed to the cat, who sat down and began to lick his injured leg.

The captain's eyes fell on the tom. "That's a cat."

"Yes. One of Crucible's more intriguing forms. I knew him as a cat before I realized he was a dragon."

"Oh. Well, that's good, because General Dockett left me to tell you: First, what is left of his forces have moved to the Scorpion Wadi. He is sending out scouts to gather any refugees or survivors they can find. Second, he asks if there are other entrances into the labyrinth from within the city, and if so, could they be used to pull out any of those trapped between the lines of fighting—especially Falaius and his forces."

The two humans shrugged, but the tomcat nodded.

"Will you help us?" Mariana asked the cat.

"I will carry you if your leg hurts too much," Linsha offered. Like bronzes, she had a weakness for small, fluffy animals.

The tom meowed and twined around her ankles. Varia guffawed as only an intelligent owl can.

"Since you are in good company," Lanther said, "I will leave you to your mission and go on one of my own. Perhaps a new prisoner or two can tell us what Thunder has done with the eggs."

He pulled his broad brimmed hat out of a small pack, threw on his tattered robe over his dirty, blood-stained clothes, and drew his long body into a compact slouch. Suddenly the tall, straight Legionnaire became the lame beggar. He leered at the women and shuffled away toward the city to find some talkative prisoners.

Linsha, Mariana, and Varia followed the cat back into the darkness of the labyrinth.

Sometime during the short summer night, the Missing City fell to attacking forces of the blue dragon. There was no official surrender or final battle. The defenders of the city just seem to give up and melt away into the darkness, leaving the streets to the Brutes and the mercenaries. Skirmishes broke out in all four districts as pockets of resistance continued to fight, but the last large companies of the militia and the Legion and its commander just disappeared. The mercenaries didn't care. They were pleased to have the city in their hands and the fighting over. Now, they felt, they could loot and celebrate and enjoy their victory as they saw fit. The Brutes, on the other hand, were puzzled. They had been impressed by the tenacity and courage of the city's defenders, and they could not understand how or why the militia had simply left.

The Brute general, commander of the overall attack, took no chances. Working with his trusted second-in-command, he set his warriors to work consolidating their hold on the city. He had his best trackers carefully sweep the streets and buildings for the wounded, for anyone wielding a weapon, or for any officers of the militia and city watch. His troops strengthened their defenses, repaired the gates and walls, and interrogated prisoners. He set up roadblocks, posted guards, and established observation posts. Then he went to see Thunder.

The great blue had already laid his claim to Iyesta's lair. He sat in the courtyard and watched while the remains of the palace roof were removed from the throne room. Prisoners from the city had been impressed by the mercenaries to do the backbreaking work of hauling out the tons of rock and debris. They worked in long lines with ropes and sledges, under the watchful eyes and cruel whips of their guards.

Thunder saw the Brute and his guard approach. His attention went back to the work on the throne room. He planned to do the last excavation himself to clear the stairs to the treasure room, and he wanted no interference.

The general made a short, almost insolent bow. "Your lordship, the city is ours."

"Good." The dragon stamped a foot on the ground in emphasis. "Soon Iyesta's defeat will be complete. Her lair and her hoard will be mine."

The Brute general nodded, his arms crossed over his bare chest. His ceremonial gold mask shone in the reflected firelight of the torches. "I hear, too, that the eggs are yours," he said casually.

The dragon was not really listening. He was too busy gloating. "Yes. On your information, I looked for them last night. They are in my keeping now."

"But you did not see fit to seal the tunnels or do anything to prevent the city's forces from escaping through the labyrinth," the general said coldly.

"Did they?" The dragon did not even look at him. "That is your problem, General. I brought you here to capture the city. You have done so. If you wish to wipe out the rest of those so-called defenders, you may chase them across the Plains. I have other things to do."

The man thought fast. He had not become general of a warrior race because of his blue skin paint. He was intelligent, strong, cunning, and merciless when the need arose. If his informant was correct, the forces that slipped out of the city were exhausted, demoralized, and nearly wiped out. However, they had found refuge in a place that would be very difficult to attack without Thunder's help, and if they stayed there long enough, they could rebuild their strength and mount a counteroffensive. What he needed was something to lure them out into the open where they could be captured or wiped out completely—including the bronze dragon. Ideally, he would like it if they could rid him of Thunder in the process, but he did not believe they were capable of such a deed. At least not without a little help.

253

He would have to speak to his informant.

He bowed briefly to the blue dragon, who did not notice, and backed out of his presence. He'd like to know the whereabouts of those eggs. The brass dragon eggs would bring those people out of their holes. If the dragon had found the eggs the night before, the general surmised, they still had to be close by. Thunder, he knew, was moving the contents of his lair in the Plains to this place, so it would be here that the dragon would hide the eggs. The dragon was stupid with overconfidence.

The general smiled beneath the mask. The campaign, he thought, was shaping up well. What he had to do now was ensure the militia knew where to look, then he would know where to find the militia.

* * *

The Scorpion Wadi lay in the stark, barren sand hills north and west of the Missing City. It had earned its name not only for the vicious little black scorpions that lived in its dry beds but also for its curved shape. Centuries ago griffin riders had reported the eroded dry river bed looked like the tail of a scorpion from the air. The name had stayed long after the elves disappeared. It was a place of overhanging ravines, washes, crumbling cliffs, undercut caves, and sculptured, narrow canyons. With the right force and enough water, it could be defended for months.

To this hot, arid sanctuary, Linsha, Mariana, Varia, and Crucible led the remnants of Iyesta's once proud militia and dragon's guard, a few battered survivors of the city watch, some civilians, the surviving Solamnics, and Falaius with a small contingent of Legionnaires. The general and the commander, the Solamnic Knights and the Legion, centaurs and civilians met in the shaded canyon at dawn. They silently gazed at one another, hollow-eyed and exhausted, unsure of what to do. They had all suffered a calamity, but this was the first time they had all gathered in one place and faced it together.

Linsha watched them, wondering if they could unite after all they had suffered. General Dockett moved forward with a smile and a cup of wine and greeted Falaius with undiguised relief. With the help of those already settled, the newcomers were treated for their wounds, fed, and given places to sleep in the shelter of a large undercut cave.

Sir Remmik ignored Linsha, a response for which she was grateful. The way she felt that morning, she was not certain she could have refrained from removing his face if he suggested putting her under arrest. The remaining Knights watched her as if they were not sure what to make of her. Sir Remmik declared she was guilty of a heinous act, and she had escaped from the cells. But oddly enough, she did not run away, she fought for the city, and she was partly responsible for their rescue and the deliverance of the nearly six hundred of the militia and city forces. These facts did not sit well on the Solamnic conscience.

Linsha didn't care. She had tramped for over fifteen hours through the dank, dark tunnels—some of which hadn't seen a two-legged walker in over four hundred years—and she was tired to the bone. She left the main group in the cave, and taking an old cloak for a blanket, she wandered into a gully nearby. The small gully was an old wash full of twisted rock formations, sandbars, and layered cliffs. A low overhang offered some shade and a sandbank made a comfortable enough bed. She spread out the cloak and fell asleep before her head hit the ground.

Varia flew to a shady perch on the ledge just over
Linsha's bed. The orange cat limped into her shelter and
stretched out beside her to rest his injured leg and side.

You will have to tell her eventually. The owl hooted
softly.

The cat understood. *I know.*

Are you afraid of her reaction?

There was silence for a moment then the cat
yawned and grumbled in his throat. *Shut up, bird. You
talk too much.*

Linsha woke just before sunset from a deep, dream-
less sleep, feeling better than she had in days. She
yawned, stretched, and crawled out from under the
overhang. Something to eat now and she might feel
human again.

"Ah, good." Lanther's voice came to her from somewhere near the ground. "You're awake. You can call off
your bodyguard now."

She scanned the ground in surprise and finally saw
him behind a nearby hump of rock and gravel. The
Legionnaire lay flat on his back in the sand while the
orange tomcat sat on his chest and growled menacingly.
Varia watched impassively from her perch.

With a chuckle, Linsha plucked the cat off the man's
chest and sat down on a rock, the cat cradled in her lap.
"He may look like a cat, but he's still a dragon," she
said, "which makes him stronger, smarter, and much
more powerful than any cat you've ever seen."

Lanther climbed to his feet and dusted off his already disheveled clothes. He leveled a glare at the

orange cat. "I won't forget that," he muttered. "Falaius has called a meeting. He sent me to find you." He wheeled, ready to stamp off.

"Lanther!" Linsha hurried to him. "Don't be angry. Crucible doesn't know you yet. These two—" she indicated Varia and the cat— "are very protective of me."

He nodded once, and his irritation seemed to fade a little from his dark blue eyes. "Falaius told me I should wake you from a distance. Next time I will follow his advice. Come on. They're meeting in the cave."

The Rose Knight fell into step beside him. "Did you find your prisoners? Do you have news?"

He was about to reply when a dazzling light shone behind them. Startled, they turned around in time to see Crucible's cat form expand outward in a glowing, glittering haze of golden colored light. They blinked in the bright light as the bronze dragon took shape in the scintillating mist. He stared down at them as the glow faded.

"My apologies, Legionnaire," the dragon said. "The next time I will simply let Varia tear your eyes out."

Lanther's mouth opened as if he planned to say something. Instead, he watched wordlessly as Varia left her perch, circled over Linsha's head, and winged silently away.

Linsha studied Lanther, a little surprised by his reaction. Something about her companions seemed to irritate the Legionnaire, but she could not imagine what.

"Shall we go?" Crucible suggested. He didn't wait for an answer but stepped out of the gully into the main canyon and headed for the cave.

Linsha thought the big bronze would have trouble manuvering through the narrow sections of the canyon, but he was as sinuous as a snake and slid his great body through like a flow of molten bronze. Only his injured wing hampered him in the tight turns.

When they arrived at the cave, Linsha learned more militia had slipped through enemy lines and made their way to the Wadi. They brought reports of Thunder and the palace, of the Brutes and their tightening hold on the city. General Dockett had interviewed each group that came in during the day, and by the time Lanther found Linsha and brought her in, the commander's face was locked in a grimace of grief and anger.

He and Falaius came out of the cave to meet the Knight and the dragon. Mariana came with them, carrying a hunk of bread and a wineskin with her good arm.

"Thought you might be hungry," she said softly to Linsha and handed her the wine and the bread. "There isn't much to be had right now."

Linsha took them gratefully. She could not remember her last meal. The two women sat down side by side on a large flat rock. Crucible lounged on his belly, placing himself behind Linsha with obvious intent. The two men and Lanther took seats by Linsha's rock. They lit no fires and brought no torches for fear of attracting attention from spies or Thunder, if he decided to fly over. They talked quietly among themselves in the growing twilight while Linsha ate and others joined them.

The newcomers stared at Crucible's bulk, dark in the shadows of the canyon floor, and they whispered quietly about the bronze and his fight with Thunder. Very few people knew the connection between the bronze dragon and the cat who had accompanied the half-elf and the Solamnic Knight through the tunnels. Crucible intended to leave it that way.

Last to come was Sir Remmik, accompanied by the next ranking officer of the circle, a man Linsha had last seen sitting on the Solamnic council in the Citadel. The

Solamnic commander fired a ferocious glare at Linsha, but he made no move toward her and took his seat at the furthest opposite side of the group from her.

Dockett made a quick head count and nodded to his commander. Falaius slowly rose to his feet. The old plainsman stood erect and tall in spite of the heavy load of sadness and danger he had been carrying. When he spoke, his deep voice remained steady and strong.

"In one day, we have lost our city and been driven from our homes. We must now make a decision. It is not one I will make for you. I am commander of what is left of the Legion. That will not change. But the militia, the city watch, Iyesta's guards, and the Solamnic circle are released from my command. You may choose to go your own ways, or you may choose to stay here and fight with us." He held up a hand to still the sudden outburst of voices. "Yes, the Legion will fight. We came here when this city was nothing but a field of ruins and phantoms. We built our headquarters here. We were here before Iyesta, before the militia, before the merchants. We will be here after Thunder is dead. I ask you to stay and fight for your homes with us, but I understand that not all of you have roots as deep as ours. You are free to go. Or free to stay. We intend to kill the dragon and drive the invaders from our city."

"And how are we supposed to get across the Plains?" someone cried. "Where are we supposed to go?"

Falaius gave a dry chuckle devoid of any humor. "If you choose to leave, you can go to Chaos for all I care. You are on your own."

Noise broke out all around him as the leaders of the various groups and curious onlookers made comments, voiced protests, and asked questions. The Legion commander let them talk for a few minutes, then he held up a hand again for silence.

"Before you make up your minds, I want you to consider two things. We have learned, much to our regret, that Iyesta was guarding a nest of eggs under the city. Somehow, Thunder learned of that nest and stole the eggs before we could save them. We don't know what he plans to do with them."

"It's not just the eggs we are worried about," Linsha said.

Falaius gestured for her to stand up. She climbed onto the flat rock and stood in front of Crucible. For a moment she gazed up at the dragon's head towering over her, one gleaming eye slightly cocked so he could see her better, and she was very glad to have him with her, even to the possible detriment of Sanction's safety. She felt a deep sense of connection with him that surprised her sometimes when she thought about it. Some of it, she knew, stemmed from their time together in Sanction. The dragon had saved her life and lent his strength and sympathy to her when she needed it most. Some of it came from their shared grief for the death of an irreplaceable dragon and friend. But the rest? It was more than friendship, more than gratitude. Perhaps it was something similar to what her brother, Ulin, felt when he flew with the gold dragon Sunrise. It was a feeling of comfort and strength and delight that she would not change for anything in the world.

"Most of you heard the rumors that Iyesta's head was missing when we found her body," Linsha began. "It was. So was Purestian's. And if we could find the bodies of the triplets, I believe we would see their skulls are missing, too."

She paced the short distance back and forth on the rock and tried to look at the faces of the people before her. Although the sun had just set and a vestige of light still remained on the plains, shadow and darkness filled the Wadi and lapped up to the top of the canyon walls. Without some form of firelight, Linsha could barely make out shapes let alone faces. She raised her voice a little to be certain everyone listened.

"Imagine if you can. Thunder—we all know what he is like—a dragon overlord increasing the power of his totem. What would he do? He could change the land like Malys or Sable. He could obliterate the city in a single afternoon. He could use his power to twist Iyesta's beloved eggs into something hideous. Worse, he could attract the attention of one of the other dragon overlords. Especially Malys."

Linsha didn't have to see the faces of the people around her to hear the quiet gasp of horror from her listeners. She pushed her point forward.

"Malys called an end to the Dragon Purge to establish the borders of the Dragon Realms. And to prevent more Great Dragons from challenging for land. What will she do when she hears Thunder has killed Iyesta, *doubled* his realm, and taken the skulls of several dragons? Will she be pleased to see an upstart claim the vast Plains of Dust?"

"What about Beryl or Sable?" a Legionnaire called out.

"What about them? I cannot believe either of them would be happy by Thunder's move. So where does that leave us?"

"Caught between the Pinnacle of Panic and the Abyss of Doom," said the same voice. Several people laughed. Most didn't. It was too close to the truth.

"An apt description. Which is why we should move quickly to destroy Thunder's totem before he can finish it. I would rather deal with a dragon like Thunder than a monster like Malys."

"But where is this totem?" shouted a man's voice.

Linsha peered through the darkness toward the speaker, but Lanther rose to his feet and answered for her. "I have spoken to several prisoners who told me Thunder has broken into Iyesta's treasure chamber. He plans to bring his collection of skulls from his lair and erect his totem in the chamber, under heavy guard."

Someone else asked, "Do you know where the dragon eggs are?"

"Not yet."

The questions, comments, and advice came faster and faster until almost everyone was talking at once. Lanther gave up trying to say anything and sat down with Mariana. Falaius and Dockett fielded questions and tried to keep order.

Standing in the darkness with Crucible beside her, Linsha felt a sudden surge of energy. She had had her say and told the people what they needed to hear. They had to make their own decision from here. In the meantime, she wanted to get out of this stifling canyon, to do something useful, to do what she was good at—gathering information.

To say they were going kill the dragon and destroy his totem was one thing. To actually do it was something else again. They needed information on his whereabouts, his guards, his preparations for the totem, his plans for the eggs. Something Lanther had said came back to her thoughts—*Find his weapon and use it against him.* Thunder had used something to kill those brasses. Neither Iyesta nor Purestian had suffered the burns characteristic of a lightning attack. Something had killed them quickly and effectively. If someone could just find that weapon, the chances of killing Thunder and living to tell about it would be much greater. She wanted to find it.

Linsha quietly edged off the rock and walked past Crucible into the darkness. She heard him turn around and come after her, she heard Lanther call her name, but she acknowledged neither of them until she had left the cave and the noise far behind and was enveloped by the solitude and darkness. She whistled a soft, lonely call and held her arm out. She felt rather than saw the owl float silently from night and land on her arm. Only then did she turn around to the bronze dragon and say, "Want to go hunting?"

ou don't have to go with me. You
hurt your leg yesterday. It needs
to heal."

Linsha crouched at the foot of a large outcropping
outside the mouth of Scorpion Wadi. Crucible lay
behind her, his long body flattened against the
ground. They had bypassed the sentries in the canyon
and now waited for Varia to return and tell them all
was clear.

"Someone has to keep you out of trouble," he whispered. "Just what do you intend to do?"

Linsha hesitated. While she felt determined to do
something and strong enough to do it, she hadn't really
considered exactly what she should do.

"I gave my word to Iyesta that I would protect her
eggs," she said after a while. "We need to find them.
But first, I want to look for the weapon Thunder used
to kill Iyesta. It's possible the enemy has not yet found
the back entrance to the labyrinth—the one in the
palace grounds. We could go there and look for—"

Crucible cut her off with a sharp sound. "Quiet! I
hear hoofbeats."

They froze, listening to the staccato rhythm of a horse approaching at a fast trot. An almost silent flutter of wings brought Varia to land on the rocks by Linsha's head. "It is the young centaur," she hooted.

"Leonidas?" Linsha's voice warmed with pleasure. She stepped out into the open where he could see her and called his name softly.

There was a clatter of hooves on stone, then silence. "Lady Linsha?" The relief in his voice almost overwhelmed the wariness of the question. He moved forward until he could see her in the starlight. "What are you doing out here?"

She heard something heavy move behind her and saw the glow of golden light illuminate the rocks around her and gleam on the centaur's pale hide, then it flashed out leaving nothing but spots dancing in her night vision. The centaur's eyes grew huge. He reared up, his hand reaching for a weapon behind his back. "No, no it's all right," she reassured him. "It's just a friend of mine."

Leonidas pranced back several steps and shook his mane. "You keep interesting friends, Lady Knight. What was that light?"

"A shapechanger. We were going to go on patrol."

"Then I am glad to find you. Once again we meet in darkness and need."

"It does seem to be a habit of ours," she agreed with a dry laugh. "Were you looking for me?"

"I came to find the militia and to tell someone what we have found."

"Who is this 'we'?"

The life seemed to drain out of him. His shoulders sagged and his hands fell to his sides. "We are all that is left of my troop—three of us, the younger ones who got thrust to the back during the heat of the fighting to

265

help the wounded, retrieve arrows, and run messages. We were running errands for our lord when our lines were overwhelmed. We found each other but no one else. We tried to go back to our position and were cut off. It wasn't until late last night that the Brutes moved on and we were able to get into the barricades to see . . . they were all dead. Uncle Caphiathus . . . everyone. The wounded, too. All killed. The Brutes left no one."

His voice sounded so grief-stricken that Linsha moved beside him and put a hand on his wither. His hide was grimy and wet with sweat, and he smelled of smoke, blood, and sweaty horse.

"No one but you three. Caphiathus would be pleased you survived."

Leonidas did not seem to hear her. "Since then we have been hiding. Watching."

Linsha's ears pricked up. "Watching what?"

"Those painted warriors mostly." He shuddered. "They are brutally efficient." He paused and looked up the trail to the Wadi. "Is anyone else still alive? Where is General Dockett? A scout found us and told us some soldiers were coming here."

"He was right. They're in the Wadi. The General and Falaius are planning a counterattack. We must try to destroy Thunder's totem."

"You mean that horrible pile of skulls?"

Linsha grabbed his arm in excitement. "Yes! Where is it?"

"In the palace. We were in the gardens this afternoon trailing the Brute general. He came to talk to Thunder and was there when the dragon brought in the first few skulls."

The Rose Knight heard an insistent meow and felt the tomcat twine around her ankles. She picked him up. "Thank you, Leonidas," she said and strode purposefully toward the feeble glow of light to the south that marked the Missing City.

Her sudden move took the centaur by surprise. "Wait! Where are you going?"

"To the palace."

"But what about the militia?"

"They are busy. They have much to do before they can attack an unarmed camp, not to mention a conquered city. What they need is information."

He swung around in front of her and offered a hand. "Then get on. I'll take you."

She took it and, clutching the cat, mounted his strong back once more. "Crucible, this is Leonidas. He has helped me several times these past ten days. Leonidas, this is Crucible. Remember what he looks like. It may be important. And don't be deceived by his size."

"Are you talking to me or him?" the centaur asked as he moved smoothly into a canter.

"Both of you."

Behind the centaur and his rider, a small shape detached from the rock outcropping and flew noiselessly after them.

The ancient elven palace was ablaze with the light of hundreds of torches and watchfires as if the images of Gal Tra'kalas had returned and were holding a gala in the gardens and courts of the long dead prince. Soldiers—mercenaries and Brutes alike—camped in the courtyard, guarded the walls, marched along the paths, and stood sentry at every observation point.

Leonidas gave the palace a wide berth and plunged into the shadows of the gardens. He found his companions on the south edge of the ruins, keeping a watch on the road from the city. After a quick introduction, the two told Linsha what they had learned so far. Their tale impressed her. These three centaurs barely out of colthood had survived the battle and managed to avoid capture while spying on the dragonlord and his minions.

Phoulos, a bay with a black mane and beard of sorts, continued. "Thunder is collecting these skulls from his lair on the Plains. We think he's putting them in the throne room, but we can't get close enough to look."

"Did he bring them all in one trip?" Linsha asked.

"No," answered the third stallion, a lighter bay named Azurale. "He won't trust anyone else to do it."

Phoulos snorted. "Or he doesn't have anyone else to do it for him. Even his own kind avoids him."

"Right. So, he's made two trips so far, and he left again just a short time ago."

Linsha rubbed her face, careful to avoid the bruise by her eye. "So the palace is empty?"

Azurale nodded. "Of him. There's guards everywhere. His journey usually takes about four hours."

"That's plenty of time. If we can get through the tunnels, we can get into the lower levels of the place and take a look at these skulls." Linsha swung her leg over Leonidas and slid to the ground where she gently put the cat down. "Let's check the door first."

She led the way to the tumbled building she knew well now. The entrance was there behind the vines and ferns and undergrowth, unguarded and still open.

The centaurs stared suspiciously at the black doorway. "Don't worry." Linsha smiled. "You don't have to go down there. I will. I just want one of you to guard the door for me."

But the orange cat hissed at her and blocked the way. *No. I will go down there. I can pass through ways you cannot and remain unseen.*

Linsha started at the words in her head. "Are you sure?"

The centaurs looked surprised. They hadn't heard the cat. For an answer, the tomcat flicked his tail and limped into the doorway. In a blink he moved out of sight.

"Interesting cat," observed Leonidas.

Linsha and the centaurs stood about the doorway in an awkward silence while they tried to decide what to do next. Around them a few insects buzzed in the grass, and a cool breeze swept through the trees. A waning moon gleamed yellow over the hills to the east.

Linsha couldn't stand the quiet. She had come here to do something, not wait around for Crucible. "Leonidas, you said the Brute general came to talk to Thunder. Is he still here?"

Phoulos answered, "Actually, yes. The Brutes set up a command headquarters in one of the other buildings. The general goes back and forth between here and the city."

"Hmm. I wonder if he knows—"

"Knows what?" Leonidas said eagerly. "What are you thinking, Lady?"

She studied the centaurs, her expression tight with concentration. "I think we'll take a look around. Would you be willing to help me?"

All three centaurs nodded vigorously. They had not planned to avenge their kin by running away.

"Good. Then listen." Talking softly, she told them what she wanted to do.

Finding a mercenary alone proved harder than Linsha expected. All the ones they found still awake and on guard either moved about in patrols or stayed at their posts with their companions. It was a long frustrating time before she and the centaurs saw a mercenary stagger out of one of the buildings and make his way into the woods to relieve himself. Fortunately for them, he had had more than his share to drink and he wandered farther into the groves than he intended. It took only a matter of moments to snatch him, break his neck, and drag him into the undergrowth. Linsha quickly pulled off his tunic with the crude blue emblem on the sleeve, his pants, which were a little too big for her but cleaner than her own filthy clothes, and his boots. He wore leather gauntlets, a broad studded belt, and a padded vest, too, which she added to her disguise. The only thing he did not have was a helmet or a hat, but Phoulos had a leather cap he gave to her to hide her curls. When she was finished dressing, Leonidas declared she looked every bit a mercenary.

Although the man had not been carrying a sword when he wandered to his death, he was armed with a dagger, several throwing knives, and a stiletto in his boot. Linsha kept the dagger and the stiletto, but she gave the slim throwing knives to the centaurs.

"You never know when a knife might come in handy," she said.

Leaving Azurale to watch the tunnel entrance for Crucible, Linsha and the other two centaurs worked their way over to the southern edge of the gardens not far from the road that led to the palace. They found the Brutes had built a strong encampment fortified with a log palisade and guarded by sentries. Within the ring sat the crumbled foundations of an old building that now supported a large and spacious tent decorated with banners and hung with lamps. Smaller tents clustered around it, leaving a clearing directly in front of the tent where the barbarians had placed a ring of spears, each holding the severed head of some hapless enemy. Guards stood at the gate, at the main tent, and all around the perimeter.

Linsha and the two centaurs looked at the encampment, impressed in spite of themselves.

"Are you sure you want to do this?" Phoulos whispered. "You might get in, but I don't see how you'll get out."

Linsha was sure. She had a strong suspicion that this general was intelligent enough to know a great deal about the dragonlord's activities. There was a good chance they could find some useful information in his tent. But was the chance of information worth the risk? She took a second look with a more discerning eye. If those guards over there had been drunk, asleep, inattentive, or fewer, her scheme might work. But they were alert and heavily armed and left not a scrap of ground within the camp unobserved from some angle. There was no way she could see to get into the general's tent and out again without being apprehended or killed. Linsha had participated in enough undercover activities to know a bad risk when she saw one.

"Maybe we'd better rethink this," she said softly.

There was a chorus of ominous creaks and a voice said in coarse Common, "That would be a good idea."

The companions froze in frightened surprise. All three knew the sound of bow strings being stretched.

"That's good," continued the voice. "You are completely covered, so don't try anything heroic. Just step out onto the path."

Linsha felt sick. She wanted to kick herself for falling so easily into their hands. She looked up at the two centaurs and gave them a nod. "Don't," she whispered.

Ever so carefully Leonidas, Phoulos, and Linsha raised their hands in plain view and walked out of the line of trees onto the path. Half a dozen Brute warriors stepped out of their hiding places, their bows drawn and arrows ready.

From a pine tree nearby, the hunting cry of an owl pierced the night. Linsha pretended not to hear it.

The leader of the Brute patrol said something in his own tongue, and the other five warriors swiftly disarmed the captives and urged them at spearpoint toward the encampment. They were taken to the open space before the large tent and forced to wait under the gruesome trophies on the spears.

Linsha refused to look at the heads for fear she might see someone she knew. She stayed close between the centaurs, keeping in their shadows so she could study the men around her without being too obvious.

The leader went into the tent and, after what seemed a lifetime to Linsha, came out again with the Brute general.

The Rose Knight pulled the leather cap further down over her face, but she needn't have bothered. The patrol leader hauled her out from between the centaurs and pushed her in front of the general. She drew herself up and stared defiantly up at the impassive gold mask. The general was a tall man, taller than Lanther, and built proportionately with wide shoulders and a chest she could crack rocks on. He wore nothing more than a kilted skirt of fine linen and leather sandals, and all of his exposed skin had been painted blue. His long hair had been plaited into dozens of small braids and twisted with white bird feathers. Dark eyes glittered through the eye holes of the gold mask as he studied her. He reached out and yanked her cap off.

"A woman. Reddish hair in curls. Green eyes like gems. Slender nose with freckles. A large bruise on her face. The description was a good one. You are the Solamnic Knight Linsha Majere." Ignoring her gasp of surprise, he turned to his warriors. "Good work. Take those two to the slave pens. Bind this one and bring her to my tent."

Linsha stiffened. Her muscles tensed, and her weight shifted as if she were preparing to run. But powerful hands clamped around her arms and pulled them behind her back. She was marched into the tent and tied with leather strips to one of the strong supporting poles in the center. The thongs bit into the raw skin and scabs around her wrists from the last time she had been bound.

"Tie her feet, too," the general ordered. "She is trained in the ways of the warrior."

The men complied and left the tent. Linsha could move nothing more than her head. She looked around and realized she and the general were alone. *Gods,* she wondered, *who has been telling him so much about me?*

The Brute moved with athletic ease to a low couch carved from black wood and cushioned with animal pelts. On his left stood a small camp table with writing implements and scrolls. To his right was a matching table with a stoneware bottle and several small cups. Behind him hung an ornate banner decorated with geometric designs surrounding a magnificent lion. A sword stood on a rack close to his hand. Hanging from the tent's roof, Linsha noticed a long, black-shafted lance, but it was muffled in shadows and she could not see it clearly.

She turned her attention back to the general. He sat on his couch and poured a dark red liquid into a cup. He held it up in a mock salute, but he did not drink.

273

When he said nothing, she glared at him. "Don't you ever take off that mask?"

"Not in the presence of outsiders," he growled. "Now tell me where the bronze dragon is. Tell me about this Scorpion Wadi. Tell me about the militia and its general. Who survived and what do they plan to do?"

"Who are you people?" she countered. "Why did you come here? Do you seriously believe Thunder will allow you to stay?"

The general swirled the drink around in his cup and laughed. "Of course he won't. He is greedy, envious, vicious, and hates anything that gets in the way of what he wants. He will kill the bronze, increase his totem, and drive us out as soon as he grows weary of our help. We, however, have other plans." He rose and strode to her, the cup still in his hand. "We are the people of Tarmak, the sons of Amarrel. We have crossed the ocean to claim this city for our own."

"But it's not your own. This city was built by the Legion, by Iyesta, and by people who came seeking peace."

"And now they are dead. The city is ours and we intend to keep it. Now, where is the dragon? What does the militia plan to do?"

Linsha pressed her back into the pole to keep away from him. The paint on his body smelled foul, and the menace in his voice sent her heart racing. His words sent her mind racing, too. She had wondered from the beginning how a dragon like Thunder had organized and planned a complicated and thorough invasion of the Missing City. Now she suspected she knew who had really planned it. From the intonation in his voice, she suspected he had not yet completed his plan. Could it be possible that he was also responsible for the death of the brass dragons?

"The bronze went back to Sanction," she said, trying not to breathe too much in his proximity.

He shook his head and held the cup closer to her face. "He is injured and cannot fly. Now, where is he?"

"How do you know all this?" she demanded. "How do you know me?"

"You are not the only one who can gather information, Lady Knight. We have had spies in this city for several years. Unfortunately, they are unavailable at this moment, and you conveniently placed yourself in my hands." He raised his other hand and placed his fingers across her face so his fingertips gripped the sides of her head. His touch felt like steel.

"How did you kill Iyesta?" she snapped.

The general's mask stared down at her, but she heard the slightest intake of breath as if her question had taken him by surprise. "You are stubborn—and as passionate as any dragon. I helped Thunder kill Iyesta and the three young ones with a gift my father received from the Highlord Ariakas himself—an Abyssal Lance." He nodded toward the black-shafted lance. "Now, I have lost patience. It is time to give me answers."

His fingers closed on her skull and a brilliant light flashed through her head, as hot and excruciating as a heated poker. Her jaws were forced open, and he poured the contents of the cup between her lips. The liquid tasted vaguely of wine and herbs, but it burned her mouth and the back of her throat. Terrified, she gagged and tried to spit it out, but she succeeded only in choking on the fiery liquid. What was it? Had he poisoned her?

"Where is the bronze dragon?" he repeated.

Linsha's body went numb and sagged in the straps holding her to the pole. Only her head remained sensitive to the pain that bore into her skull. She stifled a groan as her vision blurred and her thoughts began to run together. Inside her head, memories of dark rain and pounding thunder mingled with blurry images of the tent. She tried to force an image—any image—into focus, only to see it fade and blend and slip out of her reach.

Then the world turned black and wet. She heard the strange voices again, and this time she recognized the language they spoke. Black silhouettes swam into her vision. She saw the figure with the sword come toward her, and she saw her dagger. Clear and brilliant as a flash of lightning, a piece of her memory floated into place. Her dagger. She had stabbed the black figure in the chest. Sir Morrec had died of a knife wound to the back. As the black figure faded out of focus, the second black silhouette swam into her vision. A blow exploded behind her ear. The rainy night abruptly vanished and the tent slipped back into sight. But the steely touch of the hand on her temples was the same. The colored explosion of pain and the acrid aftertaste of magic was the same.

"The dragon," demanded the voice.

"You . . . attacked us. You killed Sir Morrec," she managed to say. She let her chin drop to her chest. Her hair was wet and her face bathed in sweat. She shook as if from a fever.

The general pressed his fingers harder. The pain grew worse. "Answer me, woman. Where do we find the bronze?"

Linsha screamed but she would not answer. Her father Palin had held out for months against the horrible tortures of the Dark Knight mystics. His daughter was made of the same stern stubbornness. She could not betray Crucible.

After a while, the Tarmak general pulled back from the Lady Knight and eyed her unconscious form. A second Tarmak officer stepped into the tent.

"Is she dead?" the man inquired in their rough, guttural language.

The general tossed the cup to the ground. "Of course not. It would take more than I gave her to kill her. She is strong."

"Will she take the bait?"

"If she is as clever as I have been told, she will take it."

"And if not?"

"Then I will give her to your men. They can kill her as they wish." He turned away from his prisoner. "Has Thunder returned from his lair?"

"No, sir. Not yet."

"Good. Then let us go make our preparations."

Together the two men walked out of the tent, leaving Linsha hanging on the pole.

I n the half light of dawn when colors had not yet become visible and the landscape was still half-hidden in grays and shadowed blacks, an owl soared out of a pine tree and circled over the tents of the Brute encampment. The few guards left in the camp paid no attention to her, and no one noticed when she swooped down to the ground near the largest tent. On the ground she was almost invisible. She hopped to a place in the back where sections of the tough fabric were stitched together. Several quick snips of her beak opened a hole large enough for her squeeze through.

Step-hopping, she made her way across the rugs on the floor to the woman's body tied to the tent pole. Varia satisfied herself that Linsha was still alive and began to climb up the Lady Knight's leg to the padded mercenary's tunic and the leather thongs that held her to the pole. The leather was tougher than the tent fabric and took some time to snip through. Finally, she nipped through the last strand, and Linsha toppled to the floor.

278

"Ouch," came a muffled protest from the prostrate woman.

"Ah, you are awake," said the owl in her whispery voice. "I am pleased they left you alive."

"Barely." Linsha groaned and tried to roll over, only to discover her feet were still tied to the pole. "Would you mind?"

Varia snapped through the last leather bindings, and Linsha pulled free. She pushed herself onto her back and lay staring at the roof of the tent as if she were trying to remember how she got there.

"Are you well?" asked the owl.

"No. That bastard knows sorcery. He used some sort of drug on me and a spell that I thought was going to shatter my skull. Gods," she groaned, "what did I tell him?"

"We need to get you out of here. The general and his officers are gone, but there are a few guards left."

Linsha did not take the hint. She lay very still, her forehead creased in thought. "It's odd. I remember he asked me questions. I don't think I answered. He knew too much about me, that's for sure. But he answered some of my questions. Why would he do that?"

The owl fussed around, pulling off the leather thongs and checking her bloody wrists. If she had been a little bigger, she would have hauled Linsha to her feet and dragged her out, but she had to be patient and wait for the Lady Knight to find her own strength.

"Varia, what is an Abyssal Lance?" Linsha asked.

The owl chirped in surprise and hooted softly. "Why?"

"The general said something about one."

"There were only a few made, as I remember. Some smiths serving the Highlord Ariakas made them as an evil variation of the dragonlance. They were dreadful weapons."

"Is that one?" Linsha raised a sluggish hand and pointed at the ceiling.

Varia cut her eyes to the roof of the tent where a long, black shaft hung on golden cords from the tent roof supports. Her dark eyes widened to pools. "So that's how they did it."

"It will kill a dragon, won't it?"

"They were not as effective as a dragonlance, but yes, they could kill a dragon."

Linsha pulled herself upright and, using the pole for support, hauled herself to her feet. "Come on, we're taking that thing with us."

She took a step toward the general's couch and fell to her knees. The tent swayed around her with a sickening spin. She took several deep breaths and put her head between her knees.

"Where are the centaurs when you need them?" she moaned.

Varia said nothing. She fluttered to her hole in the back of the tent, slipped out, and flew into the trees. Linsha did not notice. She concentrated on her breathing and her dizziness until she could bring both under control, then she sat up and climbed to her feet.

At that moment there was a shout outside, a clashing sound, and hoofbeats. Suddenly, a centaur yanked open the tent entrance.

Azurale stuck his head in. His black eyes were shining with eagerness and a crossbow dangled from his hand. "I hear you need help," he offered.

Linsha did not take the time to ask what had just happened. She accepted his help and together they lowered the black weapon down from its hangings.

In the growing light of day, Linsha was able to take a closer look at it. Varia was right. It was a dreadful weapon. It had a cruel, barbed head of rust red set in a black shaft about fifteen feet long. The handle ended in a cowl that helped protect the wielder. Linsha flinched at the touch of the thing, for it was imbued with an evil enchantment that tingled under her fingers like trapped lightning.

Azurale made a face as he helped her carry it out of the tent. "You sure you want this foul thing?"

"If it can kill Iyesta," she growled, "it will kill Thunder."

Outside the morning sun tipped the horizon and spilled across the plains in horizontal beams of yellow light. Linsha lifted her face to the sun and closed her eyes. The heat caressed her skin and touched her pale cheeks with rose.

"Varia said you had an Abyssal Lance." Crucible said behind her. "Is that it?"

She was so startled that she nearly dropped it. Belatedly, she glanced around the encampment and saw the bodies of several dead guards lying in the dirt. The smashed and mangled bodies made it evident what had happened to them. The half-dozen guards had been no match for a dragon.

The tents were empty, the headquarters deserted. That's convenient, she thought. The Brutes leave her alive in an empty camp with a weapon at hand. What was going on here?

Crucible watched her over the palisade, his dragon head gleaming with metal brilliance in the morning light.

She blinked at him. "What are you doing here? Did you find the eggs?"

"They are not in the labyrinth. I think Thunder has taken them to the treasure room. He made several trips back to his lair last night, and now he is reconstructing his skull totem."

281

Linsha flashed a worried frown. "You saw it? Is it complete?"

Crucible shook his heavy head. "I do not believe so. I think he still needs a bronze skull."

"Lady, if you don't mind," Azurale called. "This is getting heavy. What to you want to do with it?"

Linsha stared up at the bronze dragon. "I cannot carry this alone, Crucible. It is a weapon for a dragonrider. Do we leave it here or take it with us?"

He snorted that she would even ask such a question and flexed his injured wing. "Bring it. We will trap him below ground like he did Iyesta and make him feel his own weapon."

"Then you'd better hurry, before those Brutes return," Azurale suggested.

"I'll need a saddle, some rope, and—"

"A shield," Crucible added to her list.

They hurriedly gathered the items Linsha needed, and the owl, the dragon, the centaur, and the Lady Knight left the Brute encampment and, taking the evil lance with them, fled into the wild gardens.

"If we are going to lure Thunder underground, we will need bait," Linsha said as they hurried back to the hidden entrance to the labyrinth.

Crucible agreed. "A distraction would be good, too. We do not need those blue-skinned warriors chasing us down there."

"The general called them Tarmaks. Have you ever heard of that? The Dark Knights just called them Brutes."

None of the little group had heard that name. All they knew was the Brutes' reputation for ferocity and fearlessness.

It was full daylight by the time they reached the small entrance to the tunnels below the palace. Linsha, with Azurale's help, fashioned a saddle and a harness that would help her stay on Crucible's back and hold the heavy lance in place. They fastened it around the bronze, being careful of his bruised leg and his cracked wing bone, and when they were finished he declared it sturdy enough.

"Good, then take it off," Linsha said. "We'll carry it for you while you are in cat shape."

"Not this time," replied Crucible. "We need bait. Thunder needs a bronze to complete his totem. I can get him underground."

Linsha looked stunned. "How can you do that? You blocked the tunnel entrance from the treasury yourself. If you go in there, he'll kill you. And if you make it back here, you can't get through this door as a dragon."

Crucible lowered his head until his dark gold eye was level with Linsha's face. "He forgot who he was dealing with when he left it blocked with stone. I can open that entrance before he has time to draw breath. You must be waiting for me. Not in Iyesta's tomb. He might expect that. Go to the egg cavern."

Linsha reached out and touched the scaly nose that was so close to her own. His burnished scales were a darker bronze on his head and along his back, lightening to a bright golden shade along his sides and belly. His limbs were stocky but well muscled, and his tail, while not very long, was broad and had a spiny ridge linked by webbing to help him swim in water. He had a lean, elegant head and horns the color of polished steel. She didn't think she had ever seen a dragon quite so handsome as this one. She felt his breath hot on her cheeks, and when she looked into the depths of his amber eye she saw an anger burning deep as lava beneath the surface. Like all dragons, Crucible often found hatred an easy emotion to awaken.

"I will meet you there," she said, knowing it was useless to argue. "What about a diversion?"

"We can help you there, Lady Knight," Azurale said with a touch of pride. "The owl and I took word to the militia while you were a prisoner. The Legionnaires were very angry with you, but they said they would gather a force and await your word."

Linsha could just imagine Lanther's reaction to her departure last night. She shrugged it off and turned to Varia. "You are certainly losing your shyness around others. Who else have you been talking to?"

The owl ruffled her feathers. "Only those you need. I suggest we also warn Leonidas. He is with the slaves near the palace. Perhaps he can distract some of the guards as well."

Crucible nudged Linsha and said, "You'd better go. I will give you two hours. If Varia will go to Leonidas and the militia, that should give everyone enough time to set up a diversion."

Linsha found a torch inside the doorway and lit it. Bidding a hasty farewell to Crucible and Varia, she shouldered the shield and tried to lift the lance. Its full weight was more than she imagined. She staggered and would have fallen if Azurale hadn't caught the heavy handle.

"You have not told me what to do," he said, balancing the lance, "so I will go with you. You're too worn from your ordeal to carry this far."

She nodded her gratitude to the young stallion. "I didn't want to ask. I know how much centaurs loathe close, dark places."

They went their separate ways without further speech, each knowing what they had to do and each worried for the others. Linsha and the centaur carried the Abyssal Lance between them down into the tunnels of the great labyrinth, while Varia went in search of Leonidas and Lanther. Crucible found a dense grove of young pine and settled down to wait for everyone to reach their places.

This could work, Linsha told herself. It was simply a matter of timing. And if it didn't . . . well then, they wouldn't likely be alive to wallow in the failure. Time to do or die. . . .

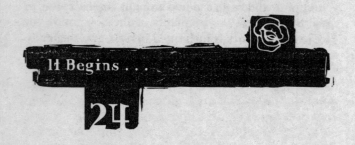

Varia flew hard to pass over the militia's forces toward Iyesta's palace. Mingled with her sense of urgency and her fear for Linsha and Crucible was a feeling of relief and approval at the remarkable speed and fortitude with which the Legion and its companion forces had answered Linsha's call. Once Varia and Azurale had convinced Lanther to listen and he recovered from his fury at Linsha's secret departure, he and Falaius had rounded up every available man and woman, put weapons in their hands, and prepared to set out. Considering how tired and ill-equipped everyone was, Varia was pleased they would respond so well.

Even the Solamnics. The owl chuckled at that memory. When Sir Remmik informed Falaius that the Knights were not going to the rescue of an exiled renegade, she'd thought the plainsman was going to strike the Knight where he stood. Instead he informed the Solamnic commander in no uncertain terms that the Knights were no longer in their snug little castle and if they wished to remain in the Scorpion Wadi, they would do as he told them. Varia chuckled again. Linsha would appreciate that little tale.

A short while ago, she had brought Linsha's word to Falaius, and now the remnants of the Solamnics, the Legion, the militia, the city watch, and the dragonguards marched the long eight miles from the Wadi toward the ruins of the Artisan's District to attack Thunder's forces from the north. If all went as planned, they would draw off enough Brutes and mercenaries to allow Linsha and Thunder to do their task.

While the militia made its move, Varia intended to find Leonidas and Phoulos.

By the position of the sun, two hours came and went without any sign of the militia. The day was growing murderously hot, and there was no wind to stir the heat. Dust and traces of smoke hung above the Missing City like a yellow veil. Crucible grew impatient. As the third hour wound toward its finish, he decided he would risk the attempt with or without Falaius's forces. He rose from his bed of pine needles and was about to step out of the grove when his sharp ears heard war horns on the wind. They were somewhere to the north of the palace, he estimated, near the slave pens. Good. If Leonidas did his work, the penned slaves were close enough to the fighting to give some added trouble to Thunder's guards. He heard the horns sound again, and his heart beat strongly. Those were not militia horns. They were the horns of the Brutes. There was nothing for it now. He had to go.

The bronze stretched his legs and folded his wings to his sides. His eyes narrowed, and his horns lay flat on his head. Focus on the rage within, his heart told him. Draw on the anger, the hatred, the frustration he had trapped within for months. Here was an outlet worthy of his fury: Thunder had killed Iyesta, his friend. Thunder had endangered Linsha. He held Iyesta's eggs captive. The big blue was a menace to everything Iyesta had worked so hard to build.

Crucible felt hate stir the power within him. Like other dragons, he had had trouble creating magic spells the past few years. Only his innate powers like shapeshifting and his breath weapon had remained with him without difficulty. But now he did not have the luxury of experimenting with unpredictable magic. He needed the power and he wanted it quickly, so he fed his hate and anger and resentment into it until the magic seethed like a volcano ready to erupt.

Crucible charged from the trees. He galloped across the magnificent garden ruins to the road, wheeled on the old stone pavings and shot like a bronze arrow for the gateway into the palace courtyard.

No one saw him coming until he was nearly to the gate. Thunder and the warriors camped in the courtyard were standing on or around the walls looking to the north. Not until the bronze's taloned claws and heavy footfalls pounded on the road by the courtyard did a few guards on the gate turn around and see him coming. They raised their swords and their voices to the garrison and died in a white-hot blast from Crucible's mouth. Thunder whipped his head around and saw his enemy, his prized desire, coming directly to him.

He moved his heavy bulk toward the palace to head off the bronze, but the smaller Crucible had too much momentum. He jumped over the blue's heavy tail and charged into the roofless throne room. Swift as light, he raced across the floor where Iyesta used to sleep and whipped down the broad stairs into her treasure room. A lightning blast exploded on the stairs behind him. He ignored it. He was moving too fast for Thunder to take good aim. His original plan had been to destroy the plug of stone and earth Thunder had used to block the entrance to the tunnels. But when he saw the gruesome pile of dragon skulls in the dim light of the treasure chamber, he skidded to a halt and stared at it in horror.

The creation of a dragon skull totem involved killing other dragons—as many as possible. It usually took years to collect enough skulls to activate the power of the pillar, because at least three or four dozen skulls were needed with the brains intact. It was not always easy to slay another dragon in such a manner that preserved the brain within the skull. From the look of Thunder's totem, Crucible guessed he had been at it for many years, in spite of the edict passed down from Malys forbidding the continued slaying of more dragons. Considering the blue's unpredictable and solitary nature and the emptiness of his realm, he must have had to work hard to collect as many skulls as he had.

But the skulls were not the worst part of the totem. Thunder had added a new element that Crucible had never imagined—the brass eggs. They lay carefully arranged between the white bones of the bare skulls in the growing pyramid of the totem, still intact and waiting for whatever vile spell Thunder had planned.

Crucible heard a roar of fury behind him that shook the walls of the palace. He hesitated no longer. He shot a beam of his breath weapon at the stone blocking the stairway down and, snatching up an egg in his mouth, he bolted for the hole that opened up before him.

Thunder pounded down the steps of the throne room. He saw Crucible steal the egg and his fury burned to blind rage. Lightning ripped from his jaws and caught the bronze on the back leg.

Crucible squealed with pain, but he did not drop the egg and he did not stop. He shot through the shattered opening and slithered down into the darkness of the labyrinth.

Like a blue avalanche, Thunder went after him. The hole blasted out of the stone plug was large enough for the smaller metallic dragon, but Thunder had to take a few minutes to rip huge chunks of rock out of his way before he could squeeze his larger body down the stairs. He did not wait for his guard to follow, nor did he try to call the Brutes. This was a battle between him and the bronze. He had killed already down in these tunnels, and he planned to kill again.

In the warm pale light of the egg chamber, Linsha paced back and forth in front of the mound where the eggs had once lain. She knew too much time had passed. She and Azurale had found the egg chamber without much difficulty, and after putting the lance out of sight in the shadow of Purestian's withered corpse, they had settled down to wait. And wait, and wait.

Something had gone wrong. She knew it. The militia had not come, or Crucible was injured, or Thunder had killed the bronze and added his skull to his magic totem. Maybe the blue was already chanting the vile spell that activated the power of the accumulated skulls. She shuddered to think about it.

To take her mind off the anxiety—and the smell of the dead dragon—she picked up three small, rounded stones and tossed them casually into the air one by one. As they came down, she caught them in one hand, tossed them to the other, and flipped them up again, around and around and around until they flew in a continuous circle. She hadn't done this in a long while, but the motions quickly became familiar again and felt good to her exhausted, overworked body.

Azurale, nervous himself, came to watch her. "Why are you doing that?" he asked.

"It's an old trick my brother taught me," she replied. "You have to concentrate to keep the rocks moving. It helps clear my mind."

The centaur watched for a few more minutes then wandered over to the entrance of the cavern. He looked tiny in the huge opening, and he felt very anxious. He did not like any part of this. Suddenly he tensed, looked at the ground, put a hand to the wall and felt the same slight vibrations he had sensed through his hooves. He pounded back to Linsha.

"Something is coming!" he said in a loud whisper. "Something big!"

Startled, she dropped the rocks on her feet. With a muffled oath, she whirled around to listen. At first she heard nothing, then a sound—a rumble growing closer and a roar like an oncoming storm—echoed down the tunnels. Her eyes widened, her pulse quickened, and she broke into a run.

Azurale wasted no time following her. They sprinted around the high mound and crouched down beside the lance that lay behind the bones of the brass dragon. They were out of sight.

Linsha felt her heart in her throat. From the sounds coming up the tunnel, the two dragons sounded like they were very close together, which was not a good sign. She and Azurale needed time to get her on Crucible's back and get the lance seated in the pommel before they had to face Thunder. Then there was no more time to think. With the sound of a tornado, Crucible burst into the cavern. He had a large, mottled globe in his mouth, and his eyes burned with an inner fire.

Linsha rose from behind the bones to get his attention. She saw him run to the mound and place the egg carefully on the warm sands, then he came toward her, favoring his back leg. She was horrified to see a long seared gash cut across the back of his hind leg.

He ran into the shadow cast by the dead dragon, and without a word he crouched to help Linsha crawl up his front leg to the saddle on his back.

As Azurale lifted her high to the dragon's bent knee, the three heard a massive growl and a roar of rage that shook the chamber.

Thunder charged into the cave.

Battle of the Dragon's Lair

25

Silent as a shadow, Varia waited in a tree close to the high wall that formed part of the slave pens built by the mercenaries. Pressed against the trunk, she was nearly invisible to all but the most intense scrutiny. She had been silent for some time except for one sleepy-sounding cry that alerted Leonidas and Phoulos to her presence. The two centaurs stood close by, their hides dark with sweat and dust. Several other captured centaurs waited with them. Varia watched them and listened.

When the sound of the war horns came, the clarion calls swept loud and long on the hot morning wind. The denizens of the pens, civilians and warriors alike, stirred and looked around at each other, at the guards, and at the thin line of trees that blocked the view to the north.

Varia saw the two centaurs lift their heads then move side by side to remove the knives hidden in each other's tails.

War horns sounded again from a different direction—Tarmak horns, sharp and fierce.

293

It was time.

Although some people knew Varia could talk, no one but Linsha knew what a virtuoso of sound the owl truly was. As soon as the sounds of the horns dissipated, she burst into a wild cacophony of shrieks, shouts, and bloodcurdling screams that burst out of the tree line as if the very skirts of battle were about to sweep over the land. She flew from tree to tree, bellowing and screeching.

In the slave pens, chaos erupted. Prisoners ran frantically, looking for a way out. The guards drew their swords and tried to restore order, but they kept looking at the trees or back to the palace as if they didn't know what to think about the uproar. Under the cover of the confusion and noise, the centaurs moved close to the big wooden gates.

Varia paused in her shrieking long enough to take a quick look toward the palace. She saw the mercenaries form ranks in the courtyard and march out to find the militia. Only a few guards remained behind. Oddly, she did not see any of the Brute warriors leave with them.

Giving one more ululating scream, Varia launched herself from the tree and shot like an arrow over the heads of the captives.

"Arise and flee!" she screeched. "War comes again!"

Only Leonidas and Phoulos knew who gave that eldrich shriek. Everyone elsed shouted and ducked as the winged shape shot overhead.

The guards at the gate also flinched and ducked from the frightening apparition. In that moment of inattention, Leonidas and Phoulos turned and proved that centaurs are well armed even without swords or crossbows. Two sets of hooves driven by powerful hindlegs slammed into the wooden gate with a resounding crash. The wooden gate held through the first blow, but a third centaur joined them, and on the second strike the gates exploded open. Leonidas took out the closest guard with his throwing knife, then the centaurs wheeled and attacked the guards.

The remaining slaves saw the open gateway and bolted for freedom. Some simply kept running into the gardens or fled back toward the city. Others, especially the captured militia and fighting men, joined the centaurs in a vicious hand to hand battle with the guards.

Varia circled overhead, watching in satisfaction. The two young centaurs fought well and led their forces slowly in the direction of the palace.

Suddenly, she saw the dark centaur rear, his front legs flailing the air. A spear protruded from his neck.

"Phoulos!" Leonidas bellowed.

Varia swooped low over the centaur as he struggled toward his friend and caught Phoulos's hand. The wounded horseman staggered to his knees.

Phoulos collapsed to his side into a growing pool of blood. The owl sadly watched Leonidas clasp his friend's hand hard. Fighting raged around him, but Leonidas took no notice. He and Varia waited until the gleam of life faded from Phoulos's eyes and the body sagged motionless on the ground. Only then did Leonidas pick up a sword and, with a yell of rage, plunge back into the fighting.

Varia sang a soft word of farewell to the spirit of the dead centaur then flapped her wings and rose high to view the palace. They were close, but they had to get inside. Time was moving swiftly, and the ragged forces of the militia were not strong enough to engage in an extended battle.

Beyond the collapsed stone walls, the green overgrowth, and the old ruined foundations that lay between the slave pens and the palace, Varia noticed new warriors had appeared—Brutes, many of them. They were not marching to the north to join the mercenaries but toward the palace. Grim and intent, they moved toward their goal with the same speed and efficiency they had shown in their invasion of the city.

The owl squawked and spiralled higher. More Brutes, led by their general, appeared from the south road. They strode into the palace courtyard. Swords flashed in the sunlight, and Varia heard the shouts of frightened men and the screams of the dying.

"Those vultures!" she hissed.

The Brutese were attacking their own allies.

* * *

Thunder's massive presence filled the great chamber. He roared again and sent a bolt of lightning searing across the roof.

"Crucible! You grubby worm! You can go no further! Come out!"

He did not see the bronze hiding behind the corpse, but he spotted the egg lying on the mound and hurried toward it. He reached for it then stopped and swept his gaze over the dead dragon in the back of the cave.

"Hurry!" rasped Crucible.

Linsha, using a strength born of terror and fury, scrambled frantically up his scaled shoulder to the saddle they had rigged between his wings. She settled herself into the seat and leaned over to reach for the lance.

Azurale handed it up to her butt first so she get it seated in the pommel.

"Here he comes!" warned Crucible.

"No!" Linsha cried, still leaning over the dragon's side. "I'm not ready!"

The heavy lance dangled precariously in her grasp. She had not yet gained a firm grip on it, and if Crucible moved now, she knew she would drop it.

Azurale knew it too, and he knew he was not tall enough to help her put it in place. All he could do was give her a moment or two. Forcing back his terror, he yanked off his crossbow and bolted out of the shadows into the open directly in the path of the blue dragon. The war cry of his clan cut through the heavy air. He fired his crossbow in the general direction of the dragon's head and charged around the mound.

Thunder leaped, thrusting his massive head to snatch the centaur in his crushing teeth, but Azurale was young, agile, and desperate. He swerved, and Thunder's fangs clashed on empty air.

Linsha watched the centaur's frantic run for just an instant, then she wasted no more of his precious gift. She closed her eyes and marshalled all of her strength, all the spiritual energy of her heart, every vestige of power she had ever had and focused it all into one final lift with her tired, aching muscles. Her hands tightened around the handle, her arm muscles cramping at the weight of the lance. The weapon rose and settled neatly into place by her right knee, the butt resting on the support by the saddle pommel, the cowl shielding her right arm, shoulder, and the right side of her torso. Now all she had to do was hold on while Crucible maneuvered them close enough to drive the point into Thunder. If it didn't work, she didn't think they need worry about a second chance.

"Hold on!" the bronze said.

Linsha could do little else. Holding on with all her strength, she clung to Crucible as he charged out from behind the dead brass into the open.

Thunder did not see them immediately. His attention was still on the fleeing centaur. Azurale had

297

reached the opposite side of the sand mound from Thunder and was dashing back and forth around the base of the high mound, trying to avoid the dragon's attack.

The blue tired of the cat and mouse game and changed tactics. Instead of lunging around the side of the mound, he threw his massive body over it. The great weight of his chest crushed the brass dragon egg into the sand, while his neck and head snaked over the edge of the mound and caught Azurale just as the young centaur wheeled to escape. The dragon's teeth closed around his human torso and crushed him. Azurale never had time to scream.

Thunder tossed back his head and ripped the centaur in half. Blood sprayed across the sand. He swallowed, snatched up the horse half, and gulped that down too. Only then did he turn his head around to see the bronze behind him.

Linsha had only a glimpse of the blue crouched on the torn and bloody mound. She saw the blood on his muzzle and the mess on his chest that was egg albumen mixed with shards of egg, sand, and the bloody gore that was once a dragon embryo. She screamed once in fury and protest, then tightened her muscles and clamped the black lance in place as Crucible sprang on the blue. They drove the rust-red tip into the dragon's back just below the base of his neck.

Thunder bellowed in agony. No one had ever inflicted such pain on him before. He twisted away and whipped his blunt tail around to slam the bronze to the ground.

Linsha, still clinging to the lance, was pulled out of the saddle. To her horror, she found herself dangling from the barbed shaft buried in the Thunder's back. The blow had been a serious one, but it obviously hadn't killed him, and now she was swinging from the back of an infuriated dragon.

"Crucible!" she screamed. She flung up her legs and wrapped them around the shaft, so she wasn't just hanging.

Thunder heard her, peered around, and recognized the curly-haired human who had flown with Iyesta. The air hissed from his nostrils, yet he did not dare use his lightning weapon. The blue's lightning was more random, and he did not want to use it so close to his own back. He tried to reach around with a taloned forefoot to snatch her off, but the lance swung out of his reach and the pain from the barbed head buried between his shoulders was agony. He flapped his wings and roared in fury.

Another pain seared across his left haunch and lower wing as Crucible ducked in close and shot a beam low against Thunder's body.

In that frantic moment after the Abyssal Lance pierced the blue's tough scales, the dark spells incorporated in the wood and steel reacted with the dragon's blood and began to work their evil purpose. It did not matter that the dragon afflicted was an evil dragon himself. Good or Evil, the lance was made to kill.

Linsha felt the change first. The wood became hot beneath her fingers and legs—so hot she could barely tolerate the pain of the heat burning into her skin. She shot a look at the sandy floor, figured her chances of surviving a fall and Thunder's attack, and decided they weren't much worse than clinging to a burning lance stuck in an enraged dragon's back.

Thunder screeched in fearful pain. Within his neck and shoulders a terrific heat spread from the barbs of the lance. He shook himself fiercely, but with every move of his mucles the barbs slid deeper and deeper

299

past his spinal chord and into his chest. Insane with pain, he lunged at Crucible, intending to crush the smaller dragon beneath his greater weight.

For Varia, the sight of the Brute warriors slaughtering the mercenary guards in the palace courtyard was enough to drive out all thoughts of sending the escaped prisoners and slaves into the throne room for a look. She would be sending them to their deaths. Instead she swooped close to Leonidas.

"Leave!" she shouted over the fighting. "Go north! Find the militia! The Brutes are attacking the palace!"

He shot her a look of bitter anger and sadness, but he nodded his understanding.

Most of the guards were dead by that time, so it took only a matter of minutes for the captives to complete their small victory, gather their mixed company, and follow Leonidas out of the ruined palace grounds toward the Artisan's District.

Varia watched them long enough to see them on their way before she flew toward the throne room. If she couldn't bring human hands and centaur muscles to help find the eggs, at least she could bring owl eyes to look for them. On noiseless wings, she swept down through the shattered roof and found a perch in a shadowy niche where several chunks of stone had fallen from the roof. She settled into her hiding place just as the Tarmak general strode into the throne room.

A few mercenaries, furious at the violent intrusion, fired arrows and crossbow bolts from behind a pile of rubble, but the Brutes swiftly dealt with them and dragged their bodies out to join their comrades in a pile by the door.

"Clear it out!" the general told his men.

The Brutes spread out into the remains of the throne room and down into the lower chamber.

"The eggs are down here," another voice called from the stairs leading down to the treasure chamber. Varia's pointed ear feathers popped up with excitement. She couldn't see into the lower chamber from where she stood, so she slowly sidled across a beam and floated down to a lower perch. From there she could dip her head down and peer down the scorched stairway into the depths of the treasure chamber. Her eyes widened. What arrogance! Did they believe Thunder was dead?

The Brutes were hard at work shoveling Iyesta's accumulated treasure into crates. Apparently they decided to help themselves rather than wait for the mercenaries to share. Other Brutes carried pickaxes and sledge hammers down the stairs. Varia wondered what they were going to do with those until she leaned a little further down and saw the edge of the dragon skull totem. The first Brute to the neatly stacked pile raised his sledge hammer and brought it down hard on the dragon skull at his feet. The bone shattered and flew in all directions.

"The eggs!" Varia cried softly. "Don't smash the eggs!"

More skulls cracked and smashed under the impact of those relentless axes. The totem began to sway; skulls toppled down with hard, cracking sounds and exploded as sledge hammers came down on the brittle bone.

Varia could only stare in astonishment. Weren't these Brutes supposed to be Thunder's allies?

"General! There's that owl!"

Varia started at the words. She hadn't realized that in her agitation, she'd crept out of her hiding place and was visible to the men in the throne room.

The Brute general stared up at her through his golden mask then said, "Kill it."

Varia did not wait to see if these soldiers would obey this order. She dove off her ledge in a hunting dive and arrowed out the wide doors before the Brutes could get an aim on her. She did not hesitate or pause to see what they would do next, but flew out of their sight as quickly as her wings could carry her.

Linsha tried to wait for the right moment to let go of the lance. She wanted to be able to control her descent, but the heat in the shaft and Thunder's frenzied movements were more than she could handle. Her hands slipped and for just a heartbeat she hung upside down by her ankles. One more strong shake of the dragon's back loosened her hold, and she broke free and fell head down along the dragon's side to the ground.

"Linsha!" Crucible sprang to meet Thunder head to head.

The huge blue felt the weight slip from the lance, but he was already moving too fast to change his intentions. He met Crucible with a thunderous clash of teeth, claws, scales and wings that smashed them both into the nesting mound and bore the smaller dragon deep into the crumbling sand. The bronze snarled with pain as his injured foreleg and wing were pressed under Thunder's greater mass. The blue snapped and tore at Crucible's head, trying to get a grip on the bronze's throat, ignoring the ferocious agony in his back.

It was the sand that saved Linsha's life. Instead of crashing headfirst into the ground, she tumbled off Thunder into a pile of sand beside his thrashing body.

She lay winded for a moment while the dragons struggled and heaved above her. She took a deep breath and scrambled up before they crushed her. Linsha fumbled for her boot with a silent plea of hope. The Brutes had disarmed her earlier but she could not remember if they had checked her boot. Her fingers sought the handle of the slim stiletto down the inside of her right boot, found it, and pulled. May the gods of the afterlife bless that dead mercenary!

She looked up at Thunder's bulk rising above her and leaped for the wing folded against his side. A grappling hook and a rope would have been better for what she intended, but the stiletto was all she had. As she reached the apex of her jump, she jammed the blade into his wing with one hand and used it to hold her weight while she scrabbled for the nearest pinion that would help her climb the struggling dragon. She had to get back on him. The lance was working—it would kill Thunder—but it was not working fast enough to save the bronze. Linsha could only hope that she could get back onto Thunder before he noticed her.

She scrambled higher, jamming her small blade into the blue's leathery wing membrane and climbing up the folds. She was so intent on her desperate climb that she did not see Crucible's eye lock on her or the dulled glow of desperation that filled his eyes. Nor did she notice that he struggled harder to keep the monstrous blue's attention away from her precarious position.

She was scrambling over Thunder's wing bone and onto the ridge of his back when she felt the dragon abruptly still. Her slight weight must have finally registered in his fevered brain, for he whipped his head around in time to see her clamber along the ridges of his back toward the black lance that bored into his shoulders. He hissed in sudden fear and hate.

Linsha focused on the black lance. She leaped and shoved it down deeper into his body. Thunder's screech almost shattered Linsha's eardrums. Sweat and tears of pain ran down her face, and she felt her hands burning around the haft of the lance. She shifted her stance and pushed on the shaft again, forcing the barbs to move faster through Thunder's lung toward his heart. Thunder's last mortal cry shook his dying body. Disbelief and terror drowned the furious glow of his eyes. His legs swayed under his weight.

Linsha stared up into the gaping holes of his nostrils and his slack mouth so close to her. She smelled the stink of his breath and thought her time had come to die.

Frantic, Crucible snapped at the blue's neck. His weakened bite caused little damage to the blue's tough scales, but he succeeded in drawing Thunder's fading attention back to himself. The blue dragon's head slammed around and pushed aside Crucible's weakening defenses. His heavy jaws closed around the bronze's neck just under the jaw, and he began to crush Crucible's throat.

Linsha pushed on the lance once more, and this time dark blood bubbled up around the wound. The barbs had torn Thunder's heart. She felt him shudder. As the life drained from the dragon's body, his wings sagged, his muscles lost their strength, and his great body slowly collapsed to the earth.

Linsha stood for a moment, hauling air into her lungs and reveling with intense relief. Then, in the sudden silence of the cavern, she heard a strange gasping, rattling noise, and her fear returned tenfold. Crucible was still underneath the massive corpse. She scrambled down Thunder's back, dropped to the ground, and hurried around the mound to the dragons' heads. Sick with fear, she found Crucible nearly buried in the sand of the nest and trapped under the dead blue. Worst of all Thunder's jaws were still locked around his throat. The bronze struggled, unable to breathe beneath the sinking dead weight of the enormous blue crushing into his chest and throat. Blood oozed from wounds on his neck and trickled down into the sand. His amber eyes darkened and bulged in his efforts to breath.

Linsha took one look and knew she could not help him alone. She had no sword to pry open Thunder's jaws, nor did she have enough strength to lift the weight of the dragon's head from Crucible's throat. He would have to do something to help himself.

"Crucible!" she cried. She grabbed Thunder's jaw and tried to wrench the head loose from the bronze's throat. It barely budged. "Listen to me! Look at me! I am here. But I need your help. I can't lift this. Crucible!"

The bronze's pain-filled eye rolled toward her. She yanked again at the blue's jaw. If she couldn't move it, maybe she could just loosen it enough for Crucible to breathe.

"Can you shapeshift? Change to a man! To a cat! Change to a shrimp for all I care! Just get out from under this!"

Would he have enough strength left? Would he have enough conscious thought left to control the magic? He could shapeshift to a cat under Thunder's body and be crushed before he knew what happened.

"Crucible!" she tried again. "Can you shapeshift to a cat? Right here? Where I can get you?"

She tugged at Thunder's huge head. The blue's dull, lifeless eye stared back her, but she thought she felt the head move slightly. She tried again and again until her vision swam and her arms trembled with fatigue. Crucible's throat rattled. She dropped down by his head and felt for some sign of life.

"No, you don't!" she yelled at the bronze. "You stay with me!"

Grasping his nose, she tugged at his head just enough to tilt it back. His nostrils twitched ever so slightly, and he took a gasp of air. It rattled down his throat into his starved lungs. All at once he began to glow with soft golden light. Linsha moved back but kept her hands ready to snatch him the moment he transformed. The spell took longer than usual, and his shape seemed to waver in the glimmering light—once long and human-like, then large, then small and four-legged. It finally settled on small and furry.

Thunder's body settled deeper into the sand as Crucible's large form disappeared and reappeared as a battered, bloody orange-striped cat pinned under Thunder's head.

That was a shape Linsha could manage. She dug the sand out from under the cat and pulled him away from the dragon. Cradling him in her arms, she began the long walk back to daylight.

Nightfall

26

She returned to the passage that led to Iyesta's treasure chamber not only because it was shorter, but she also wanted to satisfy her curiosity. Crucible had brought an egg with him into the labyrinth to enrage Thunder, and the only place she knew he had gone was the palace. For the sake of her oath to Iyesta, she tread a slow and wary path back through the darkness to the light of the stairway leading up to the treasure chamber.

She moved up the stairs until she could lift her head beyond the lintel and see into the room. The sight before her surprised her. The room was deserted, but something had left a terrible mess. Dragon skulls lay scattered across the floor—some smashed to bits, some cracked and broken. The piles and chests of treasure Iyesta had so carefully amassed over the years were ransacked, and most of it was gone. The thieves had taken the most valuable pieces—the weapons, the magic artifacts, and the chests of steel coins. They had left jewelry, gems, and piles of cheap coins scattered among the pieces of broken eyesockets, shattered jaws, and smashed brainpans. What she didn't see were the eggs. There was no sign of them—no shards, no dead embryos. Nothing.

The cat squirmed in her arms and opened his eyes. *Where are we?*

"In the treasure room," she whispered. She lifted him up so he could see.

He growled deep in his throat. *They were here. The eggs were here. He had them stacked in his totem. Who took them?*

Linsha felt her heart sink. Gods, she had tried so hard to save those eggs. Now they were gone again. She heard movement upstairs in the throne room and ducked back down into the tunnels. If the guards were returning or the thieves were still out there, she didn't want to face them. She was not sure she could fight a four year old for his toy horse. The cat sagged back into her arms and fell asleep.

Still holding the warm shape of the cat, she made her way back to the hidden entrance in the palace ruins. Late afternoon sun peeked through the vines shielding the doorway when she and Crucible came to the exit. Linsha staggered out and collapsed on the grassy patch near the door. She hoped no one was nearby, for she did not think she could walk another step. She curled her body around the cat and let her awareness sink.

Her rest lasted long enough for her eyelids to fall shut and her muscles to relax. She was drifting on the tide, gently slipping into the darkness of sleep when hoofbeats trotted through the undergrowth. She woke to dappled sunlight and the distant rumble of thunder.

Varia's voice called, "There she is!"

She looked up through bleary eyes to see the stubbled, dirty face of Sir Hugh and the young, whiskery face of Leonidas looking down at her in obvious relief.

"Lady Linsha, thank Paladine!" said Sir Hugh from his horse. "I hate to be waking you, but there are guests coming you don't want to meet."

She rolled to a sitting position and tried to focus, tried to swim back against the tide.

Varia flew down and landed on her bent knee. "Please hurry, Linsha. The Brutes ransacked the palace during the battle, and the mercenaries are furious. They're searching the entire grounds."

"Where is Azurale?" Leonidas said. "I thought he was with you."

Linsha looked at his face and noticed how much he had aged in just a short week. The boyish immaturity of his features was gone, replaced by harder, more tempered lines wrought by stress, fear, and loss. Her eyes glimmered with tears, knowing she was about to add to his grief.

"Azurale was killed by Thunder."

The centaur's expression sagged with sadness. "Phoulos is dead, too. Do you know that makes me the last of my company? The newest and the last." He turned away, too proud to show his tears.

Sir Hugh dismounted and helped Linsha to her feet. She lifted the sleeping cat and held him in her arms. It was amazing, she thought. All that size and power concentrated into a small, furry animal. The injuries were there, too: the bloody, torn neck, the broken wing bone disguised somewhere in his ribcage, the wounded foreleg, the burned gash across his backleg. Dragons were truly a marvel.

"Look who I found," Sir Hugh said. He tugged on the reins of his horse to move him closer, and for the first time Linsha took a closer look. It was Sandhawk. The Knight grinned. "I found him in a pen with other horses the mercenaries stole." He cocked his head to listen as another rumble of thunder growled somewhere to the west. "Time to get moving. You can tell us what happened while we ride."

He jumped into the saddle. He would have offered Linsha a hand onto Sandhawk's back behind him if Leonidas had not lifted her in his strong arms and placed her on his back, cat and all. Varia flew to her shoulder.

Linsha looked at the cat, the owl, the centaur, and the Knight and felt oddly comforted. She was surrounded by friends who cared for her, who looked after her, who thought enough of her to risk their own lives to help her. In spite of what might happen in the coming months, she would at least have that.

They rode westward through the gardens and toward the open plains. They evaded several mercenary patrols and slipped through a gap in the incomplete city wall that had been abandoned when the defenders fled. The mercenaries had not bothered to put up guards, and the Brutes were still consolidating their hold in the city proper. The two Knights and the centaur, cat and owl in tow, were able to escape without difficulty.

The overgrown gardens fell behind, and the small party circled their way north through the edge of the decaying ruins and out into the hills of the open plains. The centaur and the horse broke into a canter.

Linsha leaned back and gazed up at the huge sky. To the west a thunderstorm drew dark clouds and veils of rain over the grasslands, but it was a normal storm with steel blue clouds and lightning that flickered without malice. Overhead the sky was still blue, and the wind that kicked up toward the storm was cool with moisture from the ocean. She drew a deep breath of clean, salty air and told her companions about the deaths of Azurale, the unhatched brass dragonet, and Thunder.

They in turn told her about the militia, the slaves, and the battle of the Artisans's District.

"Varia brought word of your plan just after dawn," Sir Hugh said. "We attacked the mercenaries north of the palace. They came in hordes to drive us off, but there were no Brutes. They did not help at all."

Varia hooted a note of amusement. "They were too busy ransacking the palace while the mercenaries were drawn off. I saw them."

"Did they take the eggs?" asked Linsha.

"I don't know. They had many chests and crates. The eggs could have been packed in there. But why would Brutes want dragon eggs? What are they going to do with them?"

What indeed, Linsha wondered. In her mind's eye, she saw again the masked general and the dark figure in the storm. Were they the same man? Who was his informant who knew so much about her? Why had the general told her so much when he held her prisoner? "We, however, have other plans," he had said. Did those plans include using someone else to kill the blue dragon so the Brutes could have complete control of the city and the treasure without the interference of such a vicious, unpredictable partner as Thunder? Exactly who manipulated whom into attacking Iyesta's realm? Linsha stroked the cat on her lap and shook her head. She and Crucible and the militia may have won their battle this day, but she could see it would be a long time before they won the war.

It occurred to her, rather belatedly, that she should have destroyed the Abyssal Lance while she was in the chamber. Well, it was too late now. They would have to send someone in there to get it. Maybe the carrion beetles would eat it.

"What about the slaves?" she asked Leonidas. "How did you get free?"

The centaur slowed to avoid a thick patch of sage then sped up again to a canter. The wind had dried the moisture in his eyes and the companionship of the woman on his back gave him the strength to smile. "Those knives you gave us came in useful. We fought our way out, and most of the others are on their way back to the Wadi with the militia. When the mercenaries withdrew, Varia found us, and we came to find you."

"What happened to Phoulos?"

"Took a spear in the neck while we were fighting the guards," Leonidas said simply.

Linsha lapsed into silence. She didn't have the strength for more words. Her companions fell into their own thoughts, and the small company rode quietly ahead of the storm to the Scorpion Wadi.

Once in the safety of the canyon, they passed the pickets and the guards and came to the cave where people came streaming out to meet them.

Linsha looked for the faces of Falaius and General Dockett, of Lanther and Mariana, and when she found them she raised her fist in victory and thanks.

"Iyesta is avenged!" she cried. "Thunder is dead."

The cheering rose up through the canyon and vied with the voice of the storm. For that night, at least, the survivors of the Missing City were able to celebrate.

To Be Continued . . .

The Minotaur Wars

From *New York Times* best-selling author Richard A. Knaak comes a powerful new chapter in the DRAGONLANCE® saga.

The continent of Ansalon, reeling from the destruction of the War of Souls, slowly crawls from beneath the rubble to rebuild – but the fires of war, once stirred, are difficult to quench. Another war comes to Ansalon, one that will change the balance of power throughout Krynn.

NIGHT OF BLOOD
Volume I

Change comes violently to the land of the minotaurs. Usurpers overthrow the emperor, murder all rivals, and dishonor minotaur tradition. The new emperor's wife presides over a cult of the dead, while the new government makes a secret pact with a deadly enemy. But betrayal is never easy, and rebellion lurks in the shadows.

The Minotaur Wars begin June 2003.

Before the War of the Lance, there were other adventures.

Check out these new editions of the popular Preludes series!

DARKNESS & LIGHT
Sturm Brightblade and Kitiara are on their way to Solamnia
when they run into a band of gnomes in jeopardy.

KENDERMORE
Tasslehoff Burrfoot is arrested for violating the kender laws of
prearranged marriage – but his bride pulls a disappearing act of her own.

BROTHERS MAJERE
Desperate for money, Raistlin and Caramon Majere agree to take
on a job in the backwater village of Mereklar, but they soon discover
they may be in over their heads.

RIVERWIND THE PLAINSMAN
A barbarian princess and her beloved walked into the Inn of the
Last Home, and thus began the DRAGONLANCE® Saga.
This is the adventure that led to that fateful moment.

October 2003

FLINT THE KING
Flint Fireforge's comfortable life turns to chaos
when he travels to his ancestral home.

November 2003

TANIS: THE SHADOW YEARS
When an old dwarf offers Tanis Halfelven the chance to find his father,
he embarks on an adventure that will change him forever.

December 2003